THE MAD ROBOT

By
WILLIAM P. McGIVERN

I0541453

ARMCHAIR FICTION
PO Box 4369, Medford, Oregon   97501-0168

*For more information about Armchair Books and products, visit our
website at…*

www.armchairfiction.com

Or email us at…

armchairfiction@yahoo.com

KILLER ROBOTS ON JUPITER...

It seemed like a fairly simple mission. Make a routine supply run to Jupiter and plant yourself in the Earth-Mars robot experimental station. Then hang around for awhile and see if you can figure out what problems they're having with the robot development program out there. Just don't let anybody know that you're spying on them.

But when Rick Weston arrived on Jupiter, he soon found himself in a maze of hatred and intrigue. Robots were going beserk on occasion—and sometimes taking human lives! With the help of a friendly Martian scientist and a beautiful girl, it didn't take Weston long to figure out the problems with the robots weren't just mechanical.

FOR A COMPLETE SECOND NOVEL, TURN TO PAGE 77

CAST OF CHARACTERS

RICK WESTON
The largest planet in the solar system was his destination. His mission: to spy on a bunch of robots.

HO AGAR
A brilliant Martian scientist—but even he was at a loss to explain what was wrong with the Earth-Mars robot program.

DR. SIMON FARREL
He had developed a new line of robot workers, whose successful development would change the face of the Solar System.

RITA FARREL
She was torn between loyalty to her father and the grim realization that he might be guilty of treachery.

ROBOT 161
It was purely mechanical—devoid of any human characteristics. But why did it sometimes show very human traits?

CAPTAIN WILSON
Something wasn't quite right with the robot experimental program on Jupiter and he wanted answers—now.

HAWKINS
Crusty and ill tempered, this robot maintenance man really didn't care too much for newcomers.

CHAPTER ONE

RICK WESTON arrived at the Earth spaceport outside Greater New York at six o'clock in the morning. He was driven directly to the mooring tower where his slim, fast pursuit single-seater was being readied for his trip to Jupiter.

The chief mechanic, a grizzled Scotchman, who loved machinery more than he did his wife, wiped his hands on an oil-stained rag and nodded to Rick.

"She's purrin' like a cat," he said enthusiastically. "Shouldn't give you no trouble at all."

"Well, it hadn't better," Rick smiled. "If something goes wrong out there in space I can't very well drop into a convenient mooring tower and have it fixed." He glanced at his watch and then looked down the long ramp that led to the central offices of the vast sprawling field.

"Has Captain Wilson been around?" he asked MacPurdy, the chief mechanic.

MacPurdy shook his head.

"Not yet, but he sent work over that he'd be here before you left."

"Good," Rick said. "I'll go aboard and wait for him."

He had to stoop going through the door of the ship and turn his wide shoulders slightly. He was a big man with solid, capable features, but his weight was evenly distributed over his frame. There was a solemn expression on his face as he stepped into the small control cabin and began a careful, thorough check of the various panels and equipment. He was careful and deliberate in his inspection and when he finished he knew the ship was right.

He sat down then and lit a cigarette. His big frame was relaxed and his eyes were almost sleepy as they watched the smoke curl toward the ceiling in lazy blue spirals; but there was a suggestion of dormant power in his loose position and he looked as if he could move with speed if the need arose.

The cigarette had burned half its length when there was a step on the landing plank of the ship and a second later a tall, keen-eyed man in uniform appeared in the doorway of the control cabin.

"Early bird, as usual," he greeted Rick, smiling warmly. "Been here long?"

"Just a few minutes," Rick said, getting to his feet. He shook hands with Captain Wilson and said, "How soon do you want me to leave?"

"Right away," Captain Wilson said. He glanced about the small cabin with alert eyes. "Is the ship ready?"

Rick nodded.

"Fine," Wilson said. He pursed his lips and frowned at the floor. "I want to talk to you a minute, Rick. You don't know why you're being sent to Jupiter, do you?"

Rick shook his head.

"My orders were to take this ship to Jupiter. As far as I'm concerned that's all there is to the assignment."

"There's more to it than that," Wilson said. "I was asked by the divisional command to select a man for an important mission to Jupiter. I picked you, not because you're a personal friend, but because you're trustworthy, observant, and most important of all, close-mouthed."

"Thanks for the bouquets," Rick said, smiling faintly.

CAPTAIN WILSON glanced at Rick and his eyes were serious.

"You probably know," he said, "that the Earth-Mars council has for some time been conducting robot experiments on Jupiter. We have quite an extensive layout there, under the joint command of our own Doctor Simon Farrel and a brilliant scientist from Mars, Ho Agar. We aren't completely satisfied with progress to date. And our Intelligence is vitally interested in a complete report of what's going on there. You are going to compile that report, Rick. You will have no official status, other than that of pilot in the Earth Space Command. Ostensibly you are making this trip to Jupiter to deliver supplies that are needed there. The supplies are in the storage compartment of the ship now. You'll have to depend on your own ingenuity to get the information we want."

"And just what is the information you want," Rick asked.

Captain Wilson shrugged his shoulders helplessly.

"I can't tell you because we don't know. We don't suspect anyone, we aren't actually dissatisfied with the production figures and experimental reports that are sent us by Doctor Farrel, but we do want to know *if* anything is wrong. You've got to find that out."

Rick lit another cigarette slowly.

"What kind of a guy is Farrel?" he asked.

"Brilliant but eccentric," the Captain answered. "He stands for no interference, no questioning, but goes his own way in his own time. That's why you're being sent there in an unofficial capacity. If he suspected that you were spying on him I don't know what he'd do, but it wouldn't be anything calm or temperate. He'd likely destroy his formulae and tell us all to go to blue blazes."

"And how about the Martian—Ho Agar?"

"I don't know him personally," Captain Wilson said, "but his reputation as a scientist is one of the finest in the Universe. His work on metallurgy has been absolutely amazing. And from all reports he is agreeable, easy to work with and thoroughly cooperative."

"Sounds all right," Rick said. "One other thing: what excuse will I have for hanging around there after I deliver my supplies? Won't it look suspicious if I don't return immediately?"

"That's been arranged," said Captain Wilson. "Orders will be sent to you there to wait for the next ship from Earth, which will be equipped with experimental apparatus. Your orders will be to transfer that equipment to your ship for the purpose of testing it at high speed on your return trip to Earth. That should ease any suspicion that your delay in leaving might create."

"Good enough," Rick said. "You haven't given me much to go on, but I'll keep my eyes open."

"That's all I want you to do," Captain Wilson said. "Trust your common sense and observation. And if you find anything that you think should be reported immediately, don't use the communication sets at our Jupiter base. Take your ship out beyond the range of their interceptor frequency and send your message on the ship's set."

"I understand," Rick said. He glanced at his watch. "It's six-twenty now. I should probably be getting under way."

"Right," Captain Wilson said. He shook hands with Rick and stepped to the door. "Good luck. This is a big job, Rick, and you may need it."

"Thanks," Rick said. "I'll be careful."

WHEN the captain had gone, Rick seated himself at the control panel and closed the switch that hermetically sealed the doors and the hatches of the ship. Then he signaled the field's central tower for clearance and turned on the juice that set the rear rockets throbbing.

When a brilliant flare shot up from the main tower in answer to his signal, he was ready to go. He set the rocket rheostats at full power and slowly released the suction clamps that locked the ship in its mooring slot.

The atmosphere of Earth screamed past the sides of the ship as it blasted void-ward.

CHAPTER TWO

RICK WESTON arrived at the mighty planet of Jupiter seven days later. The great glowing orb of the greatest unit of the Solar System had grown steadily in his fore visi-screen with every passing hour; and now that he was within range of its atmosphere it obscured the entire surface of the screen.

He set the automatic controls and fired the fore repulsion rockets. His ship was slicing through Jupiter's heavy atmosphere and the sound of its passage was a thin high wail.

The mooring tower and group buildings of the Earth-Mars base were suddenly visible on his visi-screen and he felt his ship suddenly slide onto their beam and plummet directly toward the landing slot. He breathed a faint sigh of relief. Although he was a veteran of many such landings he never failed to feel grateful when his ship slanted onto a mechanical beam that would lead him directly and gently to the safety of a tower.

His speed was reduced to almost zero as the slim nose of the ship nuzzled softly into the tower socket. A compressed air lock snapped shut with a hiss and the ship stopped with a faint jar.

When he descended to the ground there was a short, swarthy man in uniform waiting for him. The man smiled and stuck out a hand.

"I'm Hawkins," he said, "charge of maintenance here. Have you got all the stuff we ordered?"

"I guess so," Rick said. "But I really wouldn't know. I'm just a pilot. Your supplies are in the rear storage locker of the ship."

"Fine," Hawkins said, "I'll have some of the boys get busy unloading right away. I suppose you're in a hurry to get started back."

Rick shrugged and said, "Not particularly. I feel like a little rest first."

He glanced around curiously at the vast factories and buildings that were shining under the pale cold light of the distant sun. The main building was a one-storied, duralloy structure that was at least a half-mile long. In the middle of the enclosure formed by flanking factories was a comfortable looking, four-storied building with curtained windows. Anti-grav plates throughout the compound and the surrounding area gave the entire vicinity an artificial Earth-like gravity and a 200-mile diameter electronic environmental bubble allowed for a breathable atmosphere and other weather conditions that were common on Earth.

Hawkins followed Weston's glances.

"That's the living quarters of the scientists and technicians," he explained. "The long shed houses the robot assembly line."

Rick saw only a few workers about and he commented on that fact to Hawkins.

"There's only a dozen or so of us here altogether," Hawkins said. "Most of the work is done by completed robots."

"I see," Rick said. He glanced about for a moment and then lit a cigarette and blew a cloud of smoke into the cold thin air. "These robots seem to be the coming thing," he said absently. "They'll be ready for import to Earth and Mars pretty soon, won't they?"

Hawkins looked away and Rick saw that the man's face had become expressionless. It was as if a curtain had been pulled down suddenly over a lighted window.

"I wouldn't know about that," he said.

Rick didn't push the questioning any further. He knew a blank wall when he saw one. But Hawkins' reaction was interesting and he filed it away in his mind.

"Where can I find Dr. Farrel?" he asked.

"I suppose he's in his office now," Hawkins said.

"Where would that be?"

Hawkins gestured toward the four-storied building.

"Thanks. I'll be seeing you," Rick said, as he started for the doctor's office.

Hawkins smiled but his hard bright eyes were not amused.

"Sure," he said. "I'll be seeing you."

RICK crossed the cleared ground and entered the building that housed Doctor Farrel's office. A hall extended the length of the building and an open door led from this hall to a spare office, furnished with a desk, a laboratory bench and several chairs.

Rick took off his hat and stepped into the office. It was empty. He looked around curiously and then walked toward the desk.

A door on the other side of the room opened suddenly and a stooped, gray-haired man in ill-fitting clothes appeared and his eyes narrowed angrily as he saw Rick.

"Who are you?" he snapped, limping into the room. "What do you mean by snooping around my office?"

Rick felt the blood mounting to his face. He fought down his swiftly growing anger.

"I'm Captain Weston of the Earth Space Command," he said evenly. "I presume you're Doctor Farrel."

"Yes, I'm Doctor Farrel," the gray-haired man said, limping around behind his desk and sitting down. "What do you want?"

"I just arrived from Earth with a cargo of supplies," Rick answered. "I have some papers for you to sign."

Doctor Farrel grunted and picked up a glazed communication sheet from his desk.

"You're going to be here a while, Weston," he said. "I just got a message from Earth ordering you to remain here until another ship arrives." He tossed the message back to the desk and scowled at Rick. "What's it all about?" he snapped.

"I haven't the faintest idea in the world," Rick said quietly. "It's my business to take orders. I leave their interpretation to my superiors."

Doctor Farrel chewed viciously on his lower lip and glared at Rick. Rick noticed that the man's small eyes focused on his for only a second or so. They slid off his face and shifted to the top of the desk.

"You'll stay here at this building, until your ship arrives," he said. He looked up at Rick and his watery eyes held Rick's for a second, then shifted away again. "Keep away from the robot factories and don't question my men. I'll have no snooping interference in my work. Do you understand?"

"I understand," Rick said dryly. He forced back the angry words that quivered on his lips. He turned on his heel and started for the door.

"Just a minute," Doctor Farrel snapped. "I'm not through talking to you."

Rick turned in the doorway and his face was hard as chiseled granite. His steady gaze forced the doctor's eyes down to the desk.

"What do you want?" he said in a clipped, flat voice.

"I want to remind you that I am in complete charge here," Doctor Farrel said. "If you remember that we'll get along much better."

RICK opened his mouth to reply, but before he could speak, the door opened and a tall, dark-haired girl walked into the room.

"Hello, Dad," she said to the man behind the desk. "I—"

She noticed Rick then and her words trailed off in confusion. A flush of color appeared on her slim throat and crept upward to her cheeks. "I'm sorry," she said, turning to the door. "I didn't know you were busy."

"Stay where you are," Doctor Farrel said irritably. "Our guest," he added, sarcastically, "is just leaving."

Rick glanced at the girl and was surprised at her shy, hesitant beauty. Her hair, dark and lustrous, fell in simple waves to her shoulders and her features were regular and delicate. She wore a jacket and trousers of light soft leather and a wide belt was buckled about her slim waist. The costume was severely practical and yet the simple clothes accentuated the slim, gracious lines of her body. It seemed unbelievable that this lovely girl should be the daughter of the twisted, bitter man behind the desk.

Rick saw that the doctor did not intend to introduce him, so he nodded to the girl without speaking and left the room.

Outside, in the hall, he almost bumped into a tall, slender Martian. The Martian drew back and smiled pleasantly. He was as tall as Rick but he was thin, with the delicate bone-structure that was typical of his race. His lidless eyes were amber-colored, and the only difference in his appearance from that of an average Earthman was the boneless, spatulate nose and the pale greenish cast of his skin.

"You are Rick Weston, I suppose," he said, in a high, soft voice that was not unpleasant. He extended a hand. "Hawkins told me of your arrival. I am Ho Agar. Permit me to welcome you to our base."

Rick shook hands with him and said, "Thanks." He glanced at the door that led to Doctor Farrel's office and added dryly, "Doctor Farrel doesn't seem to share your sense of hospitality."

Ho Agar chuckled and patted Rick on the arm.

"Don't mind the doctor," he said. "He's a good sort underneath all that crust. You've got to know him a while before he warms up. When I first arrived I expected to be thrown out bodily before the week was over, but we get along excellently, now. Of course," he added with a grin, "there are still occasions when I think he'd like to have me boiled in oil, but they're becoming less frequent."

Rick felt his feeling of bitter anger cooling somewhat as a result of Ho Agar's friendliness.

"Well, I'm going to be here a little while," he said, "but I think I'll just keep out of his way. I don't think we'd ever develop a sweet, lasting friendship."

"Maybe not," Ho Agar smiled, "but the doctor will have forgotten he met you by tonight. You'll have to be introduced to him again at dinner."

"That's certainly something to look forward to," Rick said ironically.

Ho Agar laughed and then a look of friendly concern appeared on his face.

"I stand here gabbing," he said ruefully, "when you probably want to get to your room and get some rest. I'll take you up and see that you have everything you need. Come along."

"I'm not tired," Rick said, "but I would like to wash and get into some clean clothes."

HE FOLLOWED the Martian down the hall to an elevator that took them to the third floor. Ho Agar led him to a large comfortable room that had a shower and bath attached.

"You'll find everything simple and plain," Ho Agar said, "but I think you'll be comfortable." He sat down on the edge of the wide bed while Rick took off his leather jacket and shirt. "I'm on the same floor, a few doors down, so if you need anything at any time just give me a call."

"Thanks," Rick said. He sat down in a chair facing the Martian and lit a cigarette. "After meeting you I don't feel quite so much like an intruder." He shook his head ruefully and stared at the glowing tip of his cigarette. "Doctor Farrel practically ordered me to stay in my room until I was ready to leave for Earth again, and he told me to keep away from the robot factories in no uncertain terms. You'd think I was a well-known saboteur, to judge from his reception."

"You mustn't let that bother you," Ho Agar said. "He treats everyone that way. His life is completely absorbed with his work here and he is often suspicious and belligerent for no reason whatsoever. If you'd like to look over our plants I would be happy to act as your guide. The work we are doing here is not secretive and much of it is very interesting. Whenever you feel like taking a tour just let me know." He smiled. "You wouldn't know it to talk to Doctor Farrel but I am equally in command on this base. We don't have any arguments about the division of authority, because I let him do pretty much as he likes. I know that he is interested solely in the production of safe, dependable robot life and that is all that matters to me."

"I certainly appreciate your offer," Rick said. "I think I'd better take advantage of it as soon as possible, because I haven't any idea when my ship will arrive."

"Fine," Ho Agar said. "We'll go immediately if you like. I don't have anything pressing to do right now, and, even if I did, I feel in the mood for a holiday." He got to his feet and walked to the door. "Will half an hour be too soon?"

"Not at all," Rick said. "I can wash and change in half that time."

CHAPTER THREE

A HALF-hour later Rick and Ho Agar walked across the cleared compound to a graveled walk that led to the long steel shed that housed the robot assembly line.

"We've made great strides here," Ho Agar said, as he noted Rick's obvious interest in the sprawling factories. "Four years ago when Doctor Farrel and I arrived, this was as desolate a place as you could imagine."

"How about the doctor's daughter?" Rick asked. "I saw her but I didn't meet her. Did she come along with the doctor on the original trip?"

"You mean Rita," Ho Agar said. "She arrived about a year later. Her mother died on Earth and she had completed her schooling, so she joined her father here."

"Not a very normal life for a young girl," Rick said.

Ho Agar shrugged. "She seems contented. She acts as her father's secretary and is very efficient. She is not an easy girl to know, but I have found her very intelligent and charming."

They had reached the steel shed, and an armed guard unbolted and opened a massive steel door as they approached. Ho Agar nodded to the man and stepped through the doorway. He waited inside until Rick joined him, then he turned and swept his arm in a gesture that took in the entire mighty plant that stretched ahead of them for an unbroken mile.

"This is your first view of robot life at work," he said, over the noise of the factory. "Someday such scenes may be familiar to the entire world."

Rick stared in fascination at the hundreds of steel robots that were working with mechanical speed and rhythm beside the two long assembly lines. There was only an occasional human being visible throughout the great plant and these men were present in a supervising capacity.

Ho Agar smiled at Rick.

"It's rather impressive, isn't it?"

"It's wonderful," Rick said.

The robot workers were fashioning others of their kind. Each robot performed a specialized operation, for he had been expressly built. Some had intricate tools bolted to their wrists, others were equipped with long, sensitive steel fingers that moved with uncanny sureness and bewildering rapidity, checking delicate equipment, making minute adjustments on complicated rheostats and gauges. The robots were not uniform in shape. There were some constructed in a crouched position, others were built with extra long arms or extra-long fingers to suit more perfectly the particular work they were doing.

The heads of the robots were simply steel balls, about eight inches in diameter, with a tiny slit in the front in which was set a high-powered lens. On the chest of each robot was a coil of fine filament wire, protected by a metal screen.

"The coils," Ho Agar explained, "are simply sensitive microphones that transmit orders to the brain of the robot. The lenses you see in their foreheads act as motion-picture cameras that impress the image of what they 'see' on the robot's brain. Those operations are simply mechanical," Ho Agar continued, as he led Rick down the long assembly line, "but the real problem has been to find some way to give robots a mechanism that would act as a human brain to interpret orders."

"You seem to have solved that problem brilliantly," Rick said.

HE WATCHED a robot assembling tiny screws on the surface of a slim metal bar. The long, deft fingers moved swiftly, unerringly through the screw container, selecting the proper size and groove, then fitting them into the metal bar and moving them under a machine that automatically tightened them into place. "This robot here," he said, "is certainly more than a machine."

Ho Agar nodded. "All the workers here are completed and have passed all their tests." He glanced at a metal tag on the assembly line directly in front of the robot, on which were stamped the numerals 18435.

"Watch," he said to Rick. He turned slightly and spoke directly to the robot. "18435 cease work."

The robot stopped working immediately and waited motionlessly.

Ho Agar said to Rick, "You see they obey perfectly. They are not automatons, by any means. They actually use intelligence and reason of a sort in obeying our commands." He nodded to the robot. "You may resume work, 18435."

The robot commenced work again without an instant's hesitation.

Ho Agar walked along, pointing out various interesting phases of the robot activity, until they reached the end of the line. Ahead of them was a massive door, bolted and protected by a combination lock.

Ho Agar twirled the dial for several seconds, then swung the door open.

"Ordinarily only Doctor Farrel and I are permitted in this laboratory, but I think we can make an exception in your case," he said.

Rick followed him into a steel-walled, windowless room about forty feet square, equipped completely with delicate laboratory apparatus. One wall of the room was covered by a chest of small drawers that extended from floor to ceiling. Each drawer, of which there were thousands, bore a small white card on which a serial number and a chemical equation were inscribed.

In the center of the room was a steel table about four feet high, with powerful spring clamps at both ends and heavy leather straps dangling from its sides. There was a raised headrest at one end of the table that was set between the cushioned jaws of a vise.

"It looks like a medieval rack," Rick said.

"Its purpose is more humane," Ho Agar smiled. "In this laboratory the robots are supplied with brains. Since the operation is highly delicate, we lock the robot into an immobile position, so that it won't inadvertently upset our work with an untimely movement. The head is secured in a vise and the arms and legs are held by these clamps."

"I see," Rick said. He was silent for a moment, then said, "I'd like to ask you a question, Ho Agar. You may consider it impertinent, but I'm going to take a chance. These robots I've seen work splendidly. Why aren't you able to export some of them to Earth and Mars, now, to take over some of the work they're able to do?"

HO AGAR shook his head slowly. "We aren't ready yet," he said.

"That's what I'm asking," Rick said. "Why aren't they ready? They look ready." He shrugged and smiled. "Of course you can tell me to go to hell; it's none of my business, but I can't help being curious."

"Yes," Ho Agar said, "your curiosity is understandable." He sighed and sat down slowly, as if he were suddenly very tired. There was a serious expression on his face that Rick hadn't seen before and his eyes were solemn.

"We are near success," he said. "Our robots are eminently satisfactory in most respects. I have no doubt that we could put a number of them into service in factories on Earth and Mars with excellent results. "But," be shrugged and smiled bitterly, "we can't be sure. Things have happened here that we have kept secret, because if they were known it might prejudice the public against ever accepting robot life. I am trying to explain to you that all the robots produced here have not been successful. Some we were forced to demobilize because they were too dangerous to have about. You see," he said, glancing up at Rick with an almost pleading expression on his face, "we can't take the chance of sending a robot from here that might, even years later, go berserk and destroy human life. We must continue our experiments until we are absolutely certain that our robots will operate favorably under all circumstances, until they wear out. There can be no compromise. We either succeed or we fail. We cannot be satisfied with anything less than perfection, because the results of imperfection would be too horrible to contemplate."

"But good lord," said Rick, "haven't you been able to figure out what causes these imperfections?"

"Not yet," Ho Agar said, with a bitter shake of his head. He was silent a moment, then added, "Do you remember when Doctor Farrel first announced his theory for the creation of practical robot life?"

Rick nodded. "That was about ten years ago, wasn't it? I was just twenty-two then, in training at the Earth space school."

"Then you probably know something of the methods we use to create intelligent robot life," Ho Agar said. "Do you remember, when Doctor Farrel's plan was adopted by the Earth-Mars Federation, that we began a universal appeal for persons of sound mental health to bequeath their brains to the Foundation after their death?"

"Yes, I remember that," Rick said, nodding. "There was considerable squeamishness on the public's part for a while, but they got over that. The idea of bequeathing brain tissue to be used in robots became as common as giving blood had been a few centuries before."

"Precisely," Ho Agar said. "Doctor Farrel collected brain tissue for five years before we actually began work on our first robot. I was selected by the doctor because of my experiments in grafting metal and flesh together. Doctor Farrel's theory is comparatively simple. He experimented for years at attempting to devise a brain of some synthetic substance that would act, in lay terminology, as a sounding board to carry commands to the robot's motor system. After trying thousands of substances he used human brain tissue, which had been kept alive electrically. The results, of course, were highly satisfactory, and he announced his plan for the collection of sufficient brain tissue to build a few hundred experimental robots. Actually in six years he received enough tissue to build millions of robots, for each robot only requires a section of brain tissue a half inch square."

"I REMEMBER the response was tremendous," Rick said. "I signed up and I don't think there was a cadet at the base who didn't. My best friend, Jimmy Haines, died shortly after, and his brain was sent to the Foundation. That's why I always had a sort of personal interest in the work here."

"Haines?" Ho Agar repeated, frowning. "He died on Mars, didn't he?"

Rick nodded. "He crashed. Forgot to set his automatic controls for landing and missed the beam."

"I remember the case," Ho Agar said. "His tissue was sent here with the first consignment. Of course, we keep no record of the various brain tissue, other than a serial number and chemical formula." He pointed to the thousands of drawers in the wall cabinet. "That's our present repository, and we have thousands more on Mars, waiting to be shipped here. But it's a safe guess that your friend's brain is at work right now somewhere on the assembly line. Of course, you understand, the will and memory and personality of James Haines ceased to exist when his brain was removed from his body."

"Yes, I know that," Rick said. But it was a peculiar feeling to realize that one of those metal creatures he had passed was being motivated through the medium of a man who had been dead for nine years and whom he had known intimately and loved like a brother.

"But the one thing Doctor Farrel hadn't foreseen," Ho Agar continued, "was that using human tissue in these metal robots would endow them with certain human qualities. And that's the way it has worked. Some of our robot products have been operating for four years, admirably. Others have been unsuccessful from the start. While still others have gone along month after month giving not the slightest trouble and then have gone wild, smashing machinery, attacking other robots within their reach and generally behaving like monsters." Ho Agar spread his hands in a helpless gesture. "Last month we had our first casualty. A robot went crazy on the line and destroyed one of our guards while the man was attempting to demobilize it. We are not ready yet to admit defeat, but unless our percentage of satisfactory robots takes a sharp upswing, we'll have to face the fact that we have failed utterly."

"I see," Rick said slowly. "I can understand, now," he said, after a moment's silence, "why Doctor Farrel hasn't got the time and energy to play the gracious host."

"Yes, it weighs on him terribly," Ho Agar said. "We all feel a sense of defeat, but the doctor holds himself responsible personally for the entire failure. His room is on our floor and many nights I hear him working hours after the rest of us have gone to bed for the night."

He stood up and smiled.

"So you see there is a real excuse for his bitterness. And now I think we had better be getting back. Dinner will be served soon and Miss Farrel likes to have everyone there on time."

When they left the laboratory Rick saw the swift darkness had fallen, and a wind had sprung up, beating against the metal sides of the buildings with cold, stinging blasts. There was the feel of rain in the air as they hurried across the cleared compound and into the four-storied building that housed their sleeping quarters.

CHAPTER FOUR

DINNER was served by candlelight in a long, wood-paneled room that was warmed by a roaring, open fire. There were eight at the table: Doctor Farrel sat at the head, flanked by Ho Agar and Hawkins, the chief of the maintenance division. Rita Farrel was at the foot of the table. Rick sat at her left beside an engineer named Webber, a gaunt, taciturn man who looked hungry. Across from him, on Ho Agar's side of the table, were two research chemists, Morgan and Blair, both men in their middle fifties. Morgan was small, red-cheeked and balding; but Blair was a huge man with fiery red hair and bushy eyebrows that shadowed his small, peculiarly expressionless eyes.

Rick ate hungrily, for the food was excellent and it had been hours since he'd had a decent meal; but despite the attention he paid his food, he couldn't help noticing the strained, unnatural silence that dominated the room. Doctor Farrel ate little and his eyes circled the faces at the table restlessly.

The silence of the room was broken only by the growing fury of the storm that was blowing over the base. Great sheets of water smashed into the side of the building with a continual booming sound and above this the thin, high wail of the wind could be heard, screaming like a tortured animal.

Rick noticed that Rita Farrel shivered involuntarily as a wind-driven sheet of water struck the side of the building like surging surf, rattling the glasses on the table.

"Good night to be inside, isn't it?" he smiled.

She turned to him gratefully.

"It isn't that there's any danger," she said, "but the noise frightens me."

"I think it does everyone," Rick said. "The only advantage to storms in the void is that you never hear a thing. I remember once seeing two meteor swarms collide just beyond Earth's Heaviside layer, and it was like something from Dante's Inferno. But the only thing I heard was the sound of my cigarette striking the floor of the control cabin."

He went on talking to the girl and her nervousness faded gradually. Finally she laughed outright at something he said, and Rick saw her father's eyes focus in their direction. The old man looked irritable.

"Pardon me for interrupting your gay chatter," he said with heavy sarcasm, "but could I have your attention for a moment, Mr. Weston?"

"Certainly," Rick said.

"I have learned," Doctor Farrel said, settling back and placing his hands on the arms of his chair, "that you chose to disregard my instructions about visiting the robot assembly line. Was there any good reason for your violation of my orders or did you just spend the afternoon there because you found time heavy on your hands?"

"I was just curious," Rick said.

Hawkins looked at him and there was no smile on his face as he said, "That seems to be a predominant characteristic of yours, doesn't it?"

MORGAN, the red-cheeked, affable little chemist, smiled nervously.

"After all, gentlemen," he said with spurious heartiness, "where would science be today if men weren't curious?"

"Shut up, Morgan!" Doctor Farrel snapped. "I'm talking to Weston. I want to know, Weston, why you disregarded my orders and went snooping about the robot assembly plant?"

"Please, just one moment, Doctor," Ho Agar interposed suavely. "Mr. Weston is a guest of ours. It was at my invitation that he visited the robot plant. You are being unfair if you suppose he used his own initiative."

Doctor Farrel banged his fist suddenly on the table.

"It doesn't matter how he went there, or with whom he went," he shouted. "He was ordered not to, yet he deliberately chose to ignore that order."

"Please, Father," Rita Farrel said quietly. She glanced around the table. "Shall we have our coffee in the lounge?"

"An excellent idea, my dear," Morgan said, rising to his feet with alacrity.

Hawkins said, "I think I'll wait here until I have Weston's answer to the doctor's question."

Rick glanced at Hawkins. The man's swarthy face was flushed with anger. He wondered why his visit to the plant should have upset the doctor and Hawkins to such an extent.

"You don't like me, do you, Hawkins?" he asked quietly.

"I don't like snooping spies," Hawkins snapped. He stood up abruptly, knocking his chair to the floor. "I don't give a damn about the other men here but I'm serving warning on you right now: Keep out of my department, if you know what's good for you."

Rick smiled thinly and his face was bitterly hard.

"If I want to go into your department, Hawkins," he said, "don't try to stop me."

"I've said my piece," Hawkins said. He glared about the room for an instant and then strode through the doorway.

There was an uncomfortable silence in the room after Hawkins left. Rita Farrel stood up and the rest of the men rose to follow her into the lounge, a comfortable living room with windows that overlooked the compound.

Farrel went directly to his office and the other men drifted away, leaving Ho Agar, Farrel's daughter and Rick alone in the room.

"You mustn't mind Father," Rita Farrel said to Rick, and there was an almost pleading note in her voice. "He's so nervous and overworked that he's snapping at everyone." Her eyes begged him to understand.

"I think," Ho Agar said in his soft voice, "that Rick understands what your father and all of us are undergoing." He moved to the window and drew the curtain aside as he spoke, and the almost continual bursts of lightning revealed the glistening, mile-long shed that housed the robot workers.

"Our robots are working harmoniously now, but none of us can guess when one or more of them might transform into a raging creature of destruction."

"Please!" Rita said, turning away from the window.

"I am sorry," Ho Agar said simply.

RICK looked over the wind-swept, rain-drenched compound at the mighty robot plant and felt a sensation that was close to terror as he thought of thousands of mighty metal creatures, working with unbroken, unchanging rhythm week after week, month after month, feeling nothing, caring for nothing but their appointed work. The realization that that limitless energy might at any instant be transformed into a blind destructive force was unnerving. Rick moved away from the window, feeling an irritation with himself for letting the tension of this place get on his nerves.

Ho Agar excused himself a while later and went to his room. Rick and Rita talked for awhile over their coffee, and he found her company charming. Before long Rick and the girl glanced at her watch and gave a low exclamation of surprise.

"Why, it's almost midnight," she said. "This is way past my bedtime." She stood up and extended her hand to Rick in a frank, impulsive gesture. "Thanks for tonight," she said. "It's been fun."

Rick smoked another cigarette after the girl had gone, then went up to his own room. He undressed slowly. The storm had increased in intensity and the blasts of lightning threw weird flickering shadows into his room. He got into bed and stretched luxuriously. He switched off the light at the side of the bed and closed his eyes. In a few minutes he was asleep.

How long he slept he didn't know. Some subtle sixth sense warned him of danger and he found himself sitting upright in bed, staring into the darkness of the room, listening with straining ears for the sound that had awakened him.

The house was silent; but an instant later Rick's flesh crawled as the quiet darkness was shattered by a high-pitched scream of mortal horror.

CHAPTER FIVE

RICK sprang out of bed and snapped on the lamp; he shoved his feet into shoes, jerked his trousers on over his pajamas and stepped into the corridor.

Doctor Farrel was just emerging from his room, fully clothed. There was a dazed, helpless look on his face as he stared at Rick.

"Rita!" he gasped feebly.

Ho Agar, the Martian, appeared in the doorway of his room. He looked as if he'd been sleeping, but his eyes were alert.

"The scream came from below," he said crisply. "Let's go down."

Rick followed him down the steps at a reckless run. When they reached the second floor, Ho Agar strode along the corridor to Rita's room. One glance told them an instant and terrible story.

The door was smashed open and was hanging crazily on one hinge. There was a hole in the center panel that could have been made only by a heavy bludgeon. Inside, the room was in wild disorder. Bedclothes were strewn about the floor, a chest of drawers had been hurled on its side, and the room was empty of life.

Rick felt a tightening in his chest as he stared dazedly at the smashed room. Rita's slippers and robe were lying on a chair, mute evidence that she had not left the room of her own will. Ho Agar touched his arm and pointed to the floor, to great gouged imprints that had been ripped and splintered in the wood.

"Those marks were made by the metal stumps of a robot," he said tensely. His fingers tightened on Rick's arm. "There's not a second to lose. One of the robots has gone berserk and taken Rita. We've got to find her before—"

Doctor Farrel appeared at the door, his eyes glazed with terror.

"Where is my daughter?" he cried wildly. He shoved past Rick into the room and stared in horror at the smashed room, the torn bedclothes.

"We don't know yet," Ho Agar said, "but we'll find her. I'm sure."

He drew Rick into the corridor.

"There are weapons downstairs," he said. "We must start the search immediately. We won't wait for the others."

Downstairs, in the lounge, Ho Agar took two powerful ray-rifles from a cabinet and handed one to Rick.

"They're loaded with maximum charges and will melt anything within fifty yards," he said.

They strode into the main corridor. The front door of the structure, a solid oaken timber three inches thick had been torn completely from its frame and was lying in a crushed, splintered heap on the floor.

Ho Agar grabbed two coats from a closet off the main corridor and handed one to Rick.

"We'll need these," he shouted over the roar of the storm, which was whipping in through the open doorway. Outside, the ground was ankle-deep with rushing rivulets and the wind lashed at their faces like stinging whips. Ho Agar bent low against the force of the storm and ran across the compound to a small steel hut built at the base of the mooring tower.

HE UNLOCKED the door and the wind snapped it open with a shattering bang. Rick had followed him across the compound and when he reached the steel hut, Ho Agar was emerging, carrying in his hands two phosphorous lamps, whose brilliant rays cut through the murk of the storm for hundreds of yards.

He handed one to Rick, then, shouting to make himself heard, he said, "Follow me. There are not many places a robot could hide in this area."

Rick nodded and set out after Ho Agar. He carried his rifle in the crook of his left arm and the lamp in his right. The glaring white rays of the latter danced ahead of him for dozens of yards, but there was nothing in its range but the lashing storm and puddled ground.

Ho Agar circled the great steel structure housing the robot assembly line and set out for the rocky wastes that surrounded the Earth-Mars base.

They struggled through ravines, waist-deep in surging water, clambered to the tops of slopes, where their powerful lamps illuminated the surrounding territory for hundreds of yards, then plunged on again, making a great, ever-widening circle about the base.

It was the lightning that eventually showed them their quarry. They were standing on the top of a slope, feet braced against the buffeting power of the storm, when a brilliant fork of lightning flashed over their heads; and by its searing light Rick saw a grotesque metal figure a few hundred yards from them, staggering crazily over the rutted, craggy ground. And in the creature's extended arms was Rita Farrel, still, white and pitifully small against the metal bulk of her captor, her dark hair streaming in the wind.

Rick grabbed Ho Agar's arm and pointed; but before the Martian could turn, the glare had faded and the darkness seemed intensified.

"Follow me!" Rick shouted.

He plunged down the slope, into a shallow valley that was half full of water, fought his way against the current and started across the uneven ground on the other side with all the speed he could force from his aching legs and laboring lungs.

He tripped and sprawled headlong half a dozen times; and he couldn't be sure he was heading in the right direction, or that the robot hadn't changed his route; but he kept going, forcing one leg in front of the other, straining his eyes into the swirling blackness of the storm for some glimpse of the robot or the girl.

He had lost his lamp, and had left Ho Agar behind, but he drove on into the darkness, sobbing for breath and cursing the rutted, uneven ground that seemed to be working against him with diabolical purpose.

Another burst of lightning showed him nothing but the ragged terrain, stretching endlessly before him like some nightmare view of Hell.

HE STOPPED for an instant, his breath coming raggedly, and tried to think. He might be hundreds of yards off his course. Any of the falls he had taken might have set him off in the wrong direction; or the robot might have circled, or changed its direction after he had first sighted it.

But he couldn't stop now. There was a chance, growing slimmer each second, that the robot was still ahead of him, so he had to keep on moving forward.

He was at the base of a small slope when he started moving again, driving himself up with legs that ached and trembled. A few feet from the top of the slope he heard a noise directly ahead, and that same instant a brilliant fork of lightning ripped apart the darkness.

By its lurid light, Rick saw a great robot facing him from the top of the slope like some wild barbaric beast, its metal body gleaming in the light, its tremendous metal hands reaching toward him, fingers opening and closing convulsively.

The robot moved toward him. Rick tried to swing his gun into position but before he could do so the robot's great arm lashed out with the force of a battering ram, striking him on the shoulder and hurling him backward as if he'd been a toy doll.

He rolled down the rocky slope and the gun slipped from his hand and clattered to the base of the hill. His shoulder ached terribly and his whole side was gradually numbing from the effect of the robot's savage blow.

He crawled to his feet at the bottom of the slope and he heard the great metal feet of the robot plunging down the hill, powdering the rocky surface with their weight.

Blinded by pain and stunned by the blow he had received, Rick staggered back from the charging robot, but his foot caught on a rock and he sprawled helplessly to the ground. He started to crawl to his feet, but he felt a slim, metal surface under his hand and he realized with a sudden wild hope that he had found the ray-rifle he had dropped.

The robot was only a dozen feet away, groping toward him, his gleaming metal body shining faintly in the blackness, when Rick snapped the rifle to his shoulder and fired four murderous blasts as fast as he could trigger the weapon.

The smoking blue beams of energy struck out from the muzzle of the gun like flaming lances and Rick saw the body of the robot suddenly transformed into a shapeless mass of molten metal. There was the acrid smell of disintegrating steel in the air for an instant and then the body of the robot crashed to the rocky ground, arms and legs flailing in a last desperate convulsion.

Rick carefully circled the destroyed creature and struggled to the top of the slope. He found the girl lying beside a great boulder. Her eyes were closed but he saw that she was still breathing.

The flimsy nightdress she was wearing was wet and tattered and her face was blue with cold.

Rick removed his own coat and wrapped it about the unconscious girl, then he lifted her in his arms and started down the slope.

At the base of the slope he saw a phosphorous light in the distance coming in his direction, and a few seconds' later Ho Agar appeared, drenched and muddy, his face anxious.

He glanced quickly at the girl in Rick's arms, then felt her pulse.

"She's all right," he said. "Nothing but shock and exposure. Where is the robot?"

Rick nodded toward the shapeless mass of twisted metal and Ho Agar swung his light on the molten remains of the robot. He moved to the side of the creature and removed a metal identification plaque from one of the arms.

He read the numerals and then glanced at Rick, an ironic smile on his face.

"This was 18435," he said quietly. "The model of industry we saw working so perfectly earlier today." He shrugged and tossed the metal plaque to the ground. "After this," he said, his eyes bitter, "we can never be sure."

CHAPTER SIX

"I CAN'T understand it," Doctor Farrel said, for the dozenth time. "I can't understand it." He was sitting in his office and his eyes were glazed and unseeing. "Robot 18435 has been operating perfectly for three and a half years. I can't understand this thing tonight."

Rick sipped his hot drink and pulled the blanket about his shoulders closer to his body. Ho Agar and Hawkins were seated on the opposite side of the room. The girl had been sleeping for an hour, now, under the effects of a powerful sedative her father had given her.

"You might understand," he said dryly, "if you'd been with me when that wild monster started charging." He shook his head and took another sip from his drink. "You know your work, Doctor, but if 18435 is as close as you can come to perfection in the creation of robots, you'd better stop trying."

"I'll never stop trying," the doctor said fiercely. His hand closed over a paper on his desk and crushed it to a shapeless ball. He glared at Rick. "There was something wrong with that robot, but we'll find the trouble and remedy it if it takes us the rest of our lives."

"It may take everyone's life," Rick said pointedly. "Doesn't the fact that your own daughter was almost killed by one of your imperfect creations convince you that you're tinkering with dynamite?"

"I recognize no personal element in this incident," Doctor Farrel said coldly. "The fact that Rita was endangered is no more significant from a scientific viewpoint than if it had been an absolute stranger."

Ho Agar cleared his throat as a prelude to diplomacy.

"We all admire your zeal, Doctor Farrel," he said. "But our results are becoming more negative with each passing month. Within a very short time my superiors are going to ask me for a complete report on my work here, and if I tell them the truth they will, I am sure, withdraw their support from this activity. No one will regret this more than I, but my regret does not alter the facts."

"I don't give a damn if everybody walks out on me," Doctor Farrel snarled. "This thing tonight doesn't prove a thing; it's just one case in a million."

"I'd say one case in a million is too many," Rick said.

Hawkins looked up at him and Rick saw that his swarthy face was flushed with anger.

"You're a hero now," he said bitterly. "So you feel you've got a right to shoot you're mouth off about things here you don't know a damn thing about." He stood up and his lips were twisted in a sneer. "Well, I, for one, don't have to sit around and listen. I've got two legs and I can leave when I want to."

Rick grinned thinly at the swarthy maintenance chief. He was fed-up with Hawkins' attitude and he was determined to be pushed no further.

"You've got a lot of teeth, also," he said gently, "but if you continue to annoy me, you may find a few of them missing."

Hawkins glared at him and, for an instant, Rick thought the man was going to lunge at him. His fists were clenched at his sides and his face was flushed with anger. But Hawkins held his temper with an obvious effort, turned and strode from the office.

Rick relaxed and sipped his drink. He couldn't figure Hawkins out. The man was no coward, he'd bet on that, and he didn't seem to be a fool. With a slight shrug he dismissed the matter. A showdown was coming between Hawkins and him, but worrying about it wouldn't help.

"I think," Ho Agar said, "that you had better try and get some sleep, Rick." He smiled faintly. "You've had a busy night."

"That's a good idea," Rick said.

HE SLEPT late the next morning, then, after breakfast, he went up to see Rita Farrel. She was lying in bed, and except for the pallor of her skin and the purple shadows under her eyes she looked fairly well.

She greeted Rick with a smile, but as he sat on the edge of the bed and took her small hand in his, she stopped smiling and her face became serious.

"Ho Agar told me about last night," she said, "and there's nothing I can say to tell you how grateful I am."

Rick patted her hand gently and smiled.

"Let's forget all about it," he said. "How are you feeling?"

"Pretty good," she said. "I—Rick, there's something I want to ask you." Her eyes met his directly and her face was grave. "I feel that you're my friend and I think you'll be honest with me. Do you think my father has any right to go on with his experiments after last night?"

Rick had been afraid she might ask him that, and he'd hoped she wouldn't. "Do you mind if I smoke?" he said.

"No, but don't change the subject." Rick lit a cigarette slowly.

"I'm no scientist," he said finally. "I don't pretend to understand your father's theory, but I know it apparently works in some cases, and in some it doesn't. Now, if these imperfections were simply mechanical, if the robots would, for instance, get out of gear and fail to perform their work as they should, it wouldn't be so serious. Any machine can break down, and generally it can be fixed." He paused and blew a cloud of smoke toward the ceiling and then shook his head. "These imperfections, as I see it, aren't mechanical. They're mental. And they take violent, homicidal turns. I don't think civilization would ever want to take the chance of using robots that might break down and go on a rampage like that one did last night. So unless your father has some absolute cure figured out, I think he is endangering the lives of everyone at this base by continuing to operate the robots. I think they should all be disassembled until he has a perfect theory devised."

The girl had turned her face on the pillow as he spoke and now she said. "I was afraid you were going to say that, Rick. I realize how right you are, but," she turned to him again beseechingly, "won't you let him work along for a while longer? Your influence because of last night has grown enormously with the men. I know Moran is thinking of leaving and two of the engineers have threatened to quit. This means so much to father that it would kill him if he were forced to stop now. I don't want you to do anything actively, but if you can help him, in any small way, I'd appreciate it more than you could ever know."

Rick grinned down at the girl and there was admiration in his eyes.

"You're certainly game," he said. "I think, however, you overestimate my influence around here. But if I can help I will. Frankly, I don't like the idea, but your say-so is good enough for me."

He stood up and smoothed the soft hair back from her forehead. "I'm a sucker for a beautiful smile," he said. "Now you'd better try and rest."

HE LEFT the room and went downstairs. Ho Agar was alone.

"There's something I want you to do for me, if you will," Rick said.

"If I can," Ho Agar said.

"I'd like to spend tonight in the robot assembly laboratory," Rick said. "That's where the trouble started last night, and I'd like to be on hand tonight, in case there's a repetition. Chances are there won't be, but I want to be there just in case. Can you fix it?"

"Why, yes," Ho Agar said slowly. He looked at Rick and there was a puzzled uncertainty in his eyes. "I hope you know what you're doing, Rick. It might be very dangerous."

"I know," Rick said, "but I'm playing a hunch."

"Do you want the others to know?"

Rick shook his head. "I'll turn in early and slip out later."

"All right," Ho Agar said, "I'll arrange everything." He shook his head somberly. "But I don't like it. If anything went wrong I'd feel personally responsible. Supposing one of those robots went mad and attacked you? You wouldn't have a chance of getting out of that plant alive."

"Maybe not," Rick said, "but on the other hand, I may find out something about what causes these break-downs. The chance is worth taking."

Ho Agar argued no further. He inclined his head slightly. "I will arrange everything, Rick."

CHAPTER SEVEN

THE robot assembly factory was dark except for infrequently placed phosphorous lamps, which cast a flickering illumination over the mile-long rows of tireless metal workers. There was no sound in the plant but the rasping jar of metal and the hum of machinery; no human voices, no laughter. Seen in the weird glow of the phosphorous lamps, the vast assembly lines looked like a futuristic concept of Hell.

There was only one human being in the entire factory. Rick had been let into the plant shortly after dark by Ho Agar. He had walked up and down the line of robot workers for an hour or so, but their conduct had been exemplary. Now he was standing in the shadow of a great turbine and from that position he could command a view of the entire factory. He was beginning to feel that he had been foolish in taking the thousand-to-one chance that some trouble might develop here tonight. From what he had learned, the occasions when a robot had gone on the destructive warpath were few and far between. And he was wondering what good it would do if he did happen to be on hand when one of the robots went mad. If Doctor Farrel and Ho Agar couldn't correct the trouble, what could he hope to do?

He was idly watching the nearest group of robots, about fifty yards from him, while these thoughts were running through his head. There was one that was easily two feet taller than the others, for he had been constructed to work on an upper carriage of the line where height was essential. This robot was a giant, almost eight feet tall and probably weighing eight or nine hundred pounds.

Rick was watching this mighty creature perform his methodical task again and again with untiring strength and skill, and the sight was magnificent. The fluid, effortless flow of energy that motivated the great robot, the tireless precision of its work and its almost unimaginable power were testimonials to the genius of Doctor Farrel. Watching the mighty machine creature, Rick was forced to realize the tremendous importance of the doctor's work. If creatures like this, perfect in every detail, could ever be produced satisfactorily, civilization would advance in one giant stride to the millennium.

But suddenly his muscles tensed; the cigarette in his hand dropped to the floor.

For the giant robot had stopped work, was turning slowly, purposefully, away from its position in the line.

Rick was deep in the shadows cast by the turbine and he knew he was beyond the range of the robot's vision; but he watched tensely as the giant creature moved slowly toward him, its great hands extended gropingly.

RICK backed into the deeper shadows formed by the corner of the wall and the turbine, but as the robot continued to advance, he realized with sudden sharp horror that he was cut off from any escape, for he had trapped himself in the angle of the corner.

He cursed the thoughtlessness that had prevented him from bringing a ray-rifle; he was completely unarmed, with nothing but his bare fists to oppose the giant robot, should the mighty creature attack.

The robot was still advancing, its heavy feet striking the concrete floor with shattering force. And Rick knew then that the creature had seen him, and was closing in on him with deliberate purpose.

He had waited too long. Had he moved the instant the creature left the line he could have gotten out of the corner, but it was too late for that now. He moved tentatively to the left; but the robot moved sideways with incredible speed, blocking off his attempt.

There was no doubt now of the robot's motive.

Rick could feel the hard desperate hammering of his heart as he backed another few feet from the robot's advance; but his shoulders touched the wall and he knew he was trapped. He risked a desperate glance over his head, but he saw that the turbine extended a full thirty feet in the air, and its sides were smooth steel, offering not the slightest handhold.

He wheeled back to the robot. The creature was only a few dozen feet away, and moving closer with each passing second.

Rick felt a desperate helplessness. There wasn't one thing he could do to save himself. His fists would be ridiculously impotent against the steel power of the giant robot.

But then, from the corner of his eye, he saw that another robot had left his place at the line and was closing in rapidly on the advancing giant monster.

Rick watched the second robot breathlessly. Was it coming to the aid of the giant creature? Or was it going to attack it from the rear?

His question was answered an instant later as the second robot hurled its bulk at the unprotected back of the giant monster, toppling it to the floor with a mighty crash.

The two creatures rolled wildly on the concrete floor, their steel-thewed arms and legs threshing convulsively. The Herculean combat was madly grotesque. No sound came from the locked monsters, except the harsh rasp of steel on steel.

Rick backed away from the titanic encounter, as gradually the superior weight of the first giant robot forced the other into helplessness. Astride the second robot, its greater weight pinning it to the floor, the giant monster's huge, battering fists began to pound into its sides with sledgehammer force.

Rick watched with fascinated terror as the steel sides of the smaller robot began to bend under the terrific mauling. For a moment he was paralyzed by the horrible savagery of the giant creature's attack; then he leaped into action. He knew he might be sacrificed himself, but he couldn't stand helplessly by while the robot that had tried to save him was being pounded into a twisted, shapeless mass of metal.

THE giant robot's back was to him, and Rick lunged for the control panel that was riveted just below the creature's right shoulder. His desperate fingers had clawed the steel screen away before the giant robot realized that another antagonist had entered the struggle.

Rick jerked the screen aside and just as his hand plunged into the delicate wire apparatus that controlled the robot's actions, a great steel hand closed over his throat.

His breath stopped with a gasp, and he felt a cloud of blackness sweeping over him. With his last atom of strength his hand closed over the meshwork of filament in the robot's control section and, as he fell to the floor, his tensed fingers jerked the finely spun wires loose from their connecting rods.

He remembered striking the floor, and the feel of steel fingers about his neck, and then he passed out. How long he remained unconscious he never knew, but when he finally raised his head and pulled himself to a sitting position, he saw that the giant robot was lying motionlessly on its side, and that the smaller robot who had saved him was standing erect.

Rick stood up with an effort. He glanced at the identification tag of the standing robot and read the numerals

161. He felt his bruised throat and swallowed painfully, then turned to Robot 161. The robot's sides were pounded out of shape in several places but it looked as if it were still in a functioning condition.

"You can go back to work, 161," he said.

The robot turned slowly, moved back to its place on the assembly line and resumed its work. Rick watched it for an instant and then he walked toward the exit door of the plant. There was a grim set to his jaw and his eyes were hard. He knew, now, that Doctor Farrel's robots did not go berserk without reason. Someone was deliberately seeing to it that they went mad. And that person had tried to have him destroyed. For he realized that the giant robot that had attacked him had not done so accidentally.

It had been ordered to kill him!

CHAPTER EIGHT

RICK went directly to Ho Agar's room and entered without knocking. The Martian looked up from the book he was reading and his yellow eyes regarded Rick with surprise.

"What's the matter?" he asked anxiously, putting the book down and rising to his feet. "I thought you were going to spend the night at the plant."

Rick told him quickly what had happened. Ho Agar listened intently, his face serious.

"I was afraid something like that might happen," he said. He frowned thoughtfully. "Did you get the identification number of the robot who came to your assistance?"

Rick nodded. "It was 161. And I'm convinced that the attack of the giant robot was not accidental. I'm sure that he was ordered to kill me by someone here at the base."

Ho Agar pursed his lips and drew a slow breath through his teeth.

"What makes you believe that, Rick?" he asked.

"That creature was looking for me," Rick said flatly. "Maybe not me, personally, but it was after a human being. I was hidden in the shadows; it couldn't possibly have seen me when it left its place on the line, yet it headed directly for me. Furthermore I'm convinced, now, that Doctor Farrel's robots are all right, but that someone is deliberately making them appear to be imperfect, untrustworthy monsters. Now, here's what I want you to tell me; could someone operate the robots by a system of remote control?"

"Why, of course," Ho Agar said. His eyes narrowed thoughtfully. "Doctor Farrel developed a wireless system of communication that would direct the robot from distances of several miles. He worked on it quite extensively before you arrived but I haven't heard him mention it lately. I don't even know where the apparatus is now."

"I think," Rick said grimly, "that we may be getting warm. Do you think we could manage to search the doctor's quarters without his knowing it?"

"We could right now," Ho Agar said quickly. "He told me he intended to spend the night working in his office. His rooms are just a few doors from here, you know."

"Let's take a look," Rick said. "I hope we don't find anything, but we can't overlook the chance."

Ho Agar picked up a small flashlight and stuck a ray-revolver in his belt.

"If you're thinking what I am," he said tightly, "we may need a weapon before this night is over."

THEY went quickly to Doctor Farrel's room, opened the door and stepped inside. Rick snapped the lights on and glanced about. The room was in perfect order. The doctor's small desk was neat and bare. There were only a few letters and some pictures of himself and Rita on its clean surface. Rick winced inwardly as he saw the picture of Rita. It had been taken outdoors, and a wind was blowing the hair about her face. She was laughing, her teeth incredibly white against the tan of her face. He thought what would happen to that smile if his suspicions of her father were correct, and the thought brought him an instant of bleak misery.

But he couldn't let anything personal interfere with his work here. There had been times when he came near to forgetting that he was at this base under orders to investigate anything irregular or suspicious. He couldn't let himself forget that he had a job to do, and that Captain Wilson was depending on him.

Ho Agar had rummaged through bureau drawers and now he turned to the closet. His low, excited voice called Rick a moment later.

"Come here. I think I've found what we're looking for," he said.

Rick stepped into the closet and saw that Ho Agar had moved aside a picture that exposed a small, steel cabinet. When he opened the steel door Rick saw a control panel, covered with rheostats and gauges.

Ho Agar studied the apparatus intently. Rick watched him in silence.

"This is it," the Martian said finally. "It's the same panel the doctor built before you arrived. With it he can control the activity of every robot in his plant."

Rick stared at the equipment with hard, angry eyes.

"The man hasn't got a streak of human decency in his body," he said harshly. "He deliberately sacrificed his daughter's safety to one of his robots that was acting under his orders."

"We mustn't jump to conclusions," Ho Agar said quietly. "The existence of this apparatus is not conclusive proof that the doctor is responsible for the crimes of the robots. In itself, it proves nothing. After all, Doctor Farrel has a perfect right to install this control panel in his room, and possibly he hasn't been the one using it. Or there may be another such panel on the base, although the possibility of that is slight."

He closed the steel door and put the picture back in place.

"I think," he said, "that we had better wait until we discover more definite proof of his guilt before we say anything about this."

He stepped from the closet as he was speaking and walked to the doctor's desk. He glanced through the letters there, tossed them down and then lifted the desk blotter. A single sheet of paper was lying beneath the blotter. He picked it up and read it carefully. Finally he handed it to Rick.

"This," he said, "explains much of what has been going on here at the base."

RICK read the letter. It was addressed to the doctor, but was not signed. However, the writer, the representative of a group of financiers on Earth, was not subtle in stating the purpose of his letter. For an unspecified, but evidently large sum of money, the doctor was asked to stall the production of robots on Jupiter until the Earth authorities lost interest and abandoned the project.

Rick glanced from the letter to Ho Agar and his eyes were bitterly hard.

"I think this is all we need," he said. "There is no longer any doubt in my mind that the doctor has been responsible for the imperfect operation of the robots all along. I haven't mentioned this to anyone before, but I was sent here by the Earth authorities to investigate the situation."

Ho Agar regarded him with surprise.

"You have kept your mission well cloaked," he said.

"It was necessary," Rick said. "But now I intend to inform Earth immediately of Doctor Farrel's treachery. And I shall also tell them that they can plan to begin mass production of robots at their earliest convenience. That news should please your government too, Ho Agar."

"They will be gratified," Ho Agar said.

Rick was placing the letter on the desk when they heard heavy, jarring footsteps in the corridor and a second later the door was flung open and a robot moved into the room.

Ho Agar dropped back a pace and drew the ray weapon from his belt, but Rick caught his arm before he could fire.

"Wait!" he snapped.

The robot that stood motionless in the doorway was numbered 161, the same robot that had saved him in the plant from the attack of the giant monster. He recognized it easily from its battered, dented sides.

Ho Agar jerked his hand loose from Rick's grip.

"We can't take a chance," he said. "This robot may have been sent here by the doctor to destroy us."

"I don't think so," Rick said. "This is 161, the robot who saved my life. And it doesn't seem to have any violent intentions."

The robot lumbered forward slowly, its arms at its sides. When it reached the desk it pointed clumsily at a picture of the doctor and shook its head slowly.

"What does it mean?" Rick said to Ho Agar. He stared in bewilderment at the robot, as it pointed again to the doctor's picture and shook its head again, more emphatically this time.

"I don't know," Ho Agar said. He turned to the robot and said, "Return to your work, 161."

But the robot made no move to obey.

Ho Agar raised his gun.

"We can't take any chances," he said grimly. "When these creatures refuse to obey, there's only one thing to do."

THERE was suddenly another step in the corridor and Doctor Farrel appeared in the doorway, a gun in his hand. His eyes shifted about the room.

"What's going on here?" he cried.

He raised his gun and covered the entire group. "Don't anyone make a move until we get this thing settled."

Ho Agar moved suddenly to one side and his hand flicked out to the light switch, plunging the room into darkness. Blue bolts of energy stabbed across the blackness and Rick heard the doctor scream in agony.

Rick dropped to the floor. He saw the steel body of Robot 161 suddenly glow a cherry red, as blue blasts of energy raked across it, transforming it to a crumbling mass of molten metal.

Ho Agar said, "Are you all right, Rick?"

"Yes," Rick said.

The lights went on again and Rick saw that the doctor was lying in the doorway with two black holes in his forehead. The gun had fallen from his hand, a few inches from his distended fingers. Robot 161 was sprawled in a motionless heap on the floor, but as Rick watched its metal fingers began to move with agonizing slowness as they scratched the numeral 4 into the wooden surface of the floor.

Ho Agar was staring at the doctor's still form and there was a tight bitter set to his lips.

"I had to do it," he muttered. "It was the only thing I could do."

Rick nodded soberly and then he glanced back at the cryptic numeral 4 that Robot 161 had scratched into the flooring with its last trace of energy.

His eyes were puzzled and thoughtful.

CHAPTER NINE

TWO days later he talked to Rita Farrel for the first time since her father's death. She was sitting at the window of the lounge when he entered.

He said, "I want to talk to you for a moment, Rita."

She stood up and started for the door, but he moved his position and put his arm across the opening. "Please," he said.

She stared at him and her eyes were dark and heavy in the fragile whiteness of her face. There was no feeling or emotion for him in her expression, not even anger or hate. Her eyes were tired and indifferent.

"You can keep me here by force, I suppose," she said evenly, "but I don't see any point to that. There is nothing for us to talk about."

"You hate me because I was involved in your father's death," Rick said. "I don't blame you. I regret that it happened as it did. But there wasn't anything else Ho Agar could do."

"I see," Rita said. Her face and voice were empty of feeling. "Is that all you wanted to tell me? If you're through, I'd like to go to my room."

Rick felt a baffled feeling of exasperation at the girl's stony calmness.

"You can go to your room when I'm through talking," he said harshly. "You can't go on like this, Rita. You haven't eaten or slept in two days. The trouble here is over, you've got to realize that and stop nursing a grudge against everybody. I know how deeply you loved your father and I realize he was probably kind and wonderful to you. But that doesn't alter the fact that the evidence indicates he was a traitor to Earth."

Rita turned from him blindly, her face twisted with pain. She put a hand weakly to her forehead and said, "No—he couldn't have been a traitor! I—I won't believe that."

Rick took her hands and suddenly she was in his arms and he could feel the sobs that shook her slim shoulders.

"Oh, Rick, you didn't know him! No one really knew him," she cried.

Rick was silent until she stopped crying, then he patted her shoulders gently. "It's all right, Rita; you'll feel better now."

She moved away from him and he gave her his handkerchief.

"Will you talk to me for a few minutes now?" he asked.

SHE nodded and he led her to the divan before the fire. He lit two cigarettes, handed one to her and then shifted about to face her squarely.

"Please listen carefully," he said. "I said the evidence indicated that your father might have been a traitor. But that evidence is all circumstantial. You were closer to your father than anyone else, and I think maybe you know something that would explain his actions. Can you remember his speaking of an offer from a group of financiers on Earth who wanted him to sabotage the production of robot life?"

Rita shook her head distractedly. "Of course not, Rick," she said. "That's the most ridiculous thing in the whole setup. Father would have sacrificed his own life before allowing anything to interfere with the robot plant. And here's another thing, Rick, those robots couldn't have done these terrible things on Father's orders because they are designed only to work. They would never attack a human being under anyone's orders. Father realized in later years they might be used as soldiers, so he designed them to do only creative work."

"But one of them attacked you," Rick said.

"I know, I know," Rita said helplessly. "But there must be some other explanation for that. Father's robots wouldn't attack anyone, even under his orders. He tested them for that many, many times."

Rick stared at the girl intently.

"Are you sure of what you're saying? You mean your father actually tested these robots, ordered them to attack human beings, and they refused?"

"Yes," Rita said emphatically. "And he wasn't satisfied with one test. He tested each robot a number of times."

"I see," Rick said. He looked thoughtfully at the glowing tip of his cigarette. He was still of the opinion that Rita's father had been mixed up in the dirty business here, but a new idea had occurred to him.

"The thing that has me puzzled," he said, frowning, "is the action of Robot 161. That robot saved my life in the assembly plant, and when it came to your father's room it seemed to be trying to tell me something. It pointed to your father's picture and then shook its head. And after Ho Agar had burned it down, it scratched a number 4 on the floor. I've stewed over that until my head aches and I've gotten nowhere. What possible significance could the numeral 4 have in this business? Can you think of anything?"

"No," Rita said slowly, "I can't."

Rick heard a step in the corridor and, turning his head, he saw Ho Agar appear in the doorway. The Martian looked from the girl to Rick and said, "I beg your pardon. I'll come back later ."

"Come on in," Rick said, getting to his feet. "Rita and I are through with our discussion."

THE girl stood up and left the room without looking at Ho Agar. When they were alone, the Martian shrugged his shoulders helplessly.

"She hates me," he said, and there was a look of pain on his thin features. "She thinks of me as her father's murderer. Her reaction is understandable but that makes it no easier to bear."

"I think she'll get over it," Rick said. He lit another cigarette and flicked the match into the fire. "By the way," he said abruptly, "have you had the communication equipment repaired yet? I should have been in contact with Earth forty-eight hours ago. Strange that it had to go on the blink just when I needed it most."

"It will be ready shortly, Rick," Ho Agar said. He looked thoughtfully at the young Earthman. "Are you going to report that Doctor Farrel's robot experiments were successful?"

"Why, of course," Rick said, surprised. "I told you that a couple of days ago. We agreed it was pretty obvious that the doctor had ordered the robots to go on a destructive rampage."

"Yes, I know," Ho Agar said, "but I wonder if the robots are ready yet for export to Earth and Mars. It would be a calamity if we were wrong in our suppositions and innocently sent out a group of imperfect robots."

"But there are no imperfect robots," Rick said. "I'm convinced of that, now. And I'm going to send that information to Earth just as soon as possible."

"Well," Ho Agar shrugged, "I suppose that it is the best procedure. There have been no disturbances in the robot plant since the doctor's death, which seems fairly conclusive evidence that he was responsible for their imperfect behavior."

"When the communication set is repaired I want to get that message off immediately," Rick said. "Will you let me know when it's ready?"

"Of course," Ho Agar said.

Rick left him, then, and went up to change for dinner. When he came down again, an hour or so later, Rita was waiting for him in the lounge. She had changed to a light, knee-length dress and her hair was brushed back from her forehead in clean, shining waves.

"You look simply terrific," Rick said, smiling at her in admiration.

"Thanks, Rick," she said. "I feel better, too, since our talk. I realize now that Father's development of robot life has been successfully accomplished, and that's all that really matters. He wouldn't have cared about what people thought, as long as his dream had been realized. And I think that now, wherever he is, he knows his work has been successful and is happy."

Rick looked at her, his face serious.

"You're a very wonderful girl, Rita," he said quietly. "There aren't many who'd take that attitude and I'm proud of you."

Rita smiled and said, "You make me sound a little awe-inspiring. I'm not the type for a halo, you know. Let's change the subject. Ho Agar was here a while ago, and he asked me to tell you that the communication set isn't ready yet, but he expects to have it in working order in another hour or so."

Rick shook his head in irritation.

"Where did he go, do you know?"

"No, I don't," Rita said. She glanced up as Moran, the chemist, and two other workers entered the room. "Come in, gentlemen," she said. "Rick, here, is on edge because he can't send a message through to Earth, so maybe you can cheer him up."

"I'm just the one for that," Moran said, smiling genially. He went over to the sideboard and took up a bottle. "I'll fix you a drink that'll take your mind off everything." He mixed several drinks and passed them around. "And what is this message that can't wait until after dinner?" he asked.

"It's important," Rick said. "I want to inform Earth that Doctor Farrel's robots are in perfect working order and that they can be exported to Earth immediately."

"No wonder you're on edge," Moran said. "Good news like that can't be sent too quickly."

Rick was raising his drink to his mouth, when the door was flung open and Hawkins charged into the room. His dark features were flushed and his eyes were snapping blackly.

"What's up?" Rick asked.

Everyone in the room had turned to stare at Hawkins. A tension came over them as he stood in the doorway, legs spread wide, and stared about with hard, angry eyes.

"Hell to pay!" he snapped. "Two more robots have just gone crazy. They're on a rampage!"

The shocked silence following Hawkins' announcement was broken by a brittle, shattering sound as Rita Farrel's glass slipped from her hand to the floor.

CHAPTER TEN

RICK stood stock-still for an instant, frozen in rigid paralysis by Hawkins' words.

Moran said, "Well, I'll be damned." in a slow, incredulous voice.

"We can't just stand here," Hawkins said tersely. "I'm rounding up the men and starting for the plant. You men arm yourselves with ray rifles and then follow as soon as possible."

He turned quickly and left the room with long, decisive strides.

Rick tossed his cigarette into the fire and started for the doorway, but Rita Farrel caught his arm before he had taken three steps.

"Please, let me come with you, Rick," she said.

"No," Rick said. "This is no job for a girl. Don't worry, we'll be able to handle it all right."

Ho Agar appeared in the doorway while Rick was talking to the girl, and his eyebrows lifted questioningly as he regarded the Earthman.

"Trouble?" he asked calmly.

Rick nodded grimly. "Lots. More robots are running wild. Hawkins is taking the men down to the plant now, to stop them."

"I see...I see," Ho Agar said. He looked off in the distance and shook his head slowly. "I'm afraid this certainly destroys my last hope of producing harmless robot-life. Incidentally," he added ironically, "the communication set is repaired, but of course you can't very well send the message you intended."

"No, I can't," Rick said grimly, "but I'm going to send another equally as important."

"And that is…?"

"I'm going to ask the Earth authorities," Rick said, "to send an official investigation committee here to get to the bottom of all this robot trouble. I'm convinced now that there is something going on—something that none of us understands."

"I think you're right," Ho Agar said, "but let's attend to the imperfect robots before we do anything else."

"Rick," Rita cried, "please let me come along."

"We may need every weapon at the base before this is finally over," Ho Agar said, glancing at Rick. "And Miss Farrel is an excellent shot. I think we had better take her with us."

Rick said, "Okay, get yourself a rifle. I don't like the idea but Ho Agar may be right. We may need you before we get things under control."

FIVE minutes later the three of them had reached the entrance to the robot plant. Hawkins was waiting outside with a group of armed men.

"We're going in the front entrance," he said, when Rick, Ho Agar and Rita arrived.

"That's the plan?" Rick asked.

"That's the plan."

"Let me make a suggestion," Ho Agar said quickly. "Rick and Miss Farrel and I will go in through the rear entrance, the one that leads to the brain laboratory. You men go in the front and between us we'll have the robots caught in a cross-fire."

"Okay," Hawkins said, "but be careful of your aim. We don't want to burn each other into cinders."

Rick held Rita's arm as they hurried through the dark, moving along the side of the robot plant behind Ho Agar. The night was black and occasionally they stumbled on the rutted, hard ground.

"Watch your step," Ho Agar called from in front of them. "And keep your weapons ready for use."

They reached the end of the building in about ten minutes. Rita's breath was coming hard, but she had kept up with the stiff pace Ho Agar had set.

The Martian turned the corner of the building and stopped before a solid steel door, protected with a formidable combination lock. He worked silently in the darkness for several moments, then swung the door open and stepped through its black opening.

"Follow me," he said. "I'll have a light on in a moment."

Rick moved cautiously into the laboratory with Rita at his side. His hands, extended gropingly before him in the blackness, suddenly touched someone.

"Ho Agar," he said. "Is that you?"

There was no answer. Rick heard a footstep on the hard floor and he could dimly make out the outline of a man in the darkness.

A flashing premonition shot through him, and he stepped back quickly, but the sixth sense warning had come too late. He saw vaguely an arm swinging down in the darkness and the next instant a hard blunt object crashed with stunning force into his forehead.

His knees buckled and he started to fall. He fought against the curtain of blackness that was drawing over his consciousness, but it was no use. The last sound he heard was Rita Farrel's high, piercing scream, but that faded away too as his limp body struck the floor...

WHEN consciousness returned he was aware of a light against the lids of his eyes, and when he attempted to move he realized he was strapped to a chair in a sitting position. There was an aching pain where he had been struck on the forehead, and his stomach felt restless.

He opened his eyes, raised his head with a painful effort. Ho Agar was standing before him, a faint mocking smile brushing his lips.

"Ah..." he murmured, "I'm relieved to see that you are yourself again."

Rick stared at him stupidly. He glanced dazedly about the steel-walled laboratory and down at the leather straps that bound him securely to the chair; then he looked up at Ho Agar again, his brain reeling in helpless bewilderment.

"What's this all about?" he said thickly. He stared at the Martian's thin, mocking smile and he felt a sudden tight knot of terror in his breast. "Where's Rita?" he demanded, struggling against the tight leather straps.

"Don't waste your energy," Ho Agar said calmly. "I strapped you in that chair myself and there's no chance of your getting loose. As for Rita," he smiled and stepped aside, "she also is—ah—confined."

He pointed to the table on which robots were secured while their brains were being inserted.

Rita Farrel was lying on its steel surface, helplessly bound. Iron clamps held her ankles and wrists, and her head was secured in the padded jaws of the giant vise. Her eyes were closed but Rick could see that she was breathing.

Hot, wild anger shot through him and he twisted futilely against the straps that held him and glared at Ho Agar.

"If you hurt her I'll tear you apart with my bare hands," he raged. "You—"

"Please." Ho Agar smiled. He sat down comfortably and crossed his long legs. "I have no intention of hurting Miss Farrel. But I may be forced to, if you do not cooperate."

"What do you mean?" Rick said.

"I won't keep you in suspense any longer," Ho Agar said. "As you have probably guessed by now I have been responsible for the imperfect operation of the robot-life here on Jupiter. Poor Doctor Farrel was an innocent, industrious scientist and I found it a simple matter to throw the blame on him. Now I want you, my dear Rick, to send a message to Earth. I have a communication set in this laboratory and I wish you to inform your superiors that Doctor Farrel's robots are completely out of hand, and that his theories and robot designs are completely unfeasible. In short, that the entire experiment here has been a complete and decidedly hazardous failure."

Rick stared at Ho Agar incredulously. He couldn't make sense of what the Martian was saying so calmly.

"You were responsible for the robot destruction here?" he finally said.

"Completely," Ho Agar said quietly. "My planet needs robot-life, Rick, and it needs the processes and formulae of Doctor Farrell; but we do not intend to share robot production with Earth. When we have the sole command of robot production we will most likely become the leading planet within the Solar System." He smiled tightly. "Our relative position in the Solar System is fourth, but we will eventually transform that, in a figurative sense, to first and foremost, through the power that Doctor Farrel's robots will bring us."

RICK stared at Ho Agar with blazing eyes.

"Mars, the fourth planet of the System!" he said bitterly. "That's what Robot 161 was trying to tell me. That was what the numeral 4 meant. And that's why it came to the doctor's room that night and tried to prevent you from murdering Doctor Farrel."

Ho Agar nodded and smiled.

"Everything you say is quite true," he said. "I have only your stupidity to thank for my continued success. At first I was afraid you were going to guess the truth, but like a typical sentimental Earthman, you were unable to think of me as an enemy because I had posed as your friend. I knew from the start that you were here as an investigator. Martian Intelligence informed me of that. I staged the kidnapping of Miss Farrel, hoping that would convince you of the unreliability of the doctor's robots; but you allowed your judgment to be blinded by Miss Farrel's undeniably attractive charms.

"I then had you attacked in the assembly plant, hoping to get you out of the way, but the unfortunate intervention of Robot 161 spoiled my plans. There again your stupidity became my chief asset. Had you been thinking clearly you might have seen that I was the only one who knew of your presence that night at the robot plant, and therefore was the only person who could have arranged the attack. But that point escaped you. I didn't want to take any more chances so I showed you the apparatus in the doctor's room and then shot him when he came in to investigate the noises he had heard from below.

"Robot 161 almost upset my plans, but luck was with me and I put it out of the way at the same time. Incidentally," Ho Agar said, smiling mockingly, "it might interest you to know that the brain that motivated Robot 161 was taken from your friend whom we discussed here in this laboratory the day you arrived. I am referring to your comrade and fellow space pilot, James Haines."

Jimmy Haines!

Rick felt a bitterness that was deeper than any emotion he had ever experienced in his life. He had no conscious thoughts; his brain was too numb for that. There was only one idea in his mind and it seemed to flow through his entire body. And that was the thought of getting his hands about Ho Agar's slender neck and choking the rotten life from the man.

"I still don't understand just how Robot 161 was able to disregard my orders," Ho Agar said musingly. "You see 161 was supposed to aid the giant robot in killing you; instead 161 saved you and destroyed the giant."

RICK was beginning to think again with some calmness, and he realized that his only chance was in keeping Ho Agar talking until Hawkins and his men subdued the rampaging robots and got to the laboratory.

He forced a smile to his lips.

"You were pretty clever," he said. "And since you hold all the cards, maybe you'll tell me how you managed to control the robots. I understand they wouldn't react to any but the work commands for which they were constructed."

"Absolutely right," Ho Agar said, smiling. "But fifty of the robots are special products of mine. Each of these special robots was equipped with two brains. One brain was normal and directed their activities at work. But the second brain, which was separated from the normal brain by a thin plastic sheet, I took from a special stock of demented, paranoiac brains that were secured for me from certain institutions on Mars. When I needed a robot for a—uh—demonstration, I simply sent an electrical current from this laboratory to two poles, which I had already built into the head of each special robot, and the plastic protection sheet was burned away. This caused the normal brain to be destroyed. Then the creature began to move under the direction of a paranoiac brain, which I could control. It was really very simple."

"You're out of your mind," Rick said evenly. "You'll never get away with this. Hawkins and the men are on their way through the plant now. They'll be here any minute. You can kill me and the girl but you'll never escape, and Mars will never get the formulae and theories of Doctor Farrel."

"I beg to differ with you," Ho Agar said smoothly. He held up a slim hand and cocked his head in a listening attitude. A contented smile appeared on his features as the faint sounds of mechanical clamor became audible.

"Hawkins and his brave men," he murmured, "entered the plant to burn down two imperfect robots. That, at least, was what they thought."

HE CHUCKLED and rubbed his slim hands together in a pleased gesture. "Actually there are about forty-five paranoiac robots in the plant, and I timed their eruption so it would occur when Hawkins and his men were in the center of the plant and unable to escape to the front entrance." He listened again to the clamor that was drifting faintly to their ears. "They won't have much chance against forty-five robots, will they, Rick?"

"You cold-blooded murderer!" Rick raged. "You've worked with those men for four years and now you send them to a horrible death without batting an eye."

"Sentiment is a barbaric sort of expression," Ho Agar said idly. He shifted slightly in his chair and said, "and now, Rick, since I have been so obligingly verbose, I hope you will repay the favor and send the message I wish to Earth."

"Supposing I tell you to go to hell?" Rick said.

"That will gain you nothing," Ho Agar said. "And it might make Miss Farrel's next few minutes very uncomfortable." He raised a slim hand as Rick strained powerfully against his bonds. "Oh, I am not thinking of torturing her," he said. "I think you should credit me with more delicacy than that. I shall, however, be forced to anesthetize her and equip her with a paranoiac brain that came, I believe, from a degenerate Martian. I wouldn't like to do that, Rick, but I don't think I shall have to. I don't think you will sit there and watch me perform an operation of that sort, when two minutes at this communication set will obviate that necessity."

"You wouldn't dare," Rick said hoarsely.

"No?" Ho Agar smiled. "I think you underestimate me. I am going to give you just ten seconds to make up your mind."

"Supposing I do what you ask," Rick said. "What will you do to Rita then?"

Ho Agar shrugged. "I will probably take her to Mars with me to assist in the production of her father's robot units. But that doesn't matter. Anything, even death, would be preferable to the operation and brain substitution I propose to perform. I think you can see that."

Rita twisted slightly on the table and Rick saw that her eyelids were open.

"I've heard everything, Rick," she said clearly. "Don't send that message to Earth. It doesn't matter what happens to me. Please don't send it."

Ho Agar smiled and bowed mockingly to the helpless girl.

"A splendid sentiment, Miss Farrel," he said, "but the decision is Rick's." He turned back to Rick. "And what shall your decision be, my dear Rick?"

"I'll send the message," Rick said evenly.

"Excellent," Ho Agar said.

He walked to the wall, pulled out a portable space-communication set and rolled it to the side of Rick's chair, within easy reach.

"I shall release your right arm," he said, "but I'd advise you not to do anything foolish."

He drew a ray-revolver from his belt, then stopped and unbuckled the strap that secured Rick's right wrist. Stepping back a pace, he pointed the gun at Rick's head and said, "Now go ahead. I am familiar with your code so don't think you can fool me with a fake message." He gestured impatiently with the gun. "Get busy. There is not too much time."

RICK reached for the key but at that instant there was a sudden shattering impact against the lab door and its steel sides trembled under the effects of tremendous blows.

Ho Agar swung toward the door and his eyes lost their calm triumph, as the mighty steel door began to sag inward.

His features working with savage terror, he wheeled back to Rick.

"Send that message, damn you!" he blazed. His trigger finger whitened with pressure as he stepped closer and shoved the gun against Rick's head. "Send it!" he repeated, his voice a desperate whisper.

Suddenly the massive steel door crashed inward and two mighty robots staggered into the room. Behind them was the swarthy figure of Hawkins, a ray-revolver in his hand.

Ho Agar spun around, but before he could pull the trigger of his gun Rick swung down across his wrist with his free hand, deflecting his aim. Hawkins took in the situation with one hard glance and then raised his gun and sent three streaking bolts of energy into Ho Agar's body.

The Martian screamed horribly and his face was a twisted mask of anguish and rage as he toppled to the floor. He fell on his side and for an instant his eyes met Rick's; and there was an insane gleam in their depths that was like a glimpse into the pits of Hell. And then the light faded in his eyes forever and he rolled limply to his back.

Hawkins crossed to Rick's side and released him, then the two men freed the girl. She clung to Rick, sobbing, when he lifted her from the steel table, but after a moment she smiled weakly.

"Sorry," she said. "It—it's just relief, I guess."

Hawkins was looking down at Ho Agar's lifeless body with bitter eyes.

"I never figured him," he said, shaking his head. He glanced at Rick. "How'd he manage it?"

Rick told him the complete story.

When he finished Hawkins said, "It's just pure dumb luck that we got here in time. When we found forty of those damn devilish robots on the warpath instead of just two, we thought we were goners for sure; but I thought of something that should've occurred to us long ago. The doctor's robots were strictly conditioned not to attack human beings, but they would attack other robots under orders. Just as we were about ready to toss in the sponge I yelled for help to the hundreds of peaceful robots and they didn't hesitate for a moment. It was a total madhouse out there on the line for a while, but it wasn't too long before they cornered and wrecked the defective robots, then went back to work." He wiped his forehead with the back of his hand and then grinned at Rick. "I had you figured all wrong; Weston. You're okay."

Rick held out his hand and smiled.

"Forget it," he said. "We were both way off in our estimates, I think."

Hawkins said, "Well, I'll let the men get busy cleaning up the mess out there." He nodded to Rick and then walked away from the laboratory, a faint smile on his dark features.

RICK lit two cigarettes carefully and handed one to the girl.

"It's all over," he said. "Ho Agar was right when he said I was a sentimental fool. I should've realized he was our man, but it just never occurred to me. If it hadn't been for Robot 161, neither of us would be alive right now."

Rita said, "I still don't understand how that particular robot was able to act of its own free will. Didn't Ho Agar say that it was one of the robots that he had equipped with two brains? And when he burned away the plastic sheet between the two brains, the normal one should have been destroyed, but it wasn't—it continued to function and it tried to warn you about Ho Agar."

Rick nodded somberly.

"Yes, the numeral 4 referred to Ho Agar, the Martian, the inhabitant of the fourth planet of our Solar System. I was a fool not to have thought of that. But I think I can understand why the paranoiac brain didn't gain control of the robot's normal brain."

"Why?" Rita asked. "That's just the one point I can't understand."

"Well—" Rick smiled faintly, and his thoughts were ten years back in time, to a red-haired youngster who had fought his way through the Earth space-school on sheer guts, "—you never knew Jimmy Haines, but he was a pretty stubborn guy."

He smiled into Rita's eyes and put his arm around her shoulders and drew her close to him.

"Maybe there's some other explanation, but I prefer to believe that one."

"Ho Agar was right," Rita said gently. "You are a sentimental fool."

Rick grinned wryly. "I suppose so," he said. "Does that make any difference to you?"

"I wouldn't have you any other way," Rita smiled.

She raised herself on tiptoes and kissed him softly on the lips.

THE END

If you've enjoyed this book, you will not want to miss these terrific titles…

ARMCHAIR SCI-FI & HORROR DOUBLE NOVELS, $12.95 each

D-31   **A HOAX IN TIME** by Keith Laumer
INSIDE EARTH by Poul Anderson

D-32   **TERROR STATION** by Dwight V. Swain
THE WEAPON FROM ETERNITY by Dwight V. Swain

D-33   **THE SHIP FROM INFINITY** by Edmond Hamilton
TAKEOFF by C. M. Kornbluth

D-34   **THE METAL DOOM** by David H. Keller
TWELVE TIMES ZERO by Howard Browne

D-35   **HUNTERS OUT OF SPACE** by Joseph Kelleam
INVASION FROM THE DEEP by Paul W. Fairman,

D-36   **THE BEES OF DEATH** by Robert Moore Williams
A PLAGUE OF PYTHONS by Frederick Pohl

D-37   **THE LORDS OF QUARMALL** by Fritz Leiber and Harry Fischer
BEACON TO ELSEWHERE by James H. Schmitz

D-38   **BEYOND PLUTO** by John S. Campbell
ARTERY OF FIRE by Thomas N. Scortia

D-39   **SPECIAL DELIVERY** by Kris Neville
NO TIME FOR TOFFEE by Charles F. Meyers

D-40   **JUNGLE IN THE SKY** by Milton Lesser
RECALLED TO LIFE by Robert Silverberg

ARMCHAIR SCIENCE FICTION CLASSICS, $12.95 each

C-10   **MARS IS MY DESTINATION**
by Frank Belknap Long

C-11   **SPACE PLAGUE**
by George O. Smith

C-12   **SO SHALL YE REAP**
by Rog Phillips

ARMCHAIR SCIENCE FICTION & HORROR GEMS SERIES, $12.95 each

G-3   **SCIENCE FICTION GEMS, Vol. Two**
James Blish and others

G-4   **HORROR GEMS, Vol. Two**
Joseph Payne Brennan and others

If you've enjoyed this book, you will not want to miss these terrific titles…

ARMCHAIR SCI-FI, FANTASY, & HORROR DOUBLE NOVELS, $12.95 each

D-41   **FULL CYCLE** by Clifford D. Simak
IT WAS THE DAY OF THE ROBOT by Frank Belknap Long

D-42   **THIS CROWDED EARTH** by Robert Bloch
REIGN OF THE TELEPUPPETS by Daniel Galouye

D-43   **THE CRISPIN AFFAIR** by Jack Sharkey
THE RED HELL OF JUPITER by Paul Ernst

D-44   **PLANET OF DREAD** by Dwight V. Swain
WE THE MACHINE by Gerald Vance

D-45   **THE STAR HUNTER** by Edmond Hamilton
THE ALIEN by Raymond F. Jones

D-46   **WORLD OF IF** by Rog Phillips
SLAVE RAIDERS FROM MERCURY by Don Wilcox

D-47   **THE ULTIMATE PERIL** by Robert Abernathy
PLANET OF SHAME by Bruce Elliot

D-48   **THE FLYING EYES** by J. Hunter Holly
SOME FABULOUS YONDER by Phillip Jose Farmer

D-49   **THE COSMIC BUNGLERS** by Geoff St. Reynard
THE BUTTONED SKY by Geoff St. Reynard

D-50   **TYRANTS OF TIME** by Milton Lesser
PARIAH PLANET by Murray Leinster

ARMCHAIR SCIENCE FICTION CLASSICS, $12.95 each

C-13   **SUNKEN WORLD**
by Stanton A. Coblentz

C-14   **THE LAST VIAL**
by Sam McClatchie, M. D.

C-15   **WE WHO SURVIVED (THE FIFTH ICE AGE)**
by Sterling Noel

ARMCHAIR MASTERS OF SCIENCE FICTION SERIES, $16.95 each

MS-5   **MASTERS OF SCIENCE FICTION, Vol. Five**
Winston K. Marks—Test Colony and other tales

MS-6   **MASTERS OF SCIENCE FICTION, Vol. Six**
Fritz Leiber—Deadly Moon and other tales

If you've enjoyed this book, you will not want to miss these terrific titles…

If you've enjoyed this book, you will not want to miss these terrific titles…

ARMCHAIR SCI-FI & HORROR DOUBLE NOVELS, $12.95 each

D-61　**THE MAN WHO STOPPED AT NOTHING** by Paul W. Fairman
　　　　TEN FROM INFINITY by Ivar Jorgensen

D-62　**WORLDS WITHIN** by Rog Phillips
　　　　THE SLAVE by C.M. Kornbluth

D-63　**SECRET OF THE BLACK PLANET** by Milton Lesser
　　　　THE OUTCASTS OF SOLAR III by Emmett McDowell

D-64　**WEB OF THE WORLDS** by Harry Harrison and Katherine MacLean
　　　　RULE GOLDEN by Damon Knight

D-65　**TEN TO THE STARS** by Raymond Z. Gallun
　　　　THE CONQUERORS by David H. Keller, M. D.

D-66　**THE HORDE FROM INFINITY** by Dwight V. Swain
　　　　THE DAY THE EARTH FROZE by Gerald Hatch

D-67　**THE WAR OF THE WORLDS** by H. G. Wells
　　　　THE TIME MACHINE by H. G. Wells

D-68　**STARCOMBERS** by Edmond Hamilton
　　　　THE YEAR WHEN STARDUST FELL by Raymond F. Jones

D-69　**HOCUS-POCUS UNIVERSE** by Jack Williamson
　　　　QUEEN OF THE PANTHER WORLD by Berkeley Livingston

D-70　**BATTERING RAMS OF SPACE** by Don Wilcox
　　　　DOOMSDAY WING by George H. Smith

ARMCHAIR SCIENCE FICTION & FANTASY CLASSICS, $12.95 each

C-19　**EMPIRE OF JEGGA**
　　　　by David V. Reed

C-20　**THE TOMORROW PEOPLE**
　　　　by Judith Merril

C-21　**THE MAN FROM YESTERDAY**
　　　　by Howard Browne as by Lee Francis

C-22　**THE TIME TRADERS**
　　　　by Andre Norton

C-23　**ISLANDS OF SPACE**
　　　　by John W. Campbell

C-24　**THE GALAXY PRIMES**
　　　　by E. E. "Doc" Smith

If you've enjoyed this book, you will not want to miss these terrific titles...

ARMCHAIR SCI-FI & HORROR DOUBLE NOVELS, $12.95 each

D-71   **THE DEEP END** by Gregory Luce
            TO WATCH BY NIGHT by Robert Moore Williams

D-72   **SWORDSMAN OF LOST TERRA** by Poul Anderson
            PLANET OF GHOSTS by David V. Reed

D-73   **MOON OF BATTLE** by J. J. Allerton
            THE MUTANT WEAPON by Murray Leinster

D-74   **OLD SPACEMEN NEVER DIE!** John Jakes
            RETURN TO EARTH by Bryan Berry

D-75   **THE THING FROM UNDERNEATH** by Milton Lesser
            OPERATION INTERSTELLAR by George O. Smith

D-76   **THE BURNING WORLD** by Algis Budrys
            FOREVER IS TOO LONG by Chester S. Geier

D-77   **THE COSMIC JUNKMAN** by Rog Phillips
            THE ULTIMATE WEAPON by John W. Campbell

D-78   **THE TIES OF EARTH** by James H. Schmitz
            CUE FOR QUIET by Thomas L. Sherred

D-79   **SECRET OF THE MARTIANS** by Paul W. Fairman
            THE VARIABLE MAN by Philip K. Dick

D-80   **THE GREEN GIRL** by Jack Williamson
            THE ROBOT PERIL by Don Wilcox

ARMCHAIR SCIENCE FICTION CLASSICS, $12.95 each

C-25   **THE STAR KINGS**
            by Edmond Hamilton

C-26   **NOT IN SOLITUDE**
            by Kenneth Gantz

C-32   **PROMETHEUS II**
            by S. J. Byrne

ARMCHAIR SCIENCE FICTION & HORROR GEMS SERIES, $12.95 each

G-7   **SCIENCE FICTION GEMS, Vol. Seven**
            Jack Sharkey and others

G-8   **HORROR GEMS, Vol. Eight**
            Seabury Quinn and others

If you've enjoyed this book, you will not want to miss these terrific titles…

ARMCHAIR SCI-FI, FANTASY, & HORROR DOUBLE NOVELS, $12.95 each

D-81   **THE LAST PLEA** by Robert Bloch
         OMEGA by Robert Sheckley

D-82   **WOMAN FROM ANOTHER PLANET** by Frank Belknap Long
         HOMECALLING by Judith Merril

D-83   **WHEN TWO WORLDS MEET** by Robert Moore Williams
         THE MAN WHO HAD NO BRAINS by Jeff Sutton

D-84   **THE SPECTRE OF SUICIDE SWAMP** by E. K. Jarvis
         IT'S MAGIC, YOU DOPE! by Jack Sharkey

D-85   **THE STARSHIP FROM SIRIUS** by Rog Phillips
         FINAL WEAPON by Everett Cole

D-86   **TREASURE ON THUNDER MOON** by Edmond Hamilton
         TRAIL OF THE ASTROGAR by Henry Haase

D-87   **THE VENUS ENIGMA** by Joe Gibson
         THE WOMAN IN SKIN 13 by Paul W. Fairman

D-88   **THE MAD ROBOT** by William P. McGivern
         THE RUNNING MAN by J. Holly Hunter

D-89   **VENGEANCE OF KYVOR** by Randall Garrett
         AT THE EARTH'S CORE by Edgar Rice Burroughs

D-90   **DWELLERS OF THE DEEP** by Don Wilcox
         NIGHT OF THE LONG KNIVES by Fritz Leiber

ARMCHAIR SCIENCE FICTION CLASSICS, $12.95 each

C-28   **THE MAN FROM TOMORROW**
         by Stanton A. Cobllentz

C-29   **THE GREEN MAN OF GRAYPEC**
         by Festus Pragnell

C-30   **THE SHAVER MYSTERY, Book Four**
         by Richard S. Shaver

ARMCHAIR MASTERS OF SCIENCE FICTION SERIES, $16.95 each

MS-7   **MASTERS OF SCIENCE FICTION AND FANTASY, Vol. Seven**
         Lester Del Rey, "The Deadliest Female" and other tales

MS-8   **MASTERS OF SCIENCE FICTION, Vol. Eight**
         Milton Lesser, "'A' is for Android" and other tales

NO ONE WAS SAFE FROM THE POWERFUL FORCE!

"I can't tell you my name," the trembling man stammered out. "I'm simply a man, Mr. Munro—a man running for his life! But whether I'm able to stay alive or not, someone else must know what I know…"

And what the running man knew was incredible and horrifying. But before the night was over, the running man was dead, and with that, Jeff Munro had to believe the horrifying truth. And he had to find a way to destroy the evil power that was loose upon the world. It had come from outer space, reaching into our Solar System from a faraway star. It was a power that could invade men's minds. It was a power capable of ruling the entire universe.

CAST OF CHARACTERS

JEFF MUNRO
Finding answers about a cult was going to be more difficult than he ever bargained for—and at the peril of his own life!

MONTGOMERY HICKS
As Director of "Heralds for Peace," you'd expect to find a most kind, generous, and helpful soul…think again!

THE TOBYS
These little aliens weren't too bright, but they wanted to reach out for the stars. So they decided to make a deal…

ROGERS
He was Hick's right-hand man in Wornegon. But under that smooth talking exterior was a penchant for violence and evil.

THOMAS SULLIVAN
He was a well established man, seemingly without any real problems. Then why was he running for his life?

CORY BENNETT
Munro's best friend, he was always there to lend an ear—or sometimes even argue a point.

THE
RUNNING
MAN

By
J. HUNTER HOLLY

ARMCHAIR FICTION
PO Box 4369, Medford, Oregon 97504

*For more information about Armchair Books and products, visit our
website at…*

www.armchairfiction.com

Or email us at…

armchairfiction@yahoo.com

CHAPTER ONE

JEFF Munro hated expressways. They cut through the forests and rolling hills with a sterile path of divided lanes and monotony. They were merely concrete signboards—*Exit Here, Food and Lodging at Next Exit,* and on and on into a blank boredom that by-passed the green growth and transformed every mile into a dull sameness of gray pavement and speeding cars. He avoided them resolutely, driving the old roads that wound in a subtle pattern through the countryside of farms and forests, inching through little towns where human beings lived with no exit signs.

He chided himself for using the word, "hate." Cory would say it was characteristic of him and his too-strong opinions. Jeff supposed it was. But only short, stinging words could describe his convictions.

Driving the miles alone, Jeff wished he had Cory beside him so they could argue it out, their favorite pastime on quiet evenings. He would tell Cory that an opinion worth holding was worth shouting out, and prove that he had won his position in the world by following that rule. Associate Professor—it was a good, honorable job, but nothing noteworthy. Political Science Department at Union College—it was a good department and a good school, but still nothing spectacular. Physically, he was an average man and knew it: five-feet-ten, black hair and brown eyes, still nothing uncommon. Yet students at Union College fought to register in his classes, and joined the clubs he served as adviser in droves. Why? Because, he would tell Cory, he spoke out. He believed strongly and he spoke and wrote for his beliefs, in the college paper and the Union Town paper. People listened because he was willing to put his reputation and emotions on the line.

As he rounded a gentle curve, a sign popped up before him. Yellow green, and red, it blasted at his vision with its message: *"HFP is on the march! Join and save the world!"* From that sign on, the trees along the road were dotted with slogans or the initials, HFP, Heralds for Peace.

"Join and save the world," Jeff grumbled. "Rather, *don't* join and save the world. Save it from the fanatics."

He knew this road well, and the signs were a new nuisance. But the next town was Bolin, and from there it was less than two hours home.

He wheeled into the last curve before the straight stretch of road that cut through Bolin. "What the devil?" he muttered. For there was no road through Bolin. Where the road should have swept between the stores lining the main street, there was a mass of people, milling about, surging one way and then another. Over the road hung a red and yellow banner. *"Heralds for Peace Lecture Today. Attend, and Save the World."*

Jeff slowed his car to a crawl and approached the crowd closely, honking his horn so they would clear a path for him. But his horn hardly made a dent in the din of shouting.

"What's going on?" he yelled to a man near his right front fender. "Can't I get through?"

The man swung about, a stout man with a dirt-streaked face, and when his eyes met Jeff's, Jeff recoiled. There was pure hatred in the farmer's eyes, and murder. Their glance held for only a moment, then the farmer re-entered the crowd.

Jeff got halfway out of his car and laid on the horn. "I want through!" he yelled. But no one bothered to look at him. He left the car in the middle of the road and walked to the crowd. A boy slipped out of the mass of people, ducking under arms and running doubled over. When he stood up in the clear, Jeff caught his arm.

"What's going on?" Jeff demanded.

The boy's face was flushed bright crimson and his breath panted in his chest. "We're going to kill her!" he said, and pulled out of Jeff's grasp. He ran to the side of the road, scooped up stones and packed them into his pockets, then ducked back into the crowd.

"We're going to kill her!" he had said, and the words were cold in Jeff's mind. The boy had been so blunt, and so eager. "We're going to kill her!" And the pockets full of stones.

He left his spot on the pavement and moved ahead quickly. This was no simple demonstration. It was a mob, and a mob meant something—someone—at the center, at the victim point. He ran, reaching the outer edge of the people and shoving his way through. Shouted words hit his ears, but he could decipher very few of them. "Damn do-gooder!" he heard, and: "Give her a lesson she won't forget!"

As he pushed in from the back, it was harder going. The people were a compact wall, shoulder to shoulder, and he couldn't break through. Inside the pack, the emotion hit him full force. The people were wild with anger, and it was almost tangible in the air. He searched frantically for an opening, letting the anger around him burn and impel his body, too. The seconds lost seemed suddenly precious. This was none of his business, none of his doing or undoing, but somehow he felt that he was the only sane person in Bolin, and if he failed to act, dreadful things would happen.

A space of a few inches opened up between two bulky men in front of him, and he slammed his way between them. He was only three back from the edge now, and a new voice was added to the din, a high, shrill voice that cried out to anyone who would hear, "Leave me alone! You're children of the devil! Leave me alone!"

The voice cried in defiance and pleading and Jeff clutched at it, pushing the last way into the open by sheer force of will and elbow. And there, walking backward before the creeping crowd, was a woman. She was middle-aged, her hair graying in streaks. Her dress was cotton and simple, her face pale and shiny, devoid of makeup. Fear made a harshness about her mouth and eyes. The red fire of blood wormed down her left arm, and oozed into her hair from the back of her scalp.

Somewhere just within his peripheral vision, an arm jerked up and a stone flew over the massed heads. The woman jerked and clutched her body; then again, as another stone flew in at her. Blood gashed behind the last one, and she was a convulsing figure, dancing her way among the hurtling pebbles.

Jeff leaped across the empty stretch of pavement and threw himself in front of her, shielding her with his body. He stiffened himself, and shouted into the face of the mob, "What's going on? Are you all out of your minds? What are you people doing?"

The effect of seeing a stranger rear up before them was what he had hoped it would be. The stones stopped flying and the forward momentum of the mob halted. But how long did he have before they started again? Seconds. He had to turn them in seconds.

"Get the hell out of the way," an anonymous voice yelled.

Jeff didn't move, not a step back, nor a step forward. They were all poised, a mass on one side, a tiny blot of two on the other, and the first movement would decide it.

"Don't dirty yourself with her," another shout sounded.

"Leave the HFP-er alone. She has it coming!"

"No!" Jeff shouted back. "There are two of us here now. Two of us. What is this all about?"

The answer was garbled as they all yelled at once. He picked out a few words: "HFP-er."

"Nuisance."

"Ordered out of town."

"Name caller."

He felt the women's faltering touch on his sleeve, and he chose a sentence to jump upon, addressing himself to one man, desperately trying to bring the mob down to an individual basis again. "Why was she ordered out of town?" he cried.

"Because we didn't want no lecture." The big man accepted the challenge. "She's not going to stand on a platform and call us Communists or sinners any more. She's not going to call anybody that any more. If other towns can run them out, so can we!"

Shouts of approval rose behind the man, but the shrill voice of the woman behind Jeff cut through the noise with a scream of its own. "I shall speak the truth as loudly and as long as I can!"

A growl rose in the street, and Jeff stood solidly against it. "Stop it!" he ordered. "Since when do the people of Bolin operate in the Dark Ages? You have no right to throw—"

He was cut off by a strong forward movement in the mob. "We have every right!" came back at him. It was the same big man. "Calling my little girl the devil's child—pestering decent, God-fearing women because they wear a little lipstick—knocking on doors—we have every right to rid our town of vermin."

Suddenly the woman was no longer behind Jeff, but beside him. Her stance was stiff and unyielding. "Painted women are the devil's tools," she said, and her voice was low, bringing a hush to the street. "And they raise the devil's children. You're wicked, all of you, and infiltrated with Communists. There are only two choices—HFP or Communism. If you're against HFP, then—"

A new stone zoomed in on her and she grabbed her face. When she drew her hand away, blood was making a trail down her cheek.

"For heaven's sake, shut up!" Jeff hissed at her. "You'll get us both killed."

"I didn't ask you to stand with me." She opened her hand, showing him the blood. "Do God's children do such things?"

"You'll find out what God's children do," a new voice called from the crowd. "One more word, and you'll know."

"Where is the law in this town?" Jeff demanded.

"Right in front of you," the same big man answered.

There was no help from the law, then. The sheriff was leading them. What was left for him to do?

He watched in fascination as the same boy he had stopped in the road, the boy with the pockets full of stones, crept out from under the big bodies in the crowd to stand in the front line.

"Just let me take her away from here," Jeff asked, not chastising them any more, but begging them. "Let us walk away." It was "us" now. He was in too deep to back out, and whatever befell the woman befell him, too.

His answer was a raised arm and a stone. He clutched his face at the sting of it, and when he saw his own blood, he lost control. "Now, just a minute," he began, feeling the redness of anger in his face. "You've got to—" Another stone cut in at him, striking his calf, and he repeated the grotesque dance of the woman.

"He's one of them, himself," the boy was shouting to the mob. "He's come to save her, can't you see that? If there were two of them, then why not three?"

"Two?" Jeff whirled to the woman beside him, but she had no chance to answer. In that one sentence from the boy, he had lost any control over the mob he had gained.

The wall of people rushed forward, and the stones flew at him in a rain of stinging pains. Fear rose in his mouth, and he grabbed the woman's hand and pulled her along with him, trying to run, to get clear before the falling stones changed to hands.

But the woman stumbled, and he was dragging her along the pavement. He let go, and the mob descended on her. Hands turned to fists, and stones to fingernails, and he plowed his way through them, fighting them off. He had to reach her before she died right there, on the road through Bolin.

Blows fell on him, and he let the groans come as they would, but he fought back. He rammed his fists into stomachs and groins; he dashed for every open foot of ground. He was knocked down, but he rose up again, until he had made his way into the center. He fell beside the woman. She was covered with blood and dirt, and her eyes looked at him with a glassiness that meant her senses were gone. Semiconscious, she could never run.

The men around him beat upon his back, but he struggled to his knees and then to his feet and lifted the woman up like a sack of vegetables, heaving her over his shoulder. He ran, running square into the crowd, and his momentum knocked some of them out of the way.

Hands reached out to grab him, but he sidestepped. With his right hand flailing before him as a club, he cleared his way yard by yard. These people weren't ready to suffer pain, only to inflict it.

A stone ripped into his back, then another, and the added sting of each made him drive harder. It was a gantlet of beating fists and hands, of flying stones and damning mouths, but the path opened and he ran it. What he thought was freedom turned out to be only a store front. He rammed into the door and with the heavy weight of the woman on his left shoulder, staggered down the aisle, past the counters of yard goods and thread and buttons. The crowd was still coming behind him, but he had a start. They must have stopped outside for a moment, he thought, and never broke his stride.

He fell against the counters in the narrow aisle, and his thighs bruised, but he pushed on and at last reached the back door. Heaving a great breath, he pushed it open. Fresh air.

He turned to the left, intending to run the back way around to his car, but now he saw what had slowed the people down. He could hear them behind him, and as he neared the corner of the line of buildings, more of them dashed around to meet him head on. They were yelling and screaming, and there was murder in them.

He dreaded going among them again. He hadn't the strength or the breath. But if he didn't, it meant he was through. He shifted the woman's body on his shoulder to give it better balance, put his head down and ran, one fist before him to act as a ramrod. He felt it smash into a face, heard a high cry, and knew he had struck the boy with the stones in his pockets. Satisfaction gave his body an extra spurt of energy, and he zigzagged, dodging into every open space, ignoring the blows that fell on him. He peered up and headed straight for a woman, her mouth open in screams. Clenching his teeth, he slammed his fist hard into her chin and she toppled beside him. And for a moment, as he had prayed, he ran alone. The mob stopped to examine the woman he had knocked down, and he ran alone.

He turned the corner and made for his car. He would lose his precious gained seconds struggling with the doors, but he had to try.

As he neared, the right hand door miraculously opened, the front seat thrust itself up, and he was clear to heave the limp weight of the woman into the back seat. He hurried for his own side of the car, and even as he passed the hood, the motor sprang into life.

Then he was inside, the door was shut and locked, and his foot was on the accelerator. He stamped down hard as the mob closed in around him, and people slid off the sides of the car, and others jumped away in front of him, clearing a path as they saw he meant to run them down. Stones pelted the metal, and the side window splashed into a maze of safety glass cracks, but he sped down the street of Bolin and away. The mob was still standing in the road, but now it was a mob with its hands down at its sides.

As Bolin and the big HFP banner swept from sight behind him, he slowed down. A handkerchief thrust its way under his nose, and a voice asked, "Are you all right?"

He looked up into the face of a young woman, a pretty woman, but plain with no makeup. She said nothing more, and he took the handkerchief, applying it to his cheek. The blood had caked, mixed with dust, and the rubbing started it bleeding again. He nursed it gingerly. It didn't hurt; it was just infuriating.

"It's not deep," the woman said. "You could hurt yourself more by shaving."

"The point is, I wasn't shaving," he said between his teeth.

He raised up in the seat and looked at the woman he had so unceremoniously tossed into the back. She was lying easily on the seat, still unconscious. There was nothing he could do for her except find a doctor.

"What were you doing in my car?" he asked bluntly.

"My name is Lucille McBreen. You saved my mother."

"Your mother? If that's your mother, why are you so calm?"

"She'll be all right. I know that. We weren't sent here to die."

"Then, you're from Heralds for Peace, too."

"We were working in Bolin together," she explained. "I managed to get out the back door of the lecture hall."

"And you didn't even try to help your mother?"

"What could I have done?" the girl asked. "Besides, as I said, I knew she'd be all right."

"And if she hadn't?"

The girl sighed, and there was a weird little smile on her face. "Some of us must die in the fight. We are all willing."

"And that makes you happy, does it? It gives you a little kick?"

She glanced at him sharply. "That wasn't worthy of you."

"Sorry. But that episode in Bolin wasn't worthy of me either. I'm not usually the target of stones. How did you get them so riled?"

"We belong to Heralds for Peace," was her total explanation.

"So do a lot of people, but that's no reason for a riot."

"There is violence in many places. More all the time. Truth always meets with resistance. We should have brought someone with us, but we made an error. We mistook pride for capability. When God sent us to Bolin, we thought we could handle it alone."

"God sent you?" he couldn't keep the skepticism from his voice.

"Don't display your impurity so blatantly," she chided him. "I thought perhaps you were a little better than the rest. After all, you stood against them. You proved—" She didn't go on.

"That I'm not the devil's child?" he prodded. "I don't believe in the devil."

"It's merely a way of describing the impure. We must have unselfish, pure, moral people if we're to save the world. God leads us. He speaks to us and directs us. We are His chosen. Anyone who joins HFP can become chosen."

Jeff cleared his throat. "No converting, please. I also don't believe in fanaticism. Religious fanaticism least of all."

"Fanatic doesn't have to be a nasty word."

"It does when it causes decent people to stand in the street and throw stones at another human being."

Her snort of contempt was loud and hard. "Decent people! We worked a week with them, going from house to house, talking, threatening, pointing out the truth, and what did those decent people do? They told us to leave, without even allowing our lecture. When we tried anyway, you saw the result."

"A result *you* caused, Miss McBreen."

"A result we didn't cause, but one we should have expected. When you deal with heathens, you must expect violence."

Jeff sighed in disgust. This was why he had led his students in the ban against HFP speakers on the campus. "I don't consider the people of Bolin heathens."

"After what they just did to you?"

"*You* did that to me. Every bit of it falls upon your head. I've never paid too much attention to HFP. I've heard of meetings, and trouble connected with it, but I've written it off since it has nothing to do with me. Now, I don't *want* to hear any more."

"That's fine with me. It would be wasted on you anyway." She said out of the new silence, "What is your name? I owe you thanks, and I'd like to know your name."

"Jeffrey Munro. I teach political science at Union College."

"Oh, yes."

"You don't mean you've heard of me?"

"I have. We have," she said. "HFP is always interested in influential men."

She closed her mouth tightly then and didn't offer anything more. Jeff was glad. What she had said had been innocent enough, but because of the mob, because of the blood on his face and the stinging pains all over his body, it touched him with undertones of menace. He didn't want to be known by HFP. And he didn't see any reason why he should be.

As the next little town rolled into view, he said, "This is Kingsley. I'll help you find a doctor for your mother, but then I'll have to go on. I have classes in the morning. Do you have any money, so you can get your mother home?"

"We have enough, thank you. But we won't go home, of course. When Mother is well enough, we'll return to Bolin. There's too much unfinished business there."

"You'd go back after what happened?"

"Not alone. But we will return there. God told me it is a fertile field, and I must sow it. First we'll return to Wornegon and rally some help—a whole new approach. We have specialists for that. Psychologists and propagandists."

Wornegon was a word Jeff knew. HFP headquarters were situated at a place called Wornegon, a place in the woods, the favorite hiding place of fanatic groups. They all took their cults to Nature, and somehow warped and distorted the very Nature they worshiped.

In Kingsley, he found the local doctor. He carried Mrs. McBreen into the treating room and walked out. His own cuts and bruises could wait until he reached Union College and the medical center. Right now he merely wanted to put miles between himself and the McBreen family. He had risked his life for them, but felt no kinship with them at all. He drove out of Kingsley with undue speed, hoping the open air and fresh breeze in the windows would make him feel clean again.

CHAPTER TWO

THREE days later, as Jeff left his last class and started back to his office, he was surprised to see Cory Bennett waiting for him in front of the Music Building. He waited in the sun, tall and blond, a man who turned the heads of the coeds, but paid them no attention in return.

Today Cory's lean body was stiff with anticipation and he held a newspaper in his right hand, slapping it against his left palm. Jeff opened without a greeting. "I see disapproval on your face and I'm shaking in my shoes."

Cory didn't answer his smile. "If you're not careful, you'll be shaking more. What in the devil got into you?"

"I have no idea what you're talking about."

"This article!" Cory waved the paper at him. "It's too strong, Jeff. What made you tackle HFP—and so violently?" Cory opened the paper and read from it, walking blindly as his eyes followed the newsprint. "For instance, this juicy little part: "If the do-gooders from Heralds for Peace were sincere in their statements of brotherhood and love, they wouldn't be roaming the streets accusing their fellow men of evil; they wouldn't be pointing fingers; they wouldn't be shouting insults. They cry, "Join and save the world," yet their methods divide men. How can division work for peace? And has self-righteousness on the part of a group of fanatics ever made a world free of sin? Hasn't it, instead, spawned witch-hunts, inquisitions and hatred?" Cory crumpled the paper angrily. "Where did you get so much venom?"

"It wasn't venom. It was firsthand experience. I ran into HFP three days ago and got full up to here." Jeff told Cory briefly about the encounter in Bolin. "I can show you my scars, too. I saw it, barely lived though it, and I won't be silent about it. I have outlets and I intend to use them. Do you know how big HFP has grown? I started checking after that riot and it's frightening. Riots, mobs, general unrest—people have to wake up."

"You can't do it with a few articles."

"No, but I can raise my voice and that's a start." They turned the last corner for the building where Jeff's office was housed, and Jeff wished he could turn the subject, too. Writing the article had given him great satisfaction, as though he could make up for each sting and each cut with harsh, angry words. He had more articles in mind. And he didn't want Cory to put a shroud on them. He tried to change the subject with a teasing lightness. "I'd like to know why you're taking me to task. I'm the predictable one in this friendship. You're the one to go off on tangents."

"Things have changed," Cory was blunt. "I'm toying with the idea that you've lost your mind."

Jeff looked for Cory's grin, but Cory's face was deeply sober. "If you don't soften that with a smile, I'm going to be insulted."

"There isn't a smile in me, Jeff. Not when it comes to this. HFP is nothing to fool around with."

"I'm not fooling around."

"All right! HFP is nothing to fight either. You're chipping away at a lion's den, and whether it's innocent chipping or not, the consequences will be the same. I tell you—."

"Jeffrey Munro! Munro!"

The shout cut through Cory's sentence, punctuated with the slap of feet on cement. Before Jeff could turn to locate the voice, he was jerked nearly off his feet and whirled around by the clutch of two hands on his shoulders. When he regained his balance, he was staring into the dirty face and frantic eyes of a stranger.

"Are you Jeffrey Munro?" the man panted, and his breath brushed Jeff's face, a stinging breath that smelled of panic.

Jeff pulled the hands from his shoulders, but the man thrust them back. *"Are* you Jeffrey Munro?" he cried again. "If you are, for God's sake don't push me away. I've got to talk to you."

"Like hell you do." Jeff pushed the hot, wet hands down again. "Now get your hands off me." He brushed his shoulders as though to rid them of the feel of the man's desperate grip.

But the man didn't move. He stood before Jeff, tall and shivering, his clothes disheveled, wrinkled and splotched with mud stains. His face was the face of a wild man, and his eyes raked Jeff's frantically. "I'm sorry. I must have made a mistake," he whispered. "But you look like the man described to me."

Jeff wavered as he saw the utter exhaustion in the man's body. "What is it you want?"

"Then—are you Munro?"

"I am."

"Thank God." The man sagged suddenly, and only Cory's quick hand kept him from falling to the ground.

"Take it easy," Cory told him.

"I'm all right," the man said. "Please, Mr. Munro, I must talk to you. Privately. Don't refuse me. You're my last hope, and I just can't go any further."

Jeff glanced to Cory, but he only shrugged, unable to make any more sense out of it than Jeff could. Something about this exhausted man shouted at Jeff to back off, to leave him alone.

They were already drawing attention from passing students. But how could he simply stride away and leave the man trembling on the walk?

Cory read his thoughts and offered feebly, "I have an appointment anyway, Jeff. We can finish our talk later."

The stranger's eyes lighted with a pitiful hope, and Jeff couldn't refuse. "All right, we'll go to my office," Jeff told him.

Cory didn't wait for anything more, but walked off quickly. "He's probably the smart one," Jeff muttered.

"What?" the man asked.

"Nothing—I was talking to myself. My office isn't far. Can you make it?"

"I can make it anyplace, Mr. Munro. Anyplace, as long as you'll listen to me."

They started on along the sidewalk and the man seemed incapable of lifting his feet above a shamble, but refused Jeff's offer of support. "It would make us too conspicuous," he explained.

"You think you're not already?" Jeff grunted. "You look like you've crawled out of a sewer pipe."

"I have."

When they reached the building, the corridors were empty. Their footsteps hit the floor hollowly, Jeff's sure and strong, the stranger's limping and shuffling.

"Right in here." Jeff opened his office door.

The man staggered into the little cubbyhole of an office and collapsed into a straight chair. He closed his eyes and a great tremor shook his body. Jeff waited. His office, the little, crammed space that had been second home for eight years, was no longer secure and content. With this man in it, it had changed. He brought an aura of fear with him—and drabness.

When the man said nothing and minutes passed, Jeff took the opening upon himself. "How about starting with your name? You seem to know me, but I have no idea who you are."

"I can't tell you my name. I have no name. Not any more." He fought to explain himself before Jeff wrote him off as a lunatic. "No one must know where I am, you see, and leaving names behind is dangerous. I'm simply a man, Mr. Munro. A man running for his life."

"And why did you run to me?"

"Because you're my only help in the world. Because you wrote that article about HFP. Because you're not afraid, and because you will understand." The man's voice was high and desperate. His face never lost its panic even in the deep, safe recesses of the building and the out-of-the-way office. "I'm running for my life, Mr. Munro, and whether or not I make it, whether or not I stay alive, someone else must know what I know. The information can't die with me."

Jeff sat down.

"You've seen the implication, then," the man said. "If you hear me out, and take this information into yourself, you may be in danger, too. But—you said you'd listen!"

Jeff leaned back in his chair. "I'm listening."

The man faced him squarely. "Something unholy is going on at Wornegon!"

"That place again," Jeff sighed in disgust. "It haunts me every place I go."

"It always will. You've cast your lot, and now it always will."

"I can do without the voice of doom," Jeff said gruffly, needing anger to cover the shivers the man's words sent down his spine. "What do you know about HFP?"

"I've been inside Wornegon for the last few days. I tried to join HFP, and that's what I know about it."

"Were you *sent* to see me?" Jeff's suspicion jumped, remembering Lucille McBreen's comment about his being known at Wornegon.

"Do I look like I was sent?"

"I don't know what you look like. You come in on me, claiming to be running for your life and looking like the devil, but you don't tell me why."

"Just listen," the man said. "I'll hurry. I don't have much time. They may be right here, right on the campus by now. They're never far behind me. So—I can only say this once. Please listen closely." His speech was disjointed; pausing and hesitating painfully, then spewing out in long, mad sentences.

"I went to Wornegon to join HFP because I'd read their pamphlets and thought maybe they had the answer to the world situation. I went to Wornegon fully intending to join, but once I got there, I held back. I can't explain why. Something struck me wrong, and I hesitated. That didn't make me too welcome. They like wholeheartedness up there. Nevertheless, I held back and kept alert. And I found things, little bits of things that added up to something unholy. The people who go there, who join HFP, are changed. And that's the only word for it."

"But that's what they promise them, isn't it? To become pure in heart, and find Truth and God?"

"It's not simply that they take up the dogma of the HFP cult, Mr. Munro. I'm trying to express something different, something more sinister. People go in one way and come out another. They go in bright and eager and come out self-righteous and hard as brass nails. But that's just one of my points. Let me get on.

"There's a curfew up there," he said. "Eleven o'clock. I never go to bed that early. I like to walk at night. So I did. I went out and walked to the left of the main residence. That's important. I went into the woods all the way to the bank of the stream that runs through the place, and on a certain rise of ground by that stream—" He broke off, coughing and struggling to breathe until tears came into his eyes.

Jeff waited the coughing fit out, then asked, "Can you go on?"

"I have to. A high rise of ground—yes. I lit a cigarette there, to smoke and think in the night, and then way ahead of me, across the stream, I saw this glow. I'd never seen anything like it. It bothered me. I crossed the stream, intending to investigate, when this hand reached out of the dark and touched my sleeve. It was a man named Rogers. He's always around up there, everyplace. Rogers. He's like a skinny watchdog, nosing around. He ordered me back to bed. I told him I wanted to investigate the light, but he wouldn't hear of it. There was something in his voice, threatening—and—I'm not a man who's afraid of much of anything, Mr. Munro, but I was afraid of him. I went back to bed."

Jeff had heard nothing yet to account for this man's condition—nothing, even, to warrant this conversation. "That glow could have been most anything. Burning refuse, some special ritual—"

"It could have been," the man agreed, "but was it? *What* was it?" He saw Jeff's skepticism and blurted almost incoherently, "There were other things, too. I saw little men—little, short men—two of them—and they didn't like my seeing them and they ran, and I lost track of them. I went into the initiation ceremony scared, but determined to see it through and fit the pieces together. I stuck it out until we were separated and led into cubicles, and I got into mine and there on the wall was this one, lighted word, *"Meditate,"* and I felt eyes on me and knew that something was going to happen to me because I had pried too deeply, and I knew that the initiation is what changes people and I couldn't sit there and have it done to me. I stared at that one lighted word, and then I broke out of the cubicle and ran. They tried to stop me, but I beat them all aside and I ran, and I'm still running. They're after me. To kill me. Because I saw too much."

He was shaking, and Jeff handed him a glass of water, sure now that his visitor with no name was more than physically exhausted. The story was incoherent and unbelievable. It was a lunatic's raving. Jeff asked feebly, "Why didn't you go to the police? Or the FBI? They're the ones to help you with this."

"I couldn't!" His answer was a shout. He lowered his voice quickly. "I couldn't. They might be there. They might be anywhere. I can't trust anyone. That's why I came to you. I can trust you after what you wrote, and with you knowing the facts, I can take the chance of going to the FBI. If they *are* there, and kill me, my information won't be lost. You'll still have it." He rubbed his eyes, then his stubbled chin, and sighed, "You see, Mr. Munro, I'm not so afraid of dying. I'm just afraid of dying without anyone knowing the truth about Wornegon."

As suddenly as he had begun his torrent of facts, he shifted, struggling to rise from his chair. "You have it all now. I know you can remember it." He stood on legs that barely held him.

"Where are you going?"

"I have to leave. I don't want to stay here too long. They might find me."

"You're too inconsistent," Jeff accused him. "You just said you weren't afraid of dying."

"I'm not thinking of myself." The blue eyes met Jeff's. "I don't want to endanger you any more than I already have."

Jeff shook his head. He didn't know what he had here—maniac, idiot or a frightened man telling the truth. But he did know what his own reaction was. Pity, a deep pity that shook with the man, panted with him and feared with him.

"Where do you plan to go?" Jeff asked him.

"Where I've been for the last four days. Limbo. Running limbo."

"That won't do. You won't even make it to the street alone. I'll drive you into town, get you situated in a hotel, and you can eat and sleep and wash yourself. Tomorrow you can go to the FBI looking believable. They'll be more likely to listen to you."

The man looked at him sharply. "Then—you don't believe me?"

"How can I say?" Jeff answered, truthfully.

"I understand. But you will believe me when I'm dead. That's all I ask."

"You're being melodramatic."

"I realize that, but I can't seem to help it. When you face death for four days in a row, words just come out that way."

"But why should HFP want to kill you?" Jeff demanded. "How could they kill you? There are laws, after all."

"They make their own laws." He moved two steps toward the door, distracted and discouraged. "You said I should go to the FBI in the morning. Why not now?"

"The office would be closed now. I suppose you could reach someone, but—"

"I'll go in the morning," the man interrupted. "You're sensible and sane and I'll follow your advice. Now we must separate. Otherwise they'll be after you, too."

"That I don't believe. And I don't think I care anyway. I'm taking you to a hotel, and you're in no shape to argue."

The man was just as stubborn. "I've already explained why I can't allow you to do that."

"Don't you want my help?" Jeff asked. The man said nothing, and Jeff saw his opening. He pushed it hard. "Wouldn't you actually like some company, some security, after four days of hell?"

The man wilted. "More than anything in this world. It's hard to be brave when someone offers comfort."

"Then, come on. We're going into town."

As Jeff drove the nearly dark streets, the man peered constantly behind them, waiting for something to happen. "You're just exciting yourself for no reason," Jeff told him, wishing that his companion would calm himself.

"Maybe you're right," the man said. "I don't see anything. It couldn't possibly be that I lost them, could it?"

There was so much hope in the question that Jeff grunted a quick "yes."

"I don't see how," he muttered. "I really don't see how. It will be a blue car—the one that follows us will be blue."

"There isn't a blue car behind us anywhere," Jeff said. "So turn around and relax. Let me look after you for a while."

The man's hand touched his sleeve fleetingly and his blue eyes were full of tears. It tore at Jeff's insides. The men he knew didn't cry. But this man did. And he could barely stand it when he realized that he was actually betraying the man's trust. He didn't believe the incoherent story about HFP, and when the man realized it, Jeff would be a traitor in his eyes.

"How can a person's world change so abruptly?" the man asked. "Five days ago I was like you, free and secure, worried enough about the world to want to do something about it, yes, but still free and secure. I would never have believed this could happen to me. Men don't run from other men in this day and age. Men don't hide in holes in this country. But I've been in holes. I wonder if I'll ever find the way out of them."

There was nothing Jeff could find to say in answer. But he did have some idea of what the man meant. The whole situation was dreamlike. His world had changed suddenly, too; from the everyday argument with Cory, he had plunged into a nightmare state, shepherding a frightened stranger, a man with no name. The running man. That was the only name he had for him. The Running Man.

"Is it much farther now?" the Running Man asked. "What?"

"Is it much farther to the hotel?"

Jeff realized with embarrassment that he had been circling, driving aimlessly, through the almost dark streets. He could have driven to the hotel and back in the time he had wasted. Why hadn't he? He looked at the man beside him and it was clear why he hadn't gone straight to the hotel. It wasn't that he believed there was danger; it was simply that he had no idea how to get the disheveled man past the desk clerk.

The Running Man gazed back at him, his trembling less apparent. "You didn't intend to take me to a hotel at all, did you? What do you have in mind, a hospital? Because, if that's it, then I want to get out right here. I'd rather take my chances with that blue car than with a bunch of psychiatrists. I'm not stupid, Mr. Munro. I know they'd lock me up."

"I didn't say a word about a hospital." Jeff was angry because the man had guessed what had just crossed his mind. "I simply can't see how I'll ever register you in any decent hotel. Not in the shape you're in."

"So where does that leave us?"

Jeff was resigned to what he knew had to be done. "There's only one thing to do. You'll have to come home with me. You can clean up, borrow some of my clothes, and then I'll take you to a hotel."

"All right," the Running Man said, but his voice was hesitant.

"What's the matter now?"

"Nothing. I was only wondering—but, of course, it wouldn't do. If I stayed with you until morning, I'd be defeating my own purpose, wouldn't I? Endangering you. I'm afraid I've let your kindness sap my reserve of strength. I have to stand alone in this thing. So do you. We both must stand alone so we won't fall together and be lost."

"Will you forget that? I'm perfectly willing to have you spend the night with me, if you'll promise to talk about something else. I can't swallow this danger business. I'm sorry. Nevertheless, I'll keep alert and watch out for your blue car, if you'll just quit talking about dying."

The man laughed a feeble laugh. "I find safety—someone to guard me even—but in order to receive it, I must forget the danger. Why do you bother with me at all if you're so certain I'm crazy?"

"I wish I knew. Maybe there's something about you that I like. Let it stand at that."

"Thank you," the Running Man said. "And from this moment on, I'll not say another word about HFP."

He was true to his promise. Jeff took the side streets home, hoping it would still his anxiety, but the Running Man, after making a great effort to watch the street ahead, was soon craning his head around again. With every corner they passed, Jeff could read the relief in the man's mind. *No blue car yet,* he would be thinking. *No blue car.*

Finally, even Jeff's gaze was more on the rear-view mirror than on the street, and he cursed himself for a fool.

"It's only four blocks now," he told the Running Man, "so, for heaven's sake, quit watching the street. There's only one car behind us, and it just turned into line. It's green! And it's not following anybody."

The Running Man faced forward and leaned his head on the seat closing his eyes in a gesture of surrender to Jeff.

Another corner passed. Jeff glanced back at the green car, and his foot lifted off the accelerator. The green car had picked up speed and seemed to be out of control, swerving from side to side and coming too fast. It suddenly cut to the right, and before Jeff could compensate, it veered toward him, sideswiping him from the rear. There was the crunch of metal, and Jeff swung hard on the wheel, his car spinning dizzily across the street, the houses careening in his vision. He hit the curb and went over it, then bounced back down, breaking to a tire-screeching halt under a light. The green car imitated his halt half a block down the street. A man climbed out.

Shaking with unused adrenalin, Jeff stepped out onto the grass on the left side of the car.

"Let me come with you," the Running Man whispered from inside. "I don't want to stay here alone."

He opened his door and stepped out onto the pavement. "Be careful, Mr. Munro," he called huskily. "This may be more than it looks."

The onrushing sound of a motor whirled Jeff around, and his warning shout stuck in his throat. Coming around the corner on two wheels, speeding under the lights, was a big blue car. It barreled down the street, then swerved, crossing the center line, heading straight for the Running Man.

"Look out!" Jeff screamed. "Jump!"

The Running Man turned, saw the blue car and froze. His arms rose to cover his eyes, but his feet didn't move from the pavement.

His scream was loud and empty. There was a heavy thud, the sound of breaking glass, and the blue car zoomed on, leaving a crumpled heap lying on the center line in front of Jeff's car.

Jeff ran to him and knelt down. "God!" Jeff moaned, as he looked closely. Blood was seeping from the man's mouth, and his body was broken, lying in impossible angles. His lips moved, forming words, and Jeff leaned close to hear them. They were more expulsions of air than tone, but he made them out.

"I never intended to—involve you like this—Mun—Munro. Now they—know who you are. They can guess—the rest. Be careful."

The eyes rolled, then glazed over, the life and image gone out of them. Jeff's breath caught sharply, and he looked up to meet the face of the man from the green, sideswiping car.

"He's dead," Jeff murmured.

"Yes," the man said, and there was no regret in it, rather an eerie satisfaction that matched the hard clench of his lips and the nasty half-smile on his face.

Jeff rose quickly, feeling vulnerable on the ground with this leering man above him. He backed away. The man followed his movements coldly. But the tension was cut by the shouts of people running to view the accident, and the high wail of a siren.

"I called an ambulance." A woman rushed up to Jeff. "I saw your friend get hit. I'll be a witness."

"He won't need an ambulance," the other man said. His voice was cold and deep, but as the siren blared onto the street and the red flash of the ambulance light set the darkness in motion, he changed. Before Jeff's startled eyes, he sagged, his face contracted in remorse, his eyes clouded, his hands went to his head. He muttered, "It was all my fault. All my fault. I forced him over."

By the time the stretcher was out and the police were ready for explanations, the man was dissolved in tears. People were comforting him, telling him that he was involved in the accident, yes, but that he hadn't *killed* the man. The blue car had done that.

Jeff rebelled against this pat plot, but held his tongue. There was nothing he could say. The driver of the green, sideswiping car gave his story, the woman witness upheld it, and he had to go along with them. He could prove nothing. But he knew, within him, that it was no accident. It was a two-car murder plot; carefully planned, brutally handled and horribly successful.

He stood in the street in a state of shock. It had all happened too quickly, and his mind was aswim with doubts, with bits of fear, and with confusion. It was a scene out of a nightmare, with the whirling, blinking red lights, the white-coated ambulance men lifting the covered stretcher, and the people standing sober-faced along the curb.

One of the policemen came over to him. "What was your friend's name?"

"What?" Jeff looked at the officer. "Oh—I don't know. He didn't tell me."

"Now, come on. He had no identification on him."

"I said he didn't tell me!" He realized that the officer would never believe him if he told the truth. So he lied quickly. "I just picked him up. He wanted a lift."

"On this back street?"

"So, I don't know why! I tell you, I didn't know the man. I just picked him up. *And now he's dead!*"

The policeman nodded. "Okay, Mr. Munro. Take it easy."

Jeff realized that the crowd was watching him. He had been shouting. He shifted, embarrassed, and all the time, in the background, he saw and heard the man from the green car, bemoaning his guilt. Where were the nasty smile, the cold, leering stare now?

"Look, officer, can I leave?" Jeff blurted.

"Do you need a tow truck for your car?"

"No. It wasn't damaged much. Just a bad dent in the right rear fender. It killed a man, but it wasn't damaged much."

The officer looked him up and down. "Do you need a doctor?"

"I need a drink!"

"Okay, you can go. I've got your name, if we need you."

Jeff didn't wait to hear anything else. He strode to his car and started the motor, going down the street past the place where the green one was parked. And the blue one? Where was the murdering blue one? Force a man to the wrong side of the street, fix it so he has to get out on the street side of his car, and then run him down. Murder!

He went into his house and turned on the lights but couldn't shake the chill that had welled over him when he stood alone with the body of his strange companion and the hard face of one of his murderers. He had to talk to someone and his house was empty. He called Cory, just to hear a voice and stop the imaginings.

He hadn't intended to rout Cory out, but Cory had his own ideas. He came over. He walked into Jeff's house, mixed two long drinks, and told Jeff to begin. It rushed out of Jeff, searching for another, sensible ear to deny it. But Cory didn't deny it. He listened with no hint of disbelief. He just shook his head.

"I told you this afternoon to leave HFP alone," he said, as Jeff finished. "I shouldn't have let you take that man in your office. You're too prone to jump in and fight for the underdog."

"You don't mean that you actually believe HFP killed him?"

"You want me to refute it, don't you? You want me to deny it could have happened?"

"Yes, I want you to deny it! When you came in here I expected you to tell me that my ideas were pure foolishness and it was all a horrible coincidence. But you don't tell me that. Instead, you believe it. All of it, Cory? The little men, too?"

"No," Cory admitted. "Not the little men, nor the strange glows in the woods. Those were the imaginings of exhaustion. But his death could have been murder. That, I do believe. You believe it, too, but you're afraid to face it. It leads to too many terrible tangents."

"Like they may be after me next, as the Running Man predicted?"

"Exactly. I've been to Wornegon, Jeff, and I think HFP is capable of murder."

"Why did *you* go?" Jeff asked. "You've never seemed to care much about saving the world."

"It wasn't that at all. They wanted my advertising firm to handle some public relations for them. Naturally I went up to have a look before I made a deal. And after I looked, I refused. I haven't felt easy in my mind since. That was what I was trying to tell you this afternoon. Leave HFP alone. It's too powerful to fight in a newspaper."

"A bunch of nuts out in the woods? Powerful?"

Cory was angry. "You're showing your ignorance. HFP isn't what you think. There are big men up there—businessmen, industrialists, and even a sprinkling of senators and governors. Would you call them a bunch of nuts?"

"No. I wouldn't call them nuts." Jeff gulped at his drink, realizing he had lost his chance to write the Running Man off as a psychopath.

"I didn't trust anybody up there," Cory went on. "I didn't like the place. It's creepy in an unexplainable way. So I turned them down and kept my mouth shut about it. I certainly didn't expect my best friend to start jabbing them with pins."

"It's more than a pin now. The article might have riled them, but that would have passed. If the Running Man was telling the truth, and they killed him because of the information he had, where does that put me? I've got that information now."

The ice cubes clinked in Cory's glass as he swallowed the last of his drink. He crossed to the bottle and poured himself a stiff shot of whiskey. He said softly, "You'd better go to the FBI."

"They'd lock me up for a lunatic. I can't prove anything."

"I knew you'd say that, but I was hoping," Cory sighed.

Cory was again right. After eight years of friendship, of close kinship, they could almost predict each other's reactions. He waited for the next question he knew would come.

"What course does that leave you?" Cory asked. "Just to sit tight and maybe be a target?"

"Not that either. If I'm a target, I want to know about it." He set his glass down, letting that action underline the seriousness of his decision. "I'm going to Wornegon." He waved Cory's protest aside. "I have to follow through. If the Running Man was right, then something has to be done, some investigation made into HFP. Even if his story was the result of exhaustion, his death was still murder, and no organization can be allowed to get away with that. So I'm going to see for myself, and then I'm going to the authorities—*then,* when I have something concrete to tell them, when I can say I saw it with my own eyes."

He waited, but Cory wouldn't answer him one way or another.

"Well?" Jeff prodded. "Isn't it the only course open to me?"

"No! You're crazy to take the chance. Don't involve yourself any more and nothing will come of it. It will all pass over."

"You sound almost sure, and how can you be?"

"But, Jeff, the target doesn't walk right into the barrel of the gun!"

"Then you think I'm probably a target, too."

"Yes, I do."

Jeff bobbed his head, putting the period to his decision.

"If you had really wanted me to stay home, you shouldn't have admitted that fact. I'm going to Wornegon. I'm nobody's sitting duck." He stared into his empty glass. "I don't really believe any of this. It's play-acting, melodrama. It will probably just turn into another wasted weekend."

"I'll waste it with you," Cory said.

"This time I say no."

"Argue all you want, but I'm going. If I'm at all responsible for making you go up there, then I've got to follow through with you."

Cory straightened to his full height, and his face set itself firmly. Arguing would do no good. Cory had exchanged his usual casual attitude for one of his infrequent moods of solid purpose, and there was no changing his mind.

CHAPTER THREE

JEFF took Friday off from his classes by the simple method of writing a note to his students on the blackboard of the classroom and assigning extra outside reading. The campus legend that had grown up about him credited him with a quick wit, a fast mind and vibrant energy. As he drove with Cory, completing the last of the two hundred miles to Wornegon, he wondered if this, like all legends, was now proving to be a distortion.

"Turn off here," Cory said from beside him.

Jeff barely made the turn in time. His eyes caught the retreating sight of a small sign, hidden among the wayside shrubbery. "You'd think they'd advertise themselves better."

"Not at Wornegon. Everyplace else their signs are blatant and obnoxiously big. But here the atmosphere is supposed to be one of reverence and humility."

"Of course. Pure in heart and body and mind—and little signs to cover big evils."

The road they traveled now curved through trees and undergrowth, penetrating the heart of a great forest. It was obviously a private road, for it went on and on and on.

"How much farther?" Jeff asked.

"Not much. Wornegon's big, remember. Three hundred acres is no camping area."

Three hundred acres! Jeff grunted his surprise. The grunt was followed by an audible cry of astonishment as he navigated another curve and broke into open ground. Facing the car was an enormous parking lot surrounded by chain link fences. And surrounding the fences was an ocean of green grass, cropped and iridescent, leading up a gentle rise to a mammoth glass and metal building.

"Wow!" was all Jeff could muster. The building was beautiful. It dominated the view and towered over four equally beautiful, but smaller, structures beside it. They were landscaped as though they had carefully settled down upon the earth, disturbing nothing, tearing up nothing, in their descent.

"And I expected rustic cabins and outhouses," Jeff laughed.

"Does the wealth surprise you?"

"Where do they get this kind of money?"

"People give it to them," Cory said. "Donate it. And this isn't all. Wornegon is only one of six such centers throughout the world."

"I knew that. But are they all this luxurious?"

"All." Cory's eyes were alive with the elegance of the place. Jeff had seldom seen him so taken with anything. But this was Cory's dream-ambition, a lust for wealth that Cory never tried to hide. Cory *was* the elegant life—tailored suits, Italian shoes, sports cars. But he worked hard for every cent of it. "Park as close to the fence as you can," Cory told him. "It's a long walk up to the main building."

"Which one is that?"

"The big one. That's the one set aside for visitors and newcomers. They told me it houses meeting rooms and lodging rooms. The two to the right are a dining hall and a recreation building. The others are for permanent residents and such."

Jeff swung into a parking place and they climbed out, passed through the unguarded gate and stepped onto the springy grass.

Jeff tried to enjoy the startling beauty around him, but the very thing he was trying to enjoy gnawed at his mind. Every step on the green grass accented the possibility that the death in the street had been murder. Power went with wealth like this. And enough power, in tight hands, could induce complete disregard for law. *Could HFP commit murder?* he asked himself again. This time the answer was "Yes."

They crossed a wide terrace and entered the main hall of the building. An enormous lobby opened before them, carpeted wall to wall in turquoise, decorated with solid, clean-lined furniture, massive tables and soaring lamps. It was like a scene out of a plush movie, and Jeff paused to take it in. Then he started for the main desk.

He stopped halfway there. "Cory, I'm going to do something childish. I'm not going to register under my right name. Maybe you shouldn't either."

"But I've been here before."

"That's right. You'll have to use your own name. But I'm going into hiding."

Cory nodded. "What do you intend to call yourself?"

"I'll keep my initials. They're on my suitcase. James Miller will do."

"Okay, Jim—if I can remember."

They registered under the watery eye of the man at the desk. He smiled at them benevolently, and Jeff immediately disliked him. "Heralds for Peace," the man said, "is joyful to have you with us. I hope you will join and march with us to save the world."

Jeff swallowed hard, gulping down a sarcastic answer.

But Cory carried the ball. His voice low and humble, Cory said, "Thank you most kindly. Men always respond to goodness."

Jeff took his key and left the desk, while someone spirited away their luggage. "Cory," he accused, when they were out of earshot of the clerk, "You are a dirty hypocrite."

"Aren't we all?" Cory grinned back.

"What do we do now?"

"You may go to your rooms, if you wish," a deep voice said into Jeff's ear, "or mingle with the other guests."

Jeff hadn't heard anyone come up, but a woman stood beside him belying the deep voice, a woman with a tanned face and bushy eyebrows. Not a mote of powder adorned her skin, and her lips were pale.

"It is a rule of Wornegon that everyone is welcome anywhere he chooses to go," she said. "You may walk about and join any group you see that interests you. Talking and unburdening yourself is the first step to purity. Get to know your Brothers."

"No privacy then," Jeff stated.

"Privacy is only necessary when one wishes to hide something. No one hides anything at Wornegon." She walked away from them and Jeff followed her movement closely. Her skirt was tight, and it shouldn't have been because her figure sagged and she wore no girdle.

"No bra either." Cory caught his thought. "The women up here revert to nature. Underclothes and makeup are considered impure."

Jeff mentally tagged her the Wiggler, and swiveled around to find a starting place. "Do they always creep up on you like that?"

"They did me," Cory said. "They must stand around behind the curtains or something and come out when they see anyone at a loss for activity. They want everyone to be happy."

"It's not happy-making. It's creepy."

They walked the giant room, sitting down from time to time whenever they saw a group of people in conversation. They said nothing, merely listening, then getting up to move on to another group. Jeff found it hard to accept the open eavesdropping, but no one he encountered seemed to mind. The first group was discussing their impending trips to underdeveloped nations to offer medical, agricultural and spiritual help. The second group was talking about a rock-throwing incident somewhere in Colorado and the courage of the HFP-ers in remaining nonviolent and martyring themselves.

The third group was intent on discussing the latest session of something called "Listening to God for Good," and this proved the most interesting, but the least intelligible. A young girl was saying, "Naturally I wrote it all down, but I still couldn't quite believe it. He directed me to go to Iran. Iran! Can you imagine that? I didn't think I had progressed that far."

This time Jeff did open his mouth. "Who directed you?"

"Why, God, of course," she said.

"Oh—I see," Jeff floundered.

"I don't think you do." The girl was frank. "Are you new here?"

"Just today."

"Then it's understandable. But don't fret, you'll come to it, too. No one is left out, you know. No one. No matter what you've done, you can redeem yourself, and *hear.*"

"Yes," Jeff stammered. "I'm sure." He stood, giving Cory a cue, and they moved away. This roving, listening and roving again was getting on his nerves. The whole place was getting on his nerves. It was innocent enough from all appearances, yet something rang false about it. The people talked of the things he had expected—religion and politics, purity and redemption—but the setting was all wrong.

He told Cory. "I'm not sure I was right in coming, after all."

"We haven't found out very much," Cory agreed. "From the looks of things, these are just a bunch of people living it up in style and pretending to be hunting for purity."

"And that might be why it feels so strange—because it's all pretense. A sham cult with sham members. Yet that woman in

Bolin wasn't any sham. She was stoned, and still planning to go back for more." He looked across the room. "Here comes the Wiggler again."

"Let's walk, and maybe she'll leave us alone."

"No. I want to ask her a question." Jeff waited for the woman to join them. "Just what is this business of 'Listening to God for Good?'"

"I see you've spent a profitable few hours," she said. "You've already discovered the basic activity of Heralds for Peace."

"And that is?"

"Listening to God for Good. Every morning, before anything else is done, our members sit down quietly and give themselves over to hearing the still, small voice. God speaks to them, to each of them separately, and gives them directions for the day and for their lives. He tells them what to do for the greatest service and good, and where they are most needed. It is a glorious thing."

"I'm sure it is," Jeff said. "Is it open to the public?"

The Wiggler gave him a condescending look. "That's a peculiar way of putting it, but actually, it is open to anyone who wishes to sit in. You can even try to hear for yourself, although it has never been done without the vital preliminaries—giving yourself totally to HFP and purity, and finding yourself through the initiation."

"Can we sit in tomorrow morning?"

"Be dressed and ready by a quarter to six. Just ask anyone and they'll direct you to a Listening Room. Now, is there anything I can do to make your stay more pleasant?"

"No thanks," Jeff said.

The Wiggler sauntered off and Cory's hand was hard on Jeff's arm.

"Do we really have to stay around for that session in the morning?"

"We haven't found a thing so far. I want to check that out."

"Look, buddy, if you felt as nervous in this fancy trap as I do, you'd be heading for the door right now."

Jeff eyed him soberly. "I didn't say I wasn't on edge."

"Then let's leave."

"No. First we listen in the morning—then we leave." Jeff went on to the elevators and Cory trailed him, unwilling, but sticking to his original bargain. Their rooms were on the third floor. They opened Jeff's door first. Jeff had prepared himself for anything here, either more luxury or a spartan atmosphere. It was luxury. Carpeting again, and overstuffed chairs, a mile-wide bed, fruit on the table and flowers on the dresser. The room wasn't one, but two: bedroom-sitting room and large bath. A smell of newness met his nostrils, new upholstery and rugs, mingling faintly with the odor of the flowers.

"And it's all for free," Cory said behind him.

"Why?" Jeff asked, knowing Cory didn't have the answer. "Why do they treat their members so damn well?"

"I asked that same question when I was here before, and was told that it gives a feeling of solidity; that the members can go out from here and face anything, knowing that this comfort and this wealth is behind them. Aside from the fact that they like to draw VIP's, and they can't ask VIP's to live in hovels."

"It looks like they're set up for kings. So, we'll be kings—for a while."

The awakening call came at five-thirty, and Jeff felt as though he hadn't slept at all. He had lain awake for long hours listening to the sounds of Wornegon. And that was the trouble—there were no sounds. There was the faint hum of the air conditioning, but nothing more. The building was so perfectly soundproofed that he might have been alone, the sole occupant of the mammoth place. He had finally risen, turned off the air conditioning and opened a window. Then the night came through to his ears, a woods night with owls in the distance, and rustling leaves. With those sounds to lull him, he slept.

Now, as the phone jangled beside his bed, he turned over stiffly and picked it up. A recorded voice announced that it was five-thirty, and would he please rise and be on time for the morning session of Listening to God for Good.

He shuffled into the bathroom. Funny, he thought, that even the nth degree of luxury made no difference in the early, sleepy morning. There was just a mirror, his bleary eyes and stubbled chin, and fifteen minutes. He sped through his shave, pulled on his clothes, and went down the hall to knock on Cory's door.

Cory opened it immediately. "You beat me," Cory smiled. "I was sure I'd have to drag you out of bed."

"You wide-awake, morning people make me sick," Jeff growled. "Are we supposed to go to this thing without even a cup of coffee?"

"Don't ask me. I've never been this deep in HFP before."

They took one of the four elevators down and the Wiggler was waiting for them in the lobby. "I thought I'd escort you personally," she said. "I've chosen a small group for you to sit in with. I think that way you'll have a better chance to understand."

They followed her and Jeff couldn't raise one footfall from the thick carpet. The lobby was full of people, all headed in one direction, but not a word came from any of them. He recognized some of them, faces he usually saw in newsreels, tycoons and senators.

The Wiggler turned off into a side corridor and led them a few feet to a door. It was open, and inside there were fifteen people, all sitting in straight chairs, paper and pencil in hand.

"Take a seat anywhere," the Wiggler said, "and relax. You are among Brothers here."

Jeff sat down, Cory close beside him.

By a quarter to six, five more people had come in and taken places in the little room. There were no windows, and none of the usual luxury. The room was gray and sterile, the first he had seen that adhered at all to his idea of what a cult should be.

"Why the paper and pencils?" Cory's deep voice broke the silence that Jeff had carefully left intact.

"We must write down our messages," a freckled woman answered. "We can't take the chance of forgetting a single word."

"Do you mean to say that God dictates and you record?"

"You put it too crudely," she told him.

"But," Jeff pushed on, "how can you be sure that it's God you're hearing and not just your own subconscious?"

The woman's face was pure condescension. "You'll understand that when you have joined us and can hear for yourself, Mr.—"

"Mu-Miller," Jeff stammered. "James Miller."

"I'm glad to know you, Mr. Miller. And I hope you won't take exception when I tell you that it's customary for us not to speak before we participate in this sacred ritual."

"I'm sorry. No one told me."

He sat caught in his own thoughts again, and was sorry, because in those thoughts was a question that wouldn't be put down. Why six o'clock? Why did these people believe that God would set an appointment time to speak to them? Why couldn't they listen just as well at seven, or ten, or midnight? If the voice was there, it was there all the time and not just at one appointed hour.

When he asked the question aloud, he received a shower of glances that made him want to crawl into the floor. He was obviously ignorant, the glances said, and uncouth to boot. They would tolerate him because he was a Brother, but they wouldn't answer.

Cory grinned at him sideways and whispered. "How does it feel to have a mouthful of foot?"

"Please!" someone said from the left of them. It was an old man, and he nodded toward the clock. It was three minutes of six.

As the clock counted the minutes, the people leaned back in their chairs, preparing themselves. Some of them closed their eyes, others stared into space. And always, the paper was ready, the pencil was poised on every lap.

There was a sudden tension in the room. Bodies tensed, hands tensed, and breathing quickened. The clock said six. Six and silence. Twenty people, all withdrawn, all glassy-eyed, in utter silence. And then the scratching started as pencils fluttered across paper and words scribbled out behind.

Jeff shivered and watched. It was weird. The Listeners were hearing something, but what? He closed his eyes and listened with all his might, straining to join them. But there was nothing—nothing for him, at any rate.

The minutes swept on. Around went the second hand and click went the minute hand, and Jeff began to sweat. The scene pricked at him. Something was wrong. There was nothing holy or godly about it. These people were taking notes—taking notes from God?

He wanted to leave, but knew he mustn't. He had to wait it out, the whole eerie thing. He had run full tilt into the lunatic fringe and felt sanely lost among them.

He pulled out his handkerchief and wiped the perspiration off his forehead. It was unreasoning crawliness that grasped him. He wanted nothing more to do with this place and this ritual.

He was judging the maneuvers he would have to make to reach the door without disturbing anyone when the scratching noise abruptly stopped. He glanced up and the people were present again. Their eyes held sense, and a joy, a fulfillment, that startled him. Whispers started and turned to murmurings, then rose to full voice as they read what they had scribbled, exchanging their messages with each other.

The freckled woman walked over and held out her paper. Jeff took it gingerly and read the awkward words. "You are fighting a glorious battle," it read, "and you must never forget your goal. Save the world with purity. Speak out against sin in dark places. Cry out for God in every place. You are the hope of the world. Offer yourself to spread the word. Denver is in need."

"Denver is in need?" he repeated.

"Yes, isn't it wonderful?" she said. "I'm to go to Denver and help recruit. That's what it means. I'm to go to Denver. My first real call. Now do you see?" Her face was glowing with a glory that Jeff had never seen in anyone. "Now do you see the wonder of it?" She walked away to join a little group that had formed, thrusting her paper before them and accepting their congratulations.

The old man who had cautioned Cory to silence was the only one without that special glow about him. He shambled over. "Want to read mine?" he asked. "I never get the glory any more. Oh, I used to, all right, but not any more. I'm always shunted off to do the gardening nowadays, or fertilize the lawns."

"What?" Jeff was sure he hadn't heard right.

"I'm no more than a gardener any more. Too old, I guess. Been with HFP since it started five years ago, but got in too old."

"Do you actually believe that God would tell you to go out and fertilize the lawns?" Jeff couldn't suppress his smile, or the relief from tension this idea brought him.

"Sure. Why not? Somebody's got to do it. But—" he looked over his shoulder at the rest of them and lowered his voice—"as to the other—God telling me, I mean—no, I don't think it's God. These others do. They still believe it. But like I said, I've been listening now for five years and I've got it figured out. I don't hear God at all. What I hear is a—well, what you might call an ethereal being. Know what that is? An ethereal being who lives outside Earth's atmosphere and is concerned with us down here, and takes the time to direct us toward peace and happiness. I call him Urias. Now Urias is a great being, I don't want to give the impression he's not, but he's not God."

Cory's head was shaking like a pendulum. Jeff cleared his throat, sure he was staring senility straight in the face.

"You won't tell the others I said that, will you?" The old man was grave. "They'll come to it for themselves, but let them serve their apprenticeship like I did."

"We won't breathe a word," Jeff assured him.

There was no possible sense in staying the weekend out. As Cory put it, the old man proved they were all a pack of nuts. He confessed that he had been wrong about Wornegon. It was what Jeff had thought it was, simply a cult. Aside from a firsthand basis for a series of articles on HFP, if he cared to write them, Jeff had nothing. And he wanted out of the weird atmosphere fast.

They packed, and without even going for breakfast, took the elevator down to the lobby.

Jeff walked with a new spring to his step. The week had been a strange nightmare, but that was past. HFP would never worry him again. He wasn't a target, nor would he be, because even with his firsthand stuff, he doubted if he would write any articles.

The glass doors were only ten paces away and the sunlight beckoned on the green grass where the old man toiled on directions from Urias. Jeff's attention fell on a tall, extremely thin man standing by the entrance. He was queer-looking aside from his thinness, dark and a little off-beat, like everything else at Wornegon. His face wasn't open like the rest of the culters. His eyes were sparking and mean.

As they neared the door, the man moved. He stood in the center of it in an attitude of waiting, his dark gaze on Jeff. Jeff strode on, intending to push right by and avoid any more HFP talk. His hand touched the door beside the man's arm, and the man said, "Mr. Munro, Jeffrey Munro."

The use of his correct name halted Jeff. "I'm afraid you're mistaken. The name's Miller."

"The name is Munro," the man said. "And we're sorry that you're leaving so soon."

"I'm sorry you're sorry, but I am leaving."

"I don't think so. Not yet anyway."

"What's this all about?" Cory wanted to know.

"You're not concerned in this, Mr. Bennett," the man said. "My business is solely with Mr. Munro."

Jeff fought to place the man and wondered why he thought he should be able to. Then a remembered fragment came to him, and he asked, "You couldn't be Rogers, could you?"

"Yes. How splendid that you know me. It will make my mission much simpler." The words were polite and gracious, but the man was too much the opposite for them to ring true. "I've been sent to fetch you by our beloved Director, Mr. Montgomery Hicks. He doesn't want you to leave without seeing him. He is sure you have questions to ask about Heralds for Peace, and this time he hopes your articles will contain facts, not mere prejudices."

"Oh—my articles." Jeff relaxed. The name Rogers had sprung from the story the Running Man had told him, and he had almost fled as he realized it. But this whole incident was concerned only with that nasty article he had written. It made sense. HFP would want to gloss itself over to him before he wrote anything more. "Actually, I don't intend to write any more articles."

"We can hardly believe that," Rogers answered. "You're not known as a tight-mouthed man. Surely you won't begrudge our Director a few minutes of your time."

Jeff turned to Cory for silent advice, but Cory only shrugged.

"I'm determined to bring you to him," Rogers said.

"I can see that. But I may be just as determined not to come."

"You will come." Rogers didn't change his tone or pitch, but Jeff couldn't decide if he had been threatened or if it was merely part of Rogers' strange way of talking.

"Will I get answers to my questions?" Jeff asked. "Any questions?"

"That is Mr. Hicks' intent."

"Then, I suppose…" He thrust his suitcase at Cory.

"What the hell," he said, "I may as well accept Hicks' offer. Wait for me here, will you?"

"I can't come along then?" Cory asked Rogers. Rogers hesitated. "It probably could be arranged."

"I was just testing," Cory said. "If I couldn't have gone, Jeff couldn't have gone either. I'll meet you outside when you're through, Jeff. I want to inspect some of Urias' work."

Cory went on through the door, lugging both suitcases, and Jeff jerked involuntarily as Rogers' thin hand fell on his arm to start him back toward the elevators.

CHAPTER FOUR

THE elevator ride had an aura of uneasiness, and all because of Rogers. His skinny, sharp-eyed presence disturbed Jeff. He stood tall, and a sense of violence radiated from him.

The doors whirred open at the sixteenth floor. They stepped out onto another thick carpet, and into a long hall, punctuated with massive wooden doors. Rogers thrust one of them wide. The room before Jeff was huge, and at the far end, squatting as king amid the splendor of the appointments, was a huge mahogany desk, with a huger presence behind it.

The presence was Montgomery Hicks, Director of HFP. "Come in. Come in," Hicks' bass voice sounded across the space.

Hicks was a giant. Tall, heavy and balding, he wore black-rimmed glasses and peered out of them with a penetrating stare that held no honesty. His clothes were finely tailored, cut and sewed to fit his bulky frame and bring it down from slobbishness to affluence. Jeff halted before the desk and gauged his man.

"Sit down, sit down." Hicks repeated everything twice. "We're informal here at HFP, Mr. Munro. Make yourself comfortable."

Jeff turned to find a chair, but one was already being shoved toward him, Rogers behind it.

"Would you like a drink?" Hicks asked. "Rogers, mix us a couple of drinks, please." He rose from the desk and came around to Jeff, taking the seat Rogers rushed forward. His bulk spread to cover the recesses of the chair.

"It's a little early for liquor," Jeff said.

"Ah, you're quite right. Coffee then? Rogers, send down for some coffee."

Rogers went to the phone and put through the order. As he did it, he lost his ominous appearance. He was no more than a glorified flunky, after all, and Jeff paid him little more attention.

"How do you like our little establishment?" Ricks asked. He didn't wait for an answer. "Of course, it doesn't really matter how you like it now. You'll easily come to appreciate it when you realize that you have no choice."

Jeff looked at Hicks sharply, but could decipher nothing from the calculated smile on the giant's face.

Hicks' voice lowered a good three tones to a bass that thundered in the room. "I believe in getting right to the point, Munro. And the point is simple. You know too much! You've kept bad company, you know too much, and you are dangerous to HFP! You also know *firsthand* what happens to men who are dangerous to HFP!"

Tension crept up Jeff's legs and spread through his body. Rogers' thin shadow cast itself on the wall beside the bulky form of Hicks, and they were suddenly his adversaries.

Hicks had threatened him. The threat was clear, sharp and menacingly inescapable.

Jeff started to his feet, but saw the shadow of Rogers' hands coming down to meet his shoulders before he felt their pressure. "No," Rogers said. "You will remain seated."

"I see you're not a man of action," Hicks mocked.

"He takes insults well, too," Rogers said.

Jeff felt caught between two descending hammers. Giving him no chance to orient himself, they had dropped upon him and stunned him into inaction. He was making a complete fool of himself, but what did a man do when his life was threatened so coolly? The threat still echoed, but he didn't quite believe it.

"You've understood me then," Hicks said.

"Very clearly," Jeff answered, and his voice was lonely in the room where he had no friend. "You've just threatened me with death."

"And are you shivering?" Hicks was eager, waiting for some sadistic pleasure he hoped to gain from Jeff's response.

"Not yet." Jeff wouldn't give him that pleasure.

Hicks pressed his fat hands together almost gleefully. "You come up to my expectations! To your living legend. You're giving me great satisfaction, Munro."

"*Mister* Munro, please," Jeff countered, grasping the first insignificant thing he could find to arouse his anger and fight shock. "I don't like people who use last names."

"I do," Hicks answered. "It sets a certain distinction between men. Employer and servant, for instance. Master and slave. Or wielder of power and the one to be crushed."

Jeff said nothing, so Hicks went on. "But enough of death. I don't want our relationship to come to that."

"Are you calling back your threat now?"

"Not at all. I'm simply raising the alternative." Hicks had again lost his look of a giant and was just a congenial fat man. Jeff didn't let the cordiality fool him, not when the threat was still quivering in his throat.

"You have your own opinions of HFP, Mr. Munro, garnered from our late friend, Thomas Sullivan."

"The man who died in that terrible accident."

The Running Man finally had a name. Thomas Sullivan. What else had he possessed, Jeff wondered, before he met the Wielder of Power and became the Crushed?

"Anyway," Hicks said, "since you do have Sullivan's story, I'm not going to waste time denying anything he may have told you. You can believe him as freely as you wish. I have greater things in store for you. I've already given you one side of the picture—the same fate Sullivan suffered. But there is another. I'm offering you power, Munro. Position and power. You see, we were ready to invite you to Wornegon when you came of your own accord."

"Why?"

"My dear friend, you would be invaluable to us, don't you know that? Your reputation, your influence, you'd be invaluable to us. After all, our line of endeavor is your line, too."

"I've never associated myself with a cult in any form."

"I'm not speaking of the cult, Mr. Munro. Politics—that's the key. You teach political science, you have many contacts in state politics. And at the moment, politics is HFP's main concern. Surely you've noticed the distinguished guests we have at Wornegon. And those are just a few of the men working with us." Hicks leaned forward, an eager glint in his eyes as he boasted, "We have ten United States Senators with us—ten! We expect to gain eighteen more in the fall elections. And governors—we have those, too. So, you see, HFP is in your line of work. Definitely."

A soft bell signaled the arrival of the coffee in a wellconcealed dumb-waiter. Rogers served it with an aplomb that was incongruous in him. Hicks took his cup in his hands, running his fingers about its rim, almost fondling it. He had the look of a man engaged in playing cat and mouse, and Jeff couldn't forget why.

"I see I haven't impressed you," Hicks said. "Then let me go further. In other parts of the world, we have even more influence. Think of it, Munro. We can create history—we can ferment crisis—we can even manipulate the cold war. We can do anything we set our minds to doing, and all for Good. All for HFP."

Jeff wasn't surprised or impressed. "You say, all in the name of Good. And then you say, all for HFP. Those two things don't go together."

"Then you think I'm exaggerating our power?" Hicks asked.

"How could you have such vast power? People aren't fooled that easily."

"There you're mistaken. Mr. Munro, you have no idea how much evil can be accomplished in the name of Good, if the person is fanatic enough about it."

This statement was uttered in a deeper tone, and it hit Jeff with a little shock, because he realized the truth of it. History had taught the lesson many times, but people forgot to be forewarned.

"Now you've turned the coin," Jeff said. "You're admitting that HFP is actually bent on evil."

"HFP is bent on HFP. And that is goal enough in itself."

"And your reason for telling me this when I'm already on your list of dead men?"

"Haven't you guessed?" Hicks' effort at amazement was thin. "We want you to join with HFP and share the rewards."

The Running Man's frantic fright returned to Jeff's mind; his terror of the initiation; his flight from the darkened cubicle. "I see. This is actually just a play to silence me short of murder. I've heard about your initiations. I have no urge to come out of one of them a fanatic."

"Have I asked you to join the rabble?" I'm offering you a position on the Board. And in payment for your help, I'm offering you power and wealth, more than you ever dreamed existed."

Jeff almost laughed. "Where did you get the impression I'd go for that? Whoever told you that I'd jump for power was dead wrong. Power isn't one of the motives that drives me."

"We know you all right. You'll accept power as quickly as the next man. Your position, and your struggle to procure it, told us that. And you'd be loyal to the trust. Once taken up, you never lay down a cause, you never turncoat to it."

"Thank you." Jeff bobbed his head. "Then we do know each other. The only false note is the conclusion you've drawn. I've already taken my stand on HFP." He was bluffing now, testing the lengths of Hicks' previous threat. The man held out riches and power in one hand and death in the other, and it was incongruous. There had to be a loophole somewhere.

But Hicks didn't show him any. "I've angered you with my order of business. I'm sorry, because I had planned it another way. We would have had you here for this little talk in any case, but since Sullivan got to you with his mad fears, I had to preface our conversation with a brutality which is abhorrent to me."

"As abhorrent as watching a man bleed in the street?"

"That incident was entirely unnecessary," Hicks said without remorse. "Sullivan just couldn't see it our way."

"Did you offer him this choice, too?"

"Of course not. We had no interest in him."

Jeff held himself steadfastly still, but inside the somber shell, he was spinning in the vastness of the room. Threat and offer—they were designed to balance one another, but they didn't. And, caught inside the fear of the threat, he couldn't grasp a sensible thought.

"Our friend is shocked into a stalemate," Rogers' voice leaked out into the air. "You've hit him with too much, Mr. Hicks."

"And that's just the way you planned it, isn't it?" Jeff spat. "I was told you have specialists for this sort of thing—specialists in psychology and propaganda."

"Now don't turn into an accuser," Hicks chided. "Actually this is all your fault. We went out of our way to try the other—studying you, planning for you, making you an attractive offer."

Jeff leaned back, welcoming the solid feel of the chair against his shoulders. What did Hicks want of him, besides his life? "Because I refused your offer, I am to die, is that right?"

"No, no," Hicks said quickly. "The offer still stands. Once made, it stands—just waiting for your better judgment to realize its implications. You only have to choose your alternative—cooperation or death. That choice is simple."

"I don't think so."

"But how can there be any question?"

"There is a question," Jeff accused, "and a big one. I don't know the first thing about HFP."

"I've told you everything I can. I can't let you in on our secrets until we have your sworn loyalty."

"Then, you see, there is no choice."

Hicks' answer was stubbornly hard. "You have all the choice you're going to get. We're not playing games, Munro. We have the ability to carry through the threat, as well as supply the promised rewards."

The decision was too much, and too sudden. Jeff could only ask himself, *If it comes down to it, will I be willing o die in a fight against HFP?* He didn't know the answer. He hadn't had time or opportunity to consider it. Somehow the promise of death seemed flimsy next to the preferred rewards of cooperation, as though the threat were made only to frighten him into their fold.

"You can't settle your mind," Hicks said. "I haven't asked you to. I'm willing to give you time. After all, we can't appear too cold-blooded and expect to gain trust, can we, Rogers?"

Jeff protested, "I don't believe any of this. I think you're just trying to scare me off."

"You'll find out soon enough," Rogers said.

"Will twenty-four hours do?" Hicks broke the rising tension. "It seems a reasonable amount to me. Greater decisions have been made in less time."

Jeff jumped at the reprieve.

"Of course, you'll spend those hours here at Wornegon." Hicks' inflection remained open. "I hardly need to point that out. You're an honorable man, and I'm sure we can trust you."

Jeff stood up without an answer. All that was in his mind was the looming of twenty-four solid hours; hours he could use to get far away; hours he could use to free himself; hours he could use. His one task now was to protect himself so he wouldn't be forced to choose the lesser of two evils.

Rogers moved behind him, and Jeff felt, more than heard, the movement. Rogers was an enigma; a prowling vulture, thinly fleshed and hungry for violence. He and Hicks made a good pair. The one to kill and the other to feed upon the kill.

"I'm sorry you're so anxious to part company," Hicks d oddly, "but since you are, Rogers will escort you back the lobby. Really, Munro, I think you'll be in just as much of a quandary tomorrow. Why don't you save yourself the nerve-racking experience and agree to my terms?"

"I'll take my time, thanks. And quit pretending civility. It doesn't hold after you've threatened my life." He turned, and Rogers swooped before him, leading the way unnecessarily back to the huge doors which had opened and thrust him innocently into this tiger's den.

Jeff shoved past Rogers and hurried across the lobby to the main door. Cory would be waiting outside. He stepped into the sun, squinting against the brightness of it, and let his eyes rake over the green grass. Cory wasn't in sight. Had they done something with him?

He went down the front of the building, struggling to keep from breaking into a lope and drawing unwanted attention. The grounds were alive with people, going from building to building, in and out, up and down. Wornegon was an anthill, and he wanted to remain just another ant until he had escaped it.

He rounded the corner of the building. "Cory!" he yelled.

This side of the grounds was almost empty, and the emptiness clenched Jeff's stomach with a terrible loneliness. If they had spirited Cory off somewhere…

"Cory!"

Far down the side of the building, a head popped up from behind a hedge, and then another head. Cory and the old man. Jeff laughed a quick, relieved laugh. Behind the hedge, he found the suitcases piled, and Cory back down on his knees.

"That didn't take you very long," Cory said.

That was the weirdest thing about it, Jeff thought. It had all happened so quickly, and yet a lifetime had gone by.

"We've got to get going," Jeff said, trying to prod Cory without arousing the old man.

"Have a look at this first," Cory answered. "Harvey here has found a new way to propagate these bushes by bending a branch over and covering it with earth."

"It's not new," the old man, Harvey, said. "I can't take credit."

Jeff muttered, "Come on, Cory. I want to reach home before dark."

"But Harvey offered to give us some of the new plants."

"Maybe next time, all right?" Jeff knew his voice was rising, but he couldn't control it. Cory was a nightmare man, slow-moving, unwilling to act, while a crisis lowered over his head. "Please, Cory. I want to get going."

Cory stood up and brushed his trouser legs free of earth. "Thanks anyway, Harvey. We'll pick up the plants the next time."

Jeff grabbed up the suitcases and started away. Cory ran a few yards to catch him. "What's the matter with you?"

"I can't waste time explaining. Let's just get to the car."

They crossed the lawn, making a straight, fast line for the parking lot gate. As they approached it, two figures came up from the other side, and Jeff's breath drew harder as he recognized the skinniness of Rogers. He increased his pace to beat Rogers to the gate, but they met in the center. Rogers stood on the right, his companion on the left.

They carried no weapons—none that were visible at any rate. The only weapon Rogers had was the nasty glint in his gray eyes and the cocky posture of his body.

"What's wrong?" Cory asked. "Not another delay. We want to make Union Town before dark."

"I don't think you will," Rogers said.

Jeff was silent. Cory didn't know what he was talking about and could perhaps handle this gambit better because of it.

"Is this some kind of game you folks play up here?" Cory laughed. "Everybody enter, but nobody leave?"

"You tell him, Munro," Rogers said; "if you think it's wise to include another bystander."

In answer, Jeff took a sudden step forward. The man beside Rogers reacted immediately, blocking his way. His hands never left his pockets, he said nothing menacing, but he blocked the way as certainly as though he held a gun.

Jeff backed up. "It's no use, Cory. We may as well go back."

Cory met his gaze with confusion. "But I thought—"

"Nobody thinks at Wornegon," Jeff spat. "We just do as we're told." He walked away from the gate.

Cory's steps behind him were muffled by the grass. "I wish you'd explain. What was that quiet battle?"

"I have to stay here another twenty-four hours, that's what. I'm caged. I'm too dangerous for them to let me run free." He headed around the side of the building again. "But they don't know me. They can't be everywhere, and I'm not afraid to climb fences. Are you with me?" Jeff stopped walking to face Cory with the question.

"Well—yes!" Cory didn't hesitate.

"Think it over. You can probably walk right through that gate and drive home. You don't have to stay."

"I didn't think staying was the general idea. I thought we were going to climb fences." Cory had already made his decision.

"I have another idea. How full is your suitcase?"

"Hardly half full," Cory said. "I only brought one extra shirt and some underwear."

"So did I. Here's what I want you to do. Stuff my clothes in with yours and leave my suitcase behind. Then go to the lot and get the car. They'll let you through, I'm sure. Drive away far enough so you're out of sight of Wornegon's buildings, then wait. I'll try the fences alone. If I make it, I'll find you and we'll be home free."

"But that leaves all the fighting to you."

"That's the way it should be. I figure you'll provide a diverting action and give me a better chance. And, I'll make it, Cory. They won't be expecting me to try the fences."

"If you don't get to me by noon, I'm coming back," Cory threatened.

"I'd rather you didn't."

"Now you sound like the Running Man."

"That's the last thing in the world I'm going to be. Get going, friend, and I'll see you in a little while."

He left Cory standing on the grass with the suitcases and went around to the front of the building. It was well that anyone watching should think he had given up, said goodbye to his friend and returned to his room. He felt like a culprit out in the night, planning strategy, stealing about. But it wasn't night, and he realized he had to face the actual danger sooner or later.

Inside the building, he barely escaped the Wiggler. He outmaneuvered her, and when her back turned, cut sideways into one of the many halls that led from the lobby.

The hall was empty and he started down it. There was bound to be an exit leading out at the side of the building if he followed the hall far enough. He passed many unexplained doors, came to another hall posted with a sign, *No Admittance,* but by-passed it, keeping straight on his course. A door finally did rear up, casting thin light into the corridor. He pushed it open.

He was between two buildings, the main one and the Recreation Center. He took advantage of his aloneness and ran across the open space, then cut behind the recreation hall and hurried the length of it.

Free of the protection of the building, he slowed to a walk. He would head into the woods that ringed Wornegon and try the fences there. With so much woods and so much fence, he couldn't miss.

The trees closed over his head and the sunlight became filtered, arcing down through the leaves in funnels of dappled yellow.

Once the buildings were out of sight, he turned left, heading for the fence he was sure was in that direction.

Time stretched as he walked, creating paths, the only human creature in the forest. Birds flew about him and squirrels chattered angrily, sassy and aggressive.

He stopped abruptly as a green barrier loomed before him. He slid behind a tree trunk to survey it. Then he realized what it was—the fence, overgrown with vines, buried beneath leaves and tendrils. He listened carefully to all the sounds about him. Birds, the rustle of animals—but no footsteps, nothing human.

He was fifty feet from it, and had a clear path, but he crept those fifty feet, using all the cover he could find. He supposed he was making a fool of himself, hiding from nothing, but he was taking no chances.

The fence was six feet high, and chain-link. He could barely see its outline through the vines. It would be hard to get a toehold, but if he jumped and grasped the top rail, he could pull himself over. He took the last three feet in one leap, and springing, caught hold of the rail. The vine leaves crumpled under the weight of his grasp and he swung his legs wildly to get enough leverage to swing himself over. His head was higher than the fence and he could see over it.

Something moved in the underbrush. Then again. He stopped his flailing and waited, hanging heavily, his hands and arms beginning to hurt. A deer? he asked himself hopefully. A gentle, melting-eyed deer?

The movement parted the bushes, and a foot thrust itself out of the undergrowth, a foot wearing a brown boot. A man emerged, another close behind him.

"You, there," the first man shouted. "Get off the fence!"

Jeff hung, wanting to be invisible, but knowing his hands showed over the top. Who was this man? He was burly, dressed in heavy work clothes, and didn't look like he belonged to Wornegon.

"In the name of HFP, get off the fence," the call came and answered his questions.

But how? How had they found him here?

He lifted himself up. He would leap this fence anyway and to hell with them. They had no weapons.

At the sound of his feet searching for a toehold, the man in the lead thrust a hand into his pocket. He didn't pull it out again, but a shape took form inside that pocket, and Jeff knew there was a gun.

He let go of the rail and fell to earth, letting his body go limp, and remained on the ground, trying to grasp the situation. He had chosen randomly. He had been quiet. And yet they had been at the fence to meet him. How?

The question echoed in his brain like a thunder clap, and he sprang to his feet and headed blindly back the way he had come. Fear ran with him now. It hadn't been easy, it hadn't been a simple escape to freedom. He was still trapped inside Wornegon, and long overdue panic seized him, pushing him forward under the trees, pounding with his feet.

When he hit the path back to the building, he turned away from it. All he could think of was the face of the Running Man. Tom Sullivan fled before him, under the trees, around the rocks, splashing across the narrow stream that rippled in the way. He was running a curve, and knew it, but didn't care. He would come to the fence again, but in a new place, one he didn't even choose, and this time he had to make it over the top—this time he had to…

You know too much! rang in his head. *You are dangerous!*

Hicks had said that to him, and he had accepted it in shock, heard it in silence, but now it was no longer silent. It screamed behind the breeze, and he ran from it. *Decide. Decide. Decide! HFP is on the march. Join and save the world!* HFP was a spider with a strong, strong web and he was helplessly entangled. He had to get out. Cory was waiting. Help was waiting.

He crashed hard into the fence and was bounced back, falling to the ground. He picked himself up and grabbed for the top rail, but fell. On the second try, he secured his place and peered over. Waiting there were two more men—not the same two, but two more, just as big, just as determined and just as hated.

He dropped to his feet. There was no more asking to be done, no more hoping. He could race the forest and leap at the fences until his heart burst inside him. Rogers was too cunning for him. Hicks was too big for him. He knew he would never get out.

He scrambled back the way he had come. He was defeated then. He had to make the choice then. His only possible hope was that Cory wouldn't return, but would go home and report this to someone who could help. And even as he hoped, he knew it wouldn't happen. He hadn't told Cory why he was being held.

He recrossed the stream, taking his direction from it. He gradually regained his composure and was ashamed of the mad dash through the woods. Yet it had been a natural thing. If he had been an animal, he would have chewed off his foot to get out of the trap. He could only run. Tom Sullivan, the Running Man, had been right. There was something unholy at Wornegon, and it was powerful enough to kill him. He had to find some way to fight it.

CHAPTER FIVE

CORY came back at noon but Jeff wasn't glad to see him. If he had to make the decision, he needed time alone, but the time was spent wrestling with his conscience over Cory; whether or not to use him, or to leave him out of it and secure his safety. If Cory knew the story, he would leave to find help. But, Jeff asked himself, would that help do any good? Could he prove the threat had been made, when Hicks and Rogers would stand together and deny it? And once done, Cory would be running, too.

By the time Cory knocked on his door, he had decided that much, at least. He had no right to endanger a friend who had come along to help him. So he brushed Cory's questions aside, and when Cory persisted, turned the rudeness to a plea for trust and patience which couldn't be refused.

Alone again, Jeff settled into the quiet of the room. Tomorrow he must give an answer, whether it was a true one or not. He slammed his fist angrily into the frustrating softness of the bed. He had come here with other plans, plans of investigating the Running Man's story. Now, more than before, it needed investigating.

Dinner was served in his room, and then it grew dark outside his windows. His only plan was a nebulous one. After dark, when the grounds were empty, he would sneak out of the building and find the place Tom Sullivan had said was a vantage point for the glow in the woods. He couldn't escape, but he could search the confines of his cage for any clue it contained.

He waited in the dim room and the silence was thickly sweet, but held no solace. He waited, and every hour of deeper dark stretched his nerves tighter.

A slight noise jerked him erect. Metal on metal, it clicked into the air from the direction of his door. He could just make out the sounds of footsteps going away in the hall. He looked at his watch. Eleven o'clock. Curfew time. Then he discovered what he had heard. The door was locked. From the outside.

He strode back to the bed. Locking guests in was not the practice of HFP. But, then, he wasn't a guest any more. Now even his hope of investigating the glow was gone. He couldn't get out.

Anger fired through him. He had been stupid, waiting too long to make his move. Five minutes earlier, and he could have been on the way to that rise of ground, watching for the glow. But it was too late. There was only one way out of the room.

And that's a lie, he said to himself. *There's never just one way to do anything.*

He switched off the room lights so he could see into the darkness. As his eyes adjusted to the night, he opened his window and peered down the side of the building. He was up three floors, and the drop was steep and smooth.

There were no window ledges around the buildings. It was too modern for that. But where the metal exterior slabs came together, there were seams—seams of smooth metal, but perhaps enough for a toehold. Now the question came, was he brave enough to risk the fall? The answer lay in how much he wanted out.

He pushed the window wide and eased himself onto the edge. He turned, resting his weight on his hands, and let his feet dangle. They touched the nearest seam and he held his breath. Was it wide enough? He didn't need much. He let his weight gently onto his feet, testing the width. It was enough. Balancing carefully, he could stand. And he wasn't stretched out his full length, which meant he had some leeway in getting to the next, lower, seam.

He tried for it, searching blank air with his right foot. There was nothing. He couldn't reach it. He was hanging on the side of a three-story drop and there was no way down. He heaved himself up again and sat straddling the window edge, waiting for the shakes to die out of him.

He put the lights on again and scoured the room for an idea. His gaze lit on the traverse draperies. The windows covered most of one wall, so the drapes were a sea of material, and where there were traverse drapes, there had to be a cord. He pulled it out for inspection. It was distressingly slight, but it was nylon. He couldn't be sure it was strong enough, but it was a chance. And if luck was at all with him, the cord shouldn't have to take too much weight. Perhaps the first seam-step down was the longest. Perhaps the rest were closer together.

He turned the lights out so his actions couldn't be seen from outside, then ripped the drapes down and yanked the cord out of the traverse rod. He knotted the cord securely around the center post of the window, and lowered it out. It fell against the building silently. He could barely see it in the night. It wasn't long enough, but he would somehow manage the final drop—if he made it that far.

Scrambling out of the window, he dangled his feet and found the first seam. He closed his eyes, trying to close fear out, too, and with one hand, caught hold of the cord. With two feet on a narrow seam, one hand on the slim cord, his only security was in the hand still grasping the window edge. He let go.

The cord caught his weight and stretched menacingly. He reached frantically below him in the dark, searching for the next seam, rubbing his foot madly along the building. The cord wasn't going to hold!

His toe caught the seam as he relaxed enough to bend his body and stretch his leg. He put as much weight on the lower seam as he could and eased himself down until he dared move his other foot to join it. He caught the seam he had just passed with his right hand, and leaned against the wall, shaking until his eyes blurred with tears. One down—how many to go?

He couldn't wait. Every moment lost meant the weakening of his lifeline. He dangled his foot to search for the next seam.

And there it was. These seams were closer together. He could reach without the cord. Trying to balance his weight between hands, he slid down and found a new toe-hold. And then again.

He clambered his way down the side of the building, down the sheerness and smoothness, like a descending beetle. The way grew easier as he learned the pattern. Another floor, another longer step down, and then more close-together seams.

The cord ran out. He barely realized it in time and clamped on tightly. There was no more help then. He either had to make it with finger-holds or jump.

He hazarded a look down. He was halfway between the first floor and the second, a big drop, but possible. It would be better to plan it than to fall attempting to go down another seam.

He drew a great breath, leaned against the comfort of the wall for a long minute, then threw himself backward into space.

He hit the ground and rolled. He lay still. Grass poked up at his mouth and nose as he lay there, afraid to move lest he find something painful in his body. Nothing hurt now. He squirmed a little, and still no pain.

Smiling at the darkness, he got to his feet. He was all right. Hicks and Rogers didn't know everything about "their man." They didn't know he was a fly who could walk upside down on grass, or an ant who could land on his feet and rise up again.

Confidence returned for the first time since his mad dash through the woods, and he slid along beside the building, keeping in its shadow. This afternoon he had run to the right. The Running Man had said, "Go left." Since he had crossed a stream this afternoon, it must mean that the stream circled through Wornegon, and he would find it again where Tom Sullivan had found it.

He was nearly at the left corner of the building when voices cut the night. He squatted. He spotted two figures—two men walking his way, between the buildings. They wouldn't be guests. The guests were tucked safely in bed, on their honor to stay there. These must be guards, or big HFP wheels. They would pass right by him if he waited, and the chances that they would see him were too big to take. His best choice was to run.

He crept on hands and knees for a few feet, angling for a hedge.

He thanked God that the night was cloudy and no moonlight would silhouette him. When he was within sprinting distance of the hedge, he doubled his body into a hump, and ran, awkwardly, painfully, for the cover of the bushes. He slammed into them making a loud rustle, then crouched, straining to hear whether his action had changed the tone of the voices.

They droned on in a conversational tone. He was safe.

He crawled through the hedge, accepting the scratches as they came. When open space grew before him, he took it at an upright run. The green grass that Urias directed to be so perfect cushioned his feet, and he was a silent Mercury speeding, with only the rush of air in his wake to give him away.

One building whizzed by and he by-passed the other, cutting across the lawns to the forest edge. He gained the first trees, thinly growing, and a shout screeched out in front of him.

He darted behind a tree and clasping the trunk, waited, struggling to still his noisy breath. The sound came again. It was no shout. His ears had turned it into a shout. Again it came, the eerie cry of a screech owl, somewhere ahead of him in the woods.

He moved on, staying close to the trees, dashing from one to another, using every available cover. He had been too foolhardy with that sprint across the lawns. If it hadn't been an owl...

He was soon deep in the woods, and he slowed, watching for a rise of ground, or the stream Tom Sullivan had mentioned.

He found the stream by its sound, unable to see anything in the darkness of the covered night. He edged up to the sound and felt water seep into the sole of his shoe. Now which way? There was no rise here. He decided to continue going left, because that was away from Wornegon. He walked the stream bank, anticipating the pull on his legs that would mean he was climbing.

It didn't announce itself that way. Instead, he stumbled, fell on his face, and sprawled halfway up an abrupt, rock cluttered knoll. He went to the top and pivoted slowly, waiting for the glow to spring before his eyes. But the darkness was unbroken. He could wait. The night and the aloneness held a taste of freedom that he relished. The forest surrounded him with rustlings, with the hoarse call of night hawks, the occasional screech of an owl. He sat down, hearing the stream lap below him.

After an hour, he wondered if he was again a fool. Sullivan may have been right about most things, but the glow might have been a figment, a frightened delusion.

The luminous hands on his watch pointed to one o'clock when a pressure struck his eyes. Across the stream, the trees were standing out in shaped silhouette, the trunks straight and black against a soft radiance that reared up behind them. The glow spread upward to light the sky in an arc, diffuse and beautiful, a steady, unchanging aurora.

He stood, fighting back a shiver. He couldn't turn tail now. This was what he had come to see.

Without waiting to make up his mind, he plunged off the knoll and entered the stream. It wasn't so narrow here, and he waded deeper and deeper, until his pant legs were soaked to the knees and his feet were slowed to a hard push through the water. He gained the other bank and sank back into forest.

When the glow grew so bright that he knew he was close to its source, he took to the tree trunks again, inching up warily, keeping himself covered. One tree, and another—and then there were no more. He had found the source.

He stood, inanely hugging the tree as he gazed on a weird sight. The glow rose before him, coming from a huge clearing, created by a ring of burning lamps of a type he had never seen. And in the clearing with the lamps, casting moving shadows, were scores of men—*little men*—broad-shouldered, dark-complected, heavily muscled, but only four and a half feet tall. They moved awkwardly, their actions uncoordinated in a grotesque way. What they were doing nearly sent him flying back the way he had come.

In the clearing, sprawled three shiny machines. Saucer-like machines. And the little men were going in and out of them, loading one, unloading another.

Jeff grasped the tree harder. Then here was proof for the deluge of saucer reports that had come from this area over the years. Actual proof! The people who reported them hadn't been wrong; only the officials who pooh-poohed the people.

The third ship had no activity around it, and as he watched, the little men stood away, leaving it in a wide area by itself. The glow went abruptly dark, and the hum of a hundred muted bumblebees replaced it. Blinded by the sudden darkness, Jeff imagined a shadow rising before him and he cowered back.

Quickly the glow bloomed up again, and he looked into the clearing. There were only two machines now. A shadow had risen; on bumblebee wings, it had sailed up out of the clearing, bound for some unknown, ungodly place.

He had seen enough. His mind couldn't take in any more. Fantasy and dreams were one thing, but seeing fantasy transform itself into fact was too much. He left his tree and ran through the woods, the glow lighting his path, splashing through the stream as he headed back to Wornegon. He had information he had never dared expect, information he was frightened to acknowledge. But it didn't help him. It only made his dilemma and his danger more harsh.

He hit the lawns and raced for his window, coming up against the wall and leaping for the cord. He fell short. He tried again, but he could never make it.

Now he was caged twice—caged outside of his cage. He would have to enter the building through a door. If he had to do it, he would let it be a big play, an act of defiance.

The lobby was dim with only three small lights burning, splashing against the turquoise carpet. He let the door fall shut behind him and turned for the elevators.

A figure emerged from the depths of an overstuffed chair, a tall, thin figure with biting eyes. Rogers. The man said nothing, falling into step beside Jeff. Jeff ignored him, but his skin prickled and sweat was starting to run down his legs to mingle with the dampness from the stream.

Rogers punched the elevator button, the doors opened, and he let Jeff step in first. As the car ascended, Jeff said, "Well?" expecting to open the way for a tirade.

Rogers didn't answer. His lips were tight, locking the words inside his mouth. At the third floor, he led the way to Jeff's room, pulled out a key and unlocked the door. He was a stiff rod of a man, and Jeff wished he would break down and accuse him, wished he would say one word. His silence was a terror in itself.

But Rogers simply waited. Shrugging, Jeff stepped across the threshold into the darkness of his room, the door shut softly behind him, and again the click of metal on metal told him the lock was secured from outside.

On a hunch, he returned to his window and gazed down. His slim cord still blew against the wall, but the scene below it had changed. Two men stood upon the grass, looking back at him. He wouldn't escape that way again.

CHAPTER SIX

MORNING touched Jeff's windows and he met it wide awake. The night had passed with no sleep, for there had been a decision to make. Not Hicks' decision, but his own. Now that he had glimpsed the clearing, the men and the three ships, he had a duty greater than escape, and he had to keep alive to perform it.

The main consideration was to get more information, because HFP was no longer just a cult, no longer even a power-hungry, brutal group of men; there was something more unholy behind it than even the Running Man had guessed, and he had to discover what it was. Since secrets were only given to members, he had to agree to join. The danger lay in whether or not he could make Hicks believe the lie of his surrender.

Then there was Cory. What to tell Cory? He had no time to think that part through. A loud knock pounded on his door and Cory was there, turning the knob that Jeff had heard unlocked at five-thirty as someone released him from his cage.

Cory was clear-eyed, although he complained of little sleep. "I hope you're not planning to skip breakfast, too," he said.

"I can't be sure. I'm not exactly my own master any more." Jeff opened noncommittally, intending to follow the line of talk wherever it took him and tell Cory only what seemed appropriate as the subject arose. "I've got some important things to do."

"And still no explanations?"

"How much do you want to know?"

"All of it!"

"That much, you can't have."

"All right, Jeff, if you want to talk in riddles, I won't bother you for answers. Something happened yesterday when you went up to interview Hicks. I can imagine a lot of things, but I've never liked to work on that level."

"Sit down and quit all the huffing," Jeff told him. "I'll tell you what I can." Jeff placed himself on the edge of the bed, wondering where to begin. With shock. Let Cory feel it, too, and then go on to the explanations. "Something did happen with Hicks yesterday. He threatened my life."

"What? How?"

"In one sentence, he just threatened my life."

"And now you're a prisoner here?"

"No. I'm being kept here until I make a certain decision. Hicks countered the threat with an offer to come in with him, to join HFP and reap some promised rewards."

"You told him where to go with that idea, of course."

"In the face of death? I told him I'd think it over."

Cory was more shocked by this last statement than by the threat.

"For heaven's sake," Jeff protested, "what would you have done? I know their threats aren't empty. I knelt beside the Running Man and learned that much. Besides—!"

"I'm sorry," Cory interrupted. "I haven't any right to judge your reactions when I can't even guess what my own might have been."

"That's just my point. I let the reaction settle in, after I ran around like a wild man trying to get away, and then I made the decision. It's not going to be easy. I'm not sure it will work out. I'm not used to throwing in with a bunch of fanatics."

"Then you've chosen to join with them," Cory stated, his voice low as though he had expected it but was disappointed.

"No, you idiot!" Jeff shouted, but only in the quiet of his mind. He didn't dare say it aloud. Not in this room. Because it might be tapped. Whatever he said here might be overheard and ruin the plan, and ruin Cory. So he said aloud, "I had to make that choice. I don't want to give my life for something I don't even know is evil."

"It killed the Running Man."

"Yes, it did. But I don't know why. Maybe that was a necessary evil." Jeff shifted, gazing down at his feet. "Then there's the other side of it—the opportunity they've offered me. HFP is a big thing, Cory. And they want me in on it, to share the power, the excitement, the bounty, if you want to call it that."

"I can't believe it." Cory stood up. "Making this choice to save your life, I can understand. But making it for power?"

"Haven't you always said that my unadmitted love for power was my real motive for writing articles?"

"Yes, I've said that, but I was only trying to hold you down a bit."

"You didn't mean it?"

"Well—" Cory's answer wouldn't come out. "I don't know. Especially not now, in the face of this."

Jeff quickly outlined Hicks' proposal, the extent of HFP's influence and wealth. "Now," he said, "admit it. You even envy me a little. And you're not as surprised as you like to pretend. This isn't really new. How many times have I complained about my salary, about the rewards I've received for hard work?"

"Hundreds of times," Cory admitted.

"Then, give me one reason why I shouldn't jump at this chance."

Cory faced him. "I haven't even one reason, Jeff. And there's an awfully good one in favor of your joining HFP. Whatever amount of weight you gave to fear in your decision, and whatever amount to greed, I won't say any more."

Jeff wanted to put an end to this conversation. "How about that breakfast? I'll take time—if you're still willing to break bread with me."

Jeff pulled on his suit coat. Once in the hall, he would set the record straight and send Cory away. But what had occurred during the last few minutes, when conveyed from prying ears to interested ears, would pave the way for his double-cross surrender to Hicks. "Come on, Cory. I'm on my way to big and better things."

Cory held back. "Maybe I should get out of the way and leave the field to you."

"Isn't everything settled between us then?" Jeff asked.

"No, because on second thought, I think I'll skip breakfast. I was going to play this quietly and staunchly, go on being a loyal friend. I can't manage it. Since you're not in danger any more, I have no business here, and even if I can't blame you for your choice, I don't have to stick around and watch you betray yourself."

Jeff was startled by the sudden change in Cory. "You're not giving me much of a chance. There was more I wanted to tell you."

"But there isn't any more I want to hear."

Jeff opened the door quickly. Cory was disappointed in him, but once in the hall he could change all that with the truth. He walked out, drawing Cory with him, and walked straight into Rogers, waiting across the corridor. There was no time for truth then. Only time to get Cory safely away before he was pushed up against the wall of HFP right beside him.

"If that's your decision, Cory, okay." Jeff pretended anger. "Run. Don't admit that there's a little of the greedy devil in all of us." He hated Cory's grim grimace, hated to send his friend home believing him to be a traitor to everything he had ever preached. But one way or another, he had to send him home. And this was, perhaps, the swiftest way. "Thanks for the worry you've expended over me, but don't give me another thought. I'm in good hands now."

He swung from Cory to Rogers, shutting his friend out with the cold turn of his back. He heard Cory's steps ebbing away down the hall, and his nerve ebbed with each of them. He was on his own now, with no friend in Wornegon, all three hundred acres of it a death trap, a dark place for dealing and double dealing.

Rogers said, "I've come to see that you have a good table for breakfast. Isn't your friend staying?"

"He's not having breakfast, and neither am I. If Mr. Hicks is open for business, I'd like another interview."

"Fine!" Rogers brightened. "I'll take you to him immediately. I'm sorry about your friend though."

"Don't be. Right at this moment, he isn't my friend—*his* choice."

Hicks extended his hand, smiling a fat, victorious smile. "I'm waiting to welcome you in with us. Since you asked to see me, I take it that you decided to join. You're an intelligent man, Mr. Munro, and when you take my hand, you'll prove it."

Jeff took the puffy hand and it was cold in his. The clasp was brief but, in a strange way, final. It marked the end of the terrible deciding and the beginning of the double-cross. He was sure now that he had guessed right and that his room had been tapped.

"I see a gleam in your eye," Hicks said, "that says you're eager for the promised information."

"You seem to be clairvoyant this morning," Jeff played at the bantering conversation, letting Hicks choose his own speed.

"Quite. Quite. But there are other things to consider, too. Now that you're with us, you'll discover how pressed we are, how we must make every moment of the day count."

"In other words, you want this interview to be short."

"I'm glad you understand. I don't want to seem rude, not after the difficult time you've just gone through, but it's enough that you're with us and we'll be working together."

Hicks' naïveté astounded Jeff. In the simple gesture of the handshake, the man accepted him as an ally. Jeff wondered if his performance with Cory had actually been so good that it dispelled all doubt. Or was it just that Hicks was so sure of his power he didn't expect anyone to be foolhardy enough to try to cross him?

"First—" Hicks sat down—"I know you're wondering why we wanted you with us, why we had you on our list of valuable men."

"That's my first question, yes."

"And it's the easiest to answer. Think of your position, Mr. Munro—Jeff, I'll call you Jeff—and you have the answer. You teach at Union College, and from our reports, you're the campus idol. Students run to you with their problems, fight to get into your classes, and belong to your political science and current events clubs with a vengeance. Are the reports correct?"

"They are. I won't be falsely modest about it because it didn't happen overnight. I earned the position I have. I've tried to be as loyal to them as they are to me."

"Exactly. And that's why you're so valuable. There are eighteen thousand students at Union College; bright, young men and women, the cream of the state, the energy and brains of the state, and those young people are what HFP wants. In our work, intelligence and stamina are basic requirements."

"And just what work is that?"

"Helping underdeveloped peoples, going into the bush, and working, spreading the word of HFP. Young idealists are our best emissaries. You have eighteen thousand of them on tap."

Jeff shifted in his chair, hunting for a way around what was coming. "Then you want me to try my influence on them, to persuade them to read your literature and visit Wornegon."

"In the long run, yes. But first you must do something even more important. You must undo what you have already done with your writings in the papers. We want you to return to Union College and give one of your frequent little talks, but this time you must speak for HFP."

"That's impossible," Jeff protested. "The students at Union College have voted to keep HFP speakers off the campus."

"That's why we haven't been able to get to them. You'll be our wedge."

"But they'll throw me out! They hate HFP."

"You don't understand human nature very well, do you, Jeff? Those students are ready for plucking, believe me, we've planned it that way. All over the world, we've let hatred build up for us. We've even *started* anti-HFP campaigns. Arousing mob emotion is easy. And that's what we need, don't you see? You take a young, intelligent mind—an open, proud mind—and then you fill it with hatred for something, and you press it and give it reason to hate, and then you turn on it. Turn on it!

"Those students hate HFP, but deep within themselves they're ashamed of that hatred because it goes against what they believe in—open minds, tolerance, all of those things. They realize their hatred is emotional. So—you shame them. They're ready to doubt themselves because they're intelligent enough to know they shouldn't hate so violently. They will listen, maybe not the first time you try, but they will listen. They'll finally bend over backwards to rid themselves of this blind prejudice, and a good many of them will come our way just out of guilt for having gone against their own principles."

"Where did you get these theories?" Jeff demanded.

"Why? Don't you believe in them?"

"That's just the trouble. They probably will work."

Hicks caught his reticence and said, "You realize that this will be a show of faith on your part. We've accepted you into HFP but you have to prove your good intentions. A man's word is only as good as his subsequent acts. You wouldn't refuse, would you?"

Jeff would never stand on a platform and speak for HFP, betray the trust of his students, become a Judas goat for their innocence and loyalty. But he could promise to do anything; he didn't have to carry through.

"I wouldn't refuse," he told Hicks. "It's not really much to ask. I expected something bigger."

"This is big enough. It's something we've been trying to do for years." Hicks uttered his next words as though they were an afterthought. "Oh, yes, I nearly forgot the other thing. In order to secure your place among the members, you'll have to participate in an initiation ceremony."

Initiation ceremony! The idea rocketed through Jeff like an explosion. Initiation—change—the Running Man. They all wheeled together in his brain. Hicks had crept up on him again, soothing first, then thrusting deep. They didn't trust him, and they would put him quietly out of the way. The initiation had grown to be the point-of-no-return in his mind.

"Naturally," Hicks filled the awkward silence, "once you have been through initiation, all of HFP's secrets will be open to you."

"Did you go through initiation?" Jeff asked bluntly.

"Of course. We all have. How else can we gain the trust of the members? We are all One, remember."

Then that way out was blocked. If he refused the ritual, Hicks would know he had been lying when he spouted all of the blah into the hidden microphones in his room. He had to agree. He could watch himself, and if things looked dangerous, he could bolt at the last minute. He wouldn't be going in unwarned. "All right," he said. "I'll agree to that, too. You made it clear yesterday that I have no choice."

"I think we're going to get along splendidly." Hicks stood up. "Rogers will escort you down."

"Down?" Jeff tensed.

"To the initiation. You'll be in time. We're sending a group of ten through this morning. You can join them and have this part of your obligation out of the way by noon, so you can return to the college and start on the other part."

He wasn't going to have time to lay any plans. The initiation was waiting for him; the point of no return was just minutes away, and he had no choice.

"I won't be seeing you again, Jeff, until you've given your speech and return for your reward," Hicks said. "So, good luck, and remember, we're going to save the world!"

Rogers didn't even stop at Jeff's floor, but led him straight through the lobby, into an unknown corridor, and up to a metal door. "The rest of them are inside already," Rogers said. "Now, please, do your best to imitate them. Try to act as though you're taking this seriously."

Rogers pushed the door open, Jeff stepped inside, and Rogers retreated. The door clicked shut, and despite the other people in the room, Jeff tried the lock. The door swung open. He wasn't trapped then.

"What's the matter?" a soft voice asked him. "Are you trying to change your mind?"

He swung to meet a girl, slim and small-boned, her hair a shiny blond, and her complexion rosy despite the lack of makeup.

"What?" he asked, not catching her meaning.

"The way you tried the door," she explained, "I thought maybe you were going to turn around and leave." The first true smile Jeff had seen in days lay on her lips, and she was pulling a white garment over her dress.

"No, nothing like that. I just have a touch of claustrophobia and I don't like to be locked in," he lied, uneasy with it.

"You musn't be nervous. This is going to be the most wonderful experience of our lives. Just think—after this, we'll be able to hear God speak."

There was the same expectant joy on her face that he had seen on so many others at Wornegon. She was happy. And that was the only word for it. Bold, eager and happy. "You've made me feel better already," he told her, and it was partly true.

"I'm Jean Tuttle. We can stick together, if you like."

"I like," he said.

There were nine others in the room, all nervously expectant, but none with the shining image of Jean Tuttle. They were ghostly, dressed in the white garments. Loose-fitting and sterile, they reminded Jeff of hospitals and operating rooms.

"We haven't much time," Jean was saying to him. "Let me help you get ready."

She came at him, carrying a mound of white, and he accepted it with a twinge. She held it for him while he slipped in under it, and then it was over him, falling to touch the floor.

"It's not very becoming," Jean said, seeing his embarrassment, "but I guess now we're all brothers under the gown, huh?"

He laughed with her, but deep inside him an anger was growing. This girl was no more than twenty. She was too much like his students, too much like the youngsters Hicks wanted him to betray.

"Do you have any special people you want to help when you're called?" she asked him.

"No. I haven't thought that far ahead. I'm a latecomer."

"They must have considered you ready."

"I don't feel it, myself, that's all. I'm a little leery."

"All of us are. We never think we're worthy—Mr. Rogers told me that himself. And it's a point in our favor. It means we're not entering this with false pride."

"You're really sold on HFP, aren't you?"

"It's something that will fill my life. Where else would I get the chance to help the world toward peace? To help people rise above their lot and find a better way?"

An opening door cut into their conversation. A man came in, silhouetted against blackness in the room behind him. He wore a white garment, too, but the cut of it was full and commanding.

"We will be quiet now," he said. He was big and broad, and the room settled to the silence of breathing at his command. "You are now going to come into your true selves, become worthy to Hear, and join in the most powerful brotherhood in the world—love for your fellows. Follow me."

Jean smiled at Jeff, a shoulder raising, then stepped in front of him to file past the big man and enter the darkness. Jeff trailed after her, pricking his senses. He had to be ready. This was the point of no return.

The room they entered was black dark. A match flared into life, touched a candle wick, and a flickering of shadows rose on the walls. Another candle jumped into light at the other end of the room, and the darkness was broken, but not much. There was no sound but the new sputtering of the wicks.

Without warning, a loudspeaker throbbed into a vibrating voice. "You have entered upon the first step of your journey into Truth. You have come into the Presence, clothed in white, sure of your ignorance, certain of your unworthiness, to stand as nothing before the Door of Light. Whether or not you emerge glorious is up to you alone. Listen—do as you are told to do—subject yourself—realize your lowliness—and pray for guidance."

The voice ebbed, and the room was eerier because of its presence. There was no feeling of reality to any of this. Jeff felt that he couldn't be standing any more alone. The others were here by choice, expecting glory, expecting something wonderful to happen and change them. But he was afraid of that change; he was painfully aware of the danger; every muscle and nerve in his body alert for signs of it, ready to flee before it.

The loudspeaker voice waxed again. "Kneel!"

The people fell to their knees around him, and he got down, too. They waited.

The voice spoke again. "Repeat these lines aloud and search for their meaning within your heart as you speak them. *I know that Heralds for Peace is more than a simple physical closeness of one man to another.*" There was a pause as the words were repeated in the darkened room. The voice continued, stopping after every line for the converts to mimic it. "*Heralds for Peace is a brotherhood of the spirit, a tie of Goodness which transcends the mortal life and glorifies the one who wears its banner. Knowing this, and aware of God in the Good and the Love in Peace, I will work, struggle, obey, deny myself, and, if required of me, I will die—I will give my life—for Heralds for Peace. I will do this gladly and willingly, knowing I am but one spoke in the vast wheel of eternity and one small tool in the hand of God.*"

The voice stopped, the last sentence repeated itself, and the big man who was shut in with them got to his feet. "You may all rise," he said. "You have taken the oath, you have given yourselves to Heralds for Peace. The glory can now be yours."

A sudden clicking arose in the room, and all around the walls, doors that had been invisible in the dimness, flew open.

"You are about to take the next step into pureness," the big man said. "Each of you will go into a cubicle alone. You will remain there one full hour. You have the oath well in mind, and you will concentrate your thoughts on the words and meanings of it. If you are chosen, if you are worthy, this hour will prove it."

His hand swept out, directing the first initiate into a cubicle. The chosen man walked in straight and tall with a tremendous dignity that Jeff had to admire. The door closed behind him. The others followed suit until Jeff was alone. Jean Tuttle had disappeared through a door close beside him, and he was the last to remain in the room. The big man gestured toward him, a sweeping movement that couldn't be misread. He walked to the nearest cubicle and stepped inside.

The door closed behind him and he was in darkness again. He had seen for a moment that the cubicle was small—nine by nine— and furnished with a bare table and a straight-backed chair. Now he couldn't see anything, and the darkness was a shroud ready to reach out and smother him. He fumbled for the chair and sat down, his back to the table.

A light flared up, nearly blinding him, but when his eyes adjusted, he saw that it wasn't a light at all, but merely a lighted word. *"Meditate!"*

It hit him like a cannon shot. Meditate! The Running Man had told him of this, and of the feeling of eyes upon him and something dire about to happen. He was on his feet, his hand against the door before he stopped himself, and retraced the few steps to the chair. He had to stay calm or he couldn't stay alert. He searched his emotions carefully for the feelings the Running Man had described, and as he consciously bent his mind to calmness, he realized he had none of those feelings. He was tense, yes, and nervously waiting, but only because of his fear of coming out of this changed into a monster. The moment for flight hadn't come.

Time inched by as he sat alone, his eyes unerringly drawn to the lighted *"Meditate!"* because it was the only light in the room. He could just barely make out the room by it and nothing was amiss.

He kept checking his watch, over and over, seeing the seconds creep into minutes and the minutes drag themselves into a quarter hour, then a half. Every minute added to his tension because there were so few of them left, and which one would be the dangerous one?

Closing his eyes, he recited bits of poorly remembered I poetry to pass the time. He couldn't spend an entire hour braced for battle. He finished with poetry and tried the Gettysburg Address, then the preamble of the Constitution. Still nothing happened.

The door slipped open.

He whirled out of the chair, but the door was just a rectangle opening back into the candlelit room. And there were people in the room; white-clad people who walked back and forth.

Moving among these people who had gone through the ordeal with him, he let himself relax. He had met the danger and found it a phantom. The Running Man, right so often, had been wrong in this instance.

Jean Tuttle came out of her cubicle and he caught her arm. When he saw her face, he was amazed. She was no longer eager. She was radiant. He couldn't ask her about it because there was a large sign in the room now that commanded, "Silence."

The man in the white gown raised his hands. "Now," he said, "for the third and last step. You will follow me into the glory of your first session of Listening to God for Good. Keep silence with you. Follow."

They filed out after him. The room he led them to was a duplicate of the one Jeff had seen when he sat in on the morning listening session. It was gray and sterile, but its atmosphere didn't dampen the radiant confidence on the faces around him.

They all sat down and the big man doled out pads of paper and pencils. "Write down all you can. If you have succeeded, and Hear, don't lose a word of it. A true Listener never does."

He took a chair himself, lowered his head, and closed his eyes. The light dramatically dimmed.

Jeff sat uncomfortably, his head bent, but his eyes open. He couldn't close himself off from the world, not yet.

Almost in unison, the people stiffened, their heads came up, the half-smiles turned to full smiles, to wonder, and to joy. Pencils started dashing across paper. They were Hearing!

Jeff was not. A tremor of fear crept inside him. He couldn't be the odd one. He tried, straining, but nothing came to him. He couldn't let them see his failure, so he pretended. He smiled as they smiled, and scribbled as fast as they did. But he wrote nothing. His only hope was that they wouldn't ask to see his message. If they did, he was sunk.

The Listening lasted three minutes, and then the people had their eyes open and were reading over what they had written.

"You may speak now," the big man said. "The initiation is done. Welcome to Heralds for Peace. May your lives now take on the purpose and joy you have struggled to attain."

The initiates all started talking at once. Jeff gravitated toward Jean Tuttle. She was standing with two other people, talking quickly, anxious to express herself.

He touched her elbow. "Jean?"

"Yes?" she turned breathlessly.

"Could I speak to you alone?"

"Of course. Come Let's sit over here."

As they went to the side of the room, he watched her closely. The Running Man had been wrong again. This girl wasn't changed. She wasn't a fanatic. She was just a girl who had fulfilled a dream.

"What is it?" she asked him.

"I thought we might compare notes, if you don't mind."

"I'd love to." She pulled her piece of paper out.

"Not those notes. I meant compare experiences, really.

I want to know what happened to you in the Meditation room."

"Oh," she refolded her paper. "It was wonderful, wasn't it? A revelation."

"Yes," he lied, "a revelation. What was your impression—what did you feel—after you went inside?"

"Well, let's see. I went in, and the lights were out, and the word lit up. I sat down. Yes, I sat down and started to think about the content of the oath I had just taken. It was warm in there, and dark. I felt good. Complete. I was trying to calm myself enough to do justice to the meditation when I smelled this wonderful odor.

A beautiful, sweet odor. Of course," she laughed a little, "that was just a hallucination. We were warned that we might have them, from the strain and the dark and all."

"After the odor, then what?" he urged.

"Well, I knew the odor wasn't real, but I grasped it anyway and took it into myself, so to speak, and let it help me meditate. After a minute or two, I heard a sound, a little click, like a door opening, but the door wasn't open, and anyway by then I was so engrossed—" She broke off. "That's all. I just kept on meditating, I guess."

"What do you mean, you guess?"

"That's the revelation. I never knew I had such powers of concentration. I spent that whole hour in deep thought. I relaxed in the beautiful odor, and I thought, and the next thing I knew the hour was up. It was marvelous. Didn't you think so?"

"Oh, yes, of course. Marvelous." He couldn't make sense out of her answers.

"And now," she said, "I'm a Listener, and I'll be able to go right into training. I've picked my area, you see, and unless God calls me somewhere else, I'm going into Africa to help the natives. To bring them some of the joy I've gained."

"And the voice this morning? May I ask what you heard?" He didn't know how far he dared pry without arousing her suspicion.

But she was anxious to share it with him. "God told me that I had proved myself worthy, and He praised me. But He was commanding, too. He reminded me never to miss a Listening session that I might lose the power to Hear, if I missed. And He reminded me to always obey. That command wasn't really necessary, because who's going to disobey God?"

"If you were ordered to die for HFP, would you give your life?"

Her eyes widened in true surprise. "Of course I would. So would you." She hesitated. "Wouldn't you?"

"Naturally," he answered quickly.

"There's only one thing in our lives now, HFP. We live for it and die for it. In the meantime, we must fight for it. We must save the world from itself, throw out the devil, and make people see Truth. 'Get thee behind me, Satan' won't do any more. We have to push him, *force* him out!" During this last statement, the softness had drained from her face and a set determination replaced it. Jeff recoiled as he saw the beginnings of Lucille McBreen in her. This sweet, shining-eyed girl wasn't far from being a fanatic. The Running Man had been right, after all.

He left her in a hurry. He didn't want to see her change before his eyes. He couldn't stand to witness the backwards metamorphosis that was taking place in her, from something fresh, poignant and beautiful to something brash, hard and ugly.

CHAPTER SEVEN

JEFF climbed out of the white robe and went back through the lobby to his room. There was no sign of Rogers. He was on his own, then, for the first time since he had entered Wornegon. On his own, and from what Hicks had said, free to leave—to go home and make that betraying speech.

The speech part he didn't intend to carry out. As for the going home part, he could scarcely wait to walk through the gate, unwatched and unstopped. Then the fight against HFP would begin.

As he repacked his suitcase, which had mysteriously reappeared in his room, he wondered why it had been so easy. Why did Hicks trust him? Yet he had to admit, he knew no real secrets. Like Tom Sullivan, he had only a shadowy glimpse of little men, of three saucer-ships, and a strong feeling of evil that emanated from Wornegon.

He crossed the lobby boldly and asked the desk clerk. "Did Cory Bennett check out?"

"He did, sir. Quite early this morning."

"Would you know what transportation he used? Did he take our car?"

"No, sir. He went by one of our chartered buses. His destination was Union Town, I believe."

Jeff shook his head. HFP grew bigger all the time. "I'm checking out. I expect to be back in a few days."

"We will welcome you."

Now for the door, the gate and the car. Freedom.

As he crossed the lobby, he realized that this was his last moment inside Wornegon. He would never be back. No one could force him back. And one thing had glued itself inside his mind on the day he had tried to jump the fences; one thing had bothered him—a *"No Admittance"* sign.

He put his suitcase down beside a chair and told himself he was foolish for even thinking such thoughts. He had risked enough. But there was frustration in him. He had come here empty-handed and was leaving with crumbs. Crumbs, moreover, that wouldn't stand up to much questioning; crumbs that would spawn disbelief. *"No Admittance"* the sign had said. Why?

No one was watching him. If the Wiggler had been approaching, or Rogers, they would have applied the brakes to his wild notion. But they weren't there. And neither were the brakes.

He left his suitcase by the chair and crossed to the side hall he had gone down before. He promised himself that if one person noticed his route, he would stop. No one noticed.

He entered the corridor. Again it was empty, and he hurried for the sign that had pricked his curiosity. It blocked the entrance to a side hall, and checking to be sure he wasn't followed, he entered it. A few feet along it was another sign. *"No Admittance,"* it said again. There were more, at corners, always at corners where another hall hooked onto the one he was traveling, always leading deeper into the insides of the building.

An odd feeling in his legs stopped him. It was a sensation he couldn't quite put his finger on, but it was queer and didn't belong. He stared back up the hall the way he had come, and realized that he actually was staring *UP*. The hall slanted downward, a gradual ramp. Too slight a decline to notice, it could only be felt in the calves of the legs. Then he was going down to the underside of the building, down into the depths.

He followed the signs as though they were direction signals, jubilant in his defiance. A door was marked, *"Keep Out,"* and he went in, but was disappointed to find only a storage closet full of medicines. Why wasn't it locked? That answer came quickly. The members of HFP could be trusted to obey signs, just as they could be trusted to keep the curfew and not wander out where they might happen upon the glow.

When the ramp ended, another warning sign led him to the right, and he came up against a door. This sign was more severe: *"Positively No Admittance!"* The exclamation mark decided him. He felt exultant as he pushed it open.

He was in a tiny room, blank-walled and bare, with only one light in the ceiling. Before him was another door. This one wasn't marked. This one was locked. He knew that without trying the handle, because there was a buzzer beside it.

He pushed down his foolish jubilation and came back to common sense. A buzzer meant there was someone on the other side of the door—someone to answer. Did he dare take the chance?

He pushed the buzzer. He hadn't come this far to turn back.

After a moment's wait, the knob turned and the door swung inward, just a bit. Jeff's gaze went down—and down—because the person who opened it was short. Too short. He was one of the little men from the clearing.

Surprise froze the boldness in Jeff's throat. The little man was dark; his skin was dusty brown and his eyes were chocolate to match his hair. Those eyes—there was a deadness to them, a dullness. He had seen it only a few times before. Blank eyes; the eyes of poor intelligence; the eyes of crippled intellect. But there was more than that. They somehow weren't human.

"Did you wish to enter?" the little man said, and his voice was soft, his enunciation slow to corroborate the fact of his slight intelligence.

Jeff only managed a nod, but that was enough, for the door swung wide and he had a clear way. The room was huge, twice the size of the lobby, and it was a room of machines. Banks of them lined the walls, and stacks of them reached to the ceiling. There were places where they sat in rows, and other places where they formed circled patterns on the floor. Computers. They could be nothing else. And all around the machines, tending them like grotesque priests, were the little men. The room swarmed with them; all busy, all engrossed in the business of pampering the monsters.

"My name is Toby, sir," the short man said. "I have little time, but I will help you however I can."

"Oh, yes." Jeff shook himself away from the sight of the machines. He decided to play it big, to bluff it out. "Mr. Hicks said you'd help me. I've come to look around. Hicks authorized it."

"I knew that," Toby said innocently. "You would not have come at all without permission. I knew you were one of the special ones anyway—from the initiation."

Jeff opened his mouth to ask for an explanation of that statement, but his question was smothered in a tinny voice that wasn't his own. Its source was the dominant thing in the room. Smack in the center of the machines stood one that set itself apart just by its size. The front of it was a great screen, circular and brightly lighted. The light pulsed spasmodically, off and on, off and on, almost keeping rhythm with the general hum of the other mechanical boxes. Now the light had grown to fill the screen entirely and was holding steady. The tinny voice was coming from it. The voice had said only two words: "Immediate attention!" It said no more.

The little men were riveted to their places, waiting, their chocolate eyes on the screen. Two little men had moved in before it.

The tinny voice intruded again. "Information. Has Cummings concluded the groundwork in Denver?"

One of the two before the screen answered by reading from a piece of paper. "From Emmett Cummings, Denver. The initial stage of development is completed. We are now waiting for word to swing into the final stage."

The words he read made no sense to Jeff. The voice from the screen said, "Permission is granted. The project must be hurried. We are almost ready to move."

Jeff listened through more questions and answers, but none of them touched on anything familiar to him. As the other little men went back to their work, he paced about, inspecting the various machines, not understanding any of them, but fascinated.

The tinny voice—could there possibly be a connection between that voice and the Listening sessions? He didn't know why the question had sprung to mind, except that this machine was so obviously the center of this room, and this room was the secret heart of Wornegon. There might be a link somewhere.

He decided to ask Toby, and let the question come out nonchalantly, careful not to arouse suspicion, if the little man was capable of suspicion. "That voice, Toby. Where does it come from?"

Toby's dusty face was dumbfounded. "The Master," he said. "You are teasing me? It is the Master."

An uneasy glimmer of doubt was growing on Toby's face, so Jeff swallowed his next question. He had wanted to ask Toby about himself and about his fellows. But it wasn't really necessary. The little men were obviously answers to themselves, no matter how farfetched that answer was. Short, awkward, alien beings and three saucer-like machines. They locked together into a fantastic result.

There was nothing creepy about Toby. Toby wasn't human, but he wasn't totally inhuman either. Even so, standing in the room, surrounded by the figures, hearing the tinny voice that had no known home, and being constantly droned upon by the hum of the giant machines, he felt a strange nausea surging in his stomach. He didn't belong here. He didn't like it here.

The emotion had no more than reached from his solar plexus to his brain, when the tinny voice halted in midsentence, then boomed out of the screen, "I sense a hostile presence in the room! An unknown! *Hostile! Hostile!*"

The busy jigsaw of activity stilled and the little men turned from their work in a body. Jeff was ringed with chocolate eyes that had hardened to brown glints.

"Not hostile," he blurted. "Not hostile. Just unidentified." He took three fast steps toward the machine, not understanding the working of it, but hoping his cry would carry to the source. "My name is Jeffrey Munro. I've been through the initiation."

"Munro," the tinny voice boomed into the iron. "I have no information on any Munro, Jeffrey. No information."

The little men were advancing, Toby in the lead. They had him encircled and they closed the space, step by short step. He pivoted, watching them come, almost hypnotized, closer and closer. What would they do to him if they ever laid their hands upon his body?

The thought of the alien hands directed by the chocolate eyes flooded hot panic through him and he ran. He hit their line and knocked them aside like marionettes, breaking through their ranks. Before he could escape through the door, he felt something new behind him, something that didn't emanate from the little men.

It was an Essence—a presence—and it was deep-soaked in menace and hate. It reached for him with intangible hands, and only the haven of the hall seemed safe. He fled for it blindly, forgetting everything but the Thing that was chasing him.

He ran the corridors, praying that it would ebb and he could escape it. Finally he came up against a wall, too tired to run further. The wall was cool on his forehead, and he rolled his head back and forth, blotting the sweat from his eyes.

The Essence was gone. It hadn't followed him. It had remained inside the room with its pulsing light and its machines. His own terror had chased him this far.

He straightened up and retraced his previous steps to the lobby. He had information now, and if he could convince the necessary people that he wasn't insane, something would be done to stop whatever was going on inside HFP.

The lobby was crowded with people, talking and reading from the stacks of HFP literature that littered the tables. Jeff picked up his suitcase.

"Jeffrey Munro!" the loudspeaker called. "Will Jeffrey Munro please come to Mr. Hicks' office. Jeffrey Munro!"

He paid it no attention, except to quicken his pace. The front doors weren't far away and this time he was going through them.

"Mr. Jeffrey Munro!" the loudspeaker called again. "Please come to Mr. Hicks' office. Jeffrey Munro!"

"What's the matter, can't you hear?" Rogers said from close beside his shoulder.

Jeff stopped, stared at the skinny man and swung for the elevators. There was no sense in trying to bolt. If Rogers was here, his armed gorillas weren't far away.

As the elevator climbed, he wondered frantically how to play this scene that was flying headlong at him. How should he react to Hicks? It was only too possible that his attempted double-cross had fallen on its face.

Hicks met him standing up, accentuating his bigness. "Well," he said from a red face, "did you enjoy your little side trip?"

"Not much," Jeff snapped. "I don't know what it is you've got down there, but I didn't think much of it. And I don't think much of this. Every time I start out the door, I'm dragged back. I want to go home, Hicks. I'm just plain sick of this place." He let the temper blow itself into an opening. He would follow it and play this scene with anger as its springboard.

Hicks laughed maddeningly. "I wouldn't say you were dragged back. I simply had you paged."

"You enforced it!"

"I'm afraid I have less and less control over Rogers. He puts his heart into his work, and where HFP is concerned, anything goes with him."

"Except me!" Jeff countered. "I never go past the fences."

"At least you still have your sense of humor. Get rid of that red face. I didn't ask you up here to chastise you."

"You mean that my prying doesn't make any difference?" Jeff watched Hicks warily.

"I was surprised that you did it, yes. I would rather you hadn't. But I'm not going to criticize the very qualities that make you so valuable to us. You have a quick, probing mind. I should have expected you to do something rash. I didn't give you enough information to satisfy your sense of proportion."

Jeff sat down, his anger subsiding in amazement. "You're blaming yourself for what I did?"

"I'm supposed to know how to handle men. I fumbled you."

"This is all very nice, I'm sure, but it doesn't solve anything. I still don't have any information," Jeff said.

"Even after what you saw?"

"What did I see? A bunch of machines, a bunch of alien men. What connection do they have with HFP? I'll lay it right on the line, Mr. Hicks. I said I'd work with you and my motives were half-greed and half-fear of refusing. But I can change my mind."

Hicks smiled weakly. "What happened to the half of your motive that was fear?"

"I've still got it. But it doesn't worry me. I think I have a better bargaining position now. I want to cooperate, and it's up to you to make it possible for me."

"All this," Rogers said, "could be just a clever grandstand play, Mr. Hicks. He's trying to go on the offensive, to force you into giving him information he hasn't earned."

"I see that, Rogers, I see that." Hicks was condescending.

"Just so you do," Rogers continued. "I wouldn't want you to believe every word he says on the basis of his flimsy promise."

"Does he have to sit in on our conversations?" Jeff demanded.

"Mr. Rogers?" Hicks asked. "I suppose he does. He's one of our Directors, too, you know."

Director Rogers. Director in charge of strong-arm tactics.

"I'm sorry," Jeff told him flatly. "I didn't realize you had so much standing."

"Few people do," Rogers answered. "I function much better when I'm able to mingle with the common members."

"I can understand that. And I've made a great blunder, haven't I? I should have been trying to win your trust."

"You can't win Rogers over to anything," Hicks said. "He's naturally suspicious."

"Especially," Rogers said pointedly, "of people who promise cooperation and then side-step into routes of their own."

"So, I made a mistake," Jeff said. "I'm not sorry, and I'd do it again. As I said, I'm not going any farther in the dark. Either I'm trusted enough to know the truth or I'm not trusted at all. Which is it, Mr. Hicks?"

"You shall have your information," Hicks answered. "To be perfectly frank, Jeff, with what you know already, you're as dangerous as you ever can be. And, in the end, you know what would happen to you if you tried to betray us."

"You've summed it up very neatly," Jeff said.

"Then we'll settle down and I'll tell you everything you want to know. Rogers, will you continue in your role of lackey long enough to mix up some highballs?"

Rogers sidled to the bar and took out three glasses. So far, so good, Jeff thought. He hadn't gained any ground, but he hadn't lost any either. The new information would send him out of this meeting the winner.

"Where shall I begin?" asked Hicks.

"You needn't waste time with what I already know or have guessed," Jeff told him. "I saw the little men and their saucers. I guessed that they're alien—from space somewhere. What I want to know is where and why?"

"The where of it isn't important. I'm not sure of that myself. As for the why, since you saw them, you must have also noticed their dullness. Their stupidity. That's a good deal of the why of it. And that leads me farther back still. You saw the machines. What did you think they were?"

"Computers. Except for the big one."

"They are not computers. They are an enormous system of amplification, of communication. The one you singled out is the speaker. A speaker that projects no voice. It projects *thoughts!* Through space. Millions of miles of space."

Jeff glanced up from his glass.

"You're startled," Hicks said. "So was I when I was first contacted. It was Toby who contacted me, incidentally. Nasty little fellow, but he gave me the chance of a lifetime. To get on— you have to forget everything you consider to be fact and truth, and try to believe something that sounds like pure fantasy. Imagine a planet, much different from Earth, where creatures of great intelligence evolved. Great intelligence."

"That's not difficult," Jeff interjected.

"No, but now imagine these great intelligences housed in an immobile body. *They can't move.* They have no hands or feet. They think, but they don't move. Don't ask me what they are, or what they look like, because I don't know. They may be treelike, or stones, or pillars of marble. But they can't move. So what value is this intelligence? They can't get together to communicate, so they evolve telepathy. Mental powers come into play. And again, I don't know the extent of these powers, but they are fantastic. Sometimes, during the night, the thought of it frightens me." Hicks paused, swallowing a great gulp from his glass. "Frightens me."

"Anyway," he continued, "you must give these creatures credit for having emotion and yearnings. Like us, they saw the stars, or sensed them, or whatever. The point is, they wanted them. Can you imagine the frustration of a great mind tied to one spot? Knowing the stars are there, and what they are, but unable to build rockets, unable to move from that damnable spot? So they compensated. They developed their mental powers to the point where they could search other planets telepathically. And, fate being with them, on a near planet they encountered our little, awkward friends."

"Toby's people," Jeff said.

"Yes. Just as you've seen them—stupid, awkward, even in movement, but human enough to have one ultimate goal: self-aggrandizement. And, in their turn, a yearning for the stars. Here we have two great forces coming into contact: immobile intelligence and mobile stupidity. Both with one motive. So they joined. It's as simple as that. The immobile beings, the Masters, unraveled the principles of physics and discovered how to build spacecraft. They directed the Tobys in the step-by-step work until the craft were a reality. The Tobys jumped at the chance. They know their limitations, you see, but they won't accept them. And here was their chance to fulfill their dreams by riding on someone else's intelligence."

"I see," Jeff said. "Toby's people exchanged mobility for brains and vice versa."

"Yes, but the Masters weren't content. Would you be content with such hands and feet—slow, awkward and having to be shown every step of every thing you wanted done? The Masters' search wasn't over. Next, they led the Tobys to their home world and directed them in fabricating and setting up powerful transmitters that could send the telepathic powers of the Masters farther into space, searching for intelligence to equal their own. They found Earth, and while our intelligence doesn't equal theirs by any means, we are so far better than the Tobys that they had to have us. So the Tobys set up receivers and boosters on our Moon. Then, after careful investigation, they made contact. I was one of the first. I admit, they chose me for my selfishness, my greed, if you like. But it has paid off, and will payoff even more."

"Then, you're working with the Masters, the minds."

"For great reward. We have a deal much like Toby's people have. In return for recruiting on Earth, we are given power. Power and wealth here, and promised power and wealth on other worlds."

Hicks was red-faced with this news. The promise was enervating to him. He reveled in it, wallowed in it.

"You are recruiting," Jeff took up the statement. "What does this mean?"

"HFP, of course! HFP is a gigantic recruiting operation. The Masters want bright, sturdy people to send to the stars as explorers, miners, settlers and conquerors—all for the Masters, of course—and HFP supplies them. We will conquer worlds, Jeff! And we will rule those worlds, because the Masters can't. They are tied to their own, so we will rule in their stead."

Jeff struggled to rise out of the swamp of facts. "Then these people, people like Jean Tuttle, who think they're going to Africa to help natives, are actually going into space?"

"Precisely! It's wonderfully clever, isn't it? They come here and train in languages they think belong to Earth, but don't. They train in hard, rough living. And then they go out—some have gone already, four ships full—and they wind up in space. They work for *us.*"

"But you can't get away with that. As soon as they realize how they've been tricked, they'll revolt."

"They have realized, and they have revolted. But we've regained their loyalty simply by threatening retaliation upon their families left behind on Earth. It's an old ruse. And it works."

"But what about those families? Don't they wonder when they don't receive letters from their children?"

"Of course, and they storm into Wornegon, demanding to know what has become of their darlings." Hicks was smiling gleefully. "We tell them. The whole truth. And *they* join HFP."

"No," Jeff protested.

"But they do! Because, when we tell them where their children are, we also tell them that their only hope of ever having them back is their silence and cooperation. They can't talk. They can't refuse to cooperate."

Jeff sat still. The nausea he had felt before was returning, but now it wasn't the nausea of alienness, it was just plain sickness at the horrible art of blackmail Hicks had described.

"It shocks you," Hicks said. "Don't be afraid to admit it. I was shocked at first. I refused them, do you know that? Then I thought it over, and accepted. Just as you are doing now. After all, what harm can it do these youngsters? And Earth will be ours as payment. We're almost ready for our Big Push. It won't be much longer before Earth will be on her knees to us. We have a grand, grand army, and no one can resist us once we make our move."

Jeff finished his drink and set down the empty glass. He had to pretend to go along with it. He wasn't free yet.

"Well," Hicks asked. "What do you think? First reaction?"

"It makes me sick," Jeff admitted. "On the other hand, it's interesting."

"You have a big stake in it." Rogers added his thin voice. "You have the main recruiting job for this state."

"Oh, Rogers," Hicks sighed, "you always have to pull the glory back down to the level of business. Jeff knows his responsibilities."

"I do," Jeff said, heartily. "I most surely do."

"I want to be certain of that," Rogers said. "Things have changed in the last half-hour. You know the truth. The stakes are high, higher than you dreamed, so you must remember that the punishment for betrayal is also high."

"I see what you're thinking," Hicks said to Rogers, "and I agree with you. You can have your head this time."

"And just what does that mean?" Jeff asked.

"That you won't be allowed to roam around alone," Rogers said. "You're going to be followed everywhere you go, until you've proven your good faith by giving that speech. I know you pretty well, Munro, and I think the speech will be your biggest obstacle. If you can go through with it, I'll be satisfied that you're really on our side. If you try to back out, I'll be there to stop you. And I mean stop you."

"I believe it." Jeff was frank. "Tell me, Rogers, do you by any chance drive a blue car?"

"Yes, my car is blue. That fact should serve to keep you to your word."

"That fact, plus a broken headlight," Jeff countered. He stood up, not giving Rogers a chance at the last word.

CHAPTER EIGHT

JEFF drove the roads to Union Town, hardly noticing the passing scenery as the shock he had been compelled to hide in Hicks' office hit him. Earth wasn't alone any more. Earth had been invaded, and no one knew it but a few madmen. And himself.

He found it hard to overcome disbelief, even though he had seen Toby and felt the Essence of the Masters. That was probably why Wornegon was so secure. If anyone should suspect, he would never speak of it. The idea was too insane.

Today, he drove the expressways because close behind him sped the blue car with Rogers in it. As the shock wore thin, he tried to plan ahead. What should be his first move? Whatever it was, he had to take Rogers' presence into account. This was Sunday, and it would already be dark by the time he reached home. Perhaps he should let the whole thing rest for the night, lull Rogers into a feeling of calm. Tomorrow morning he could start his campaign.

In the back of his mind was the hope of help from the FBI. One of the local men, Sam Kirby, was a friend of sorts—at least an acquaintance—and he had to approach someone who knew him. If he broke in on a stranger with his story, he would wind up where Tom Sullivan thought he was going to wind up—in a hospital!

With that much set in his mind—home, a night's rest and Sam Kirby—he led Rogers in procession down the roads to Union Town.

He let the morning rise and warm the air before he stirred from his kitchen. He had checked the street when he first got up and found Rogers' car just where it had been the night before. He had managed to sleep, but Rogers hadn't, and there was pleasure in the thought of the glinty eyes bloodshot and swollen from weariness.

At nine o'clock, he walked down the front steps, waved to Rogers, and called a "Good morning" which he didn't mean. "I'm going to do some shopping," he yelled to the skinny man.

Jeff backed out of the driveway, watching the blue car creep up behind him. Down the street, crossing intersections, halting for stop signs, they drove in unison, one behind the other.

"Keep coming, Mr. Director," Jeff said between his teeth. "Once we get downtown, you'll find yourself without a leader."

He swung onto the main street and was engulfed in traffic. Women drivers hemmed him in, and progress was a crawl. There were no parking places, Rogers could see that for himself.

He went the length of the shopping district, giving Rogers a good view of the congestion, and turned a corner to drive to the parking ramp. If there was anyplace in town to lose a tail and still let it seem accidental, the ramp was the place. The FBI office wasn't far from it, down a side street.

He entered the ramp, took his pass from the attendant machine, and wheeled up the curving insides of the building. The blue car followed. Around he went—up and around, up and around—driving slowly, but still getting the sense of dizziness. Motors roared in the half-enclosed space until it sounded like a race track. He kept on, searching for the one spot he had to have.

On the fourth level, he slowed. There were no cars ahead of him now; they had all found parking places. Rogers swung in behind him, and in back of Rogers was a long line of cars, stretching down the ramp. This might be the level then. He edged ahead. If there was only the one special place left on this level— the one and no more—he was safe.

Near the end of the row, he found it. The one parking place. He smiled in the security of the car. It wasn't chance that this space was here. No one ever parked in it. It was a blind space, an impossible space, demanding careful maneuvering to get out of it. Once tried, people left it empty. There was a concrete pillar on one side, a speed limit sign on the other, and as it came out of the end of the row, it made a sharp turn necessary. But Jeff didn't care how fast he could get out. All he wanted was to get in.

Carefully blocking any chance for Rogers to go around him, he veered his car to the left and backed into the parking slot, easing his fenders past the barriers. He got out quickly, watching Rogers creep ahead, his skinny neck straining as he looked frantically for another spot on this level. There wasn't one.

Rogers stopped in the center of the traffic lane, unsure. Horns sounded, hollow and deafening around the curves, tooting Rogers out of the way. Jeff didn't wait for the outcome. Rogers would be forced to continue up the ramp to the next level, and those seconds would give the needed time. He headed for the elevator, but once Rogers was out of sight, ran back across the building and took the stairs. He pounded down them, estimating in his mind what Rogers was doing. If he had found a spot on the next level, he would be getting out of his car right now. Another flight of stairs passed, and Rogers would be at the elevators.

Jeff hit ground level and ran onto the sidewalk. Rogers would leave the elevator in a minute or two, but he would be way across the building, lost. Jeff hurried along the street, hiding himself among the women shoppers, the taste of minor victory sweet in his mouth.

After a block, he cut to a side street and went to the FBI office. It was up one flight of noisy stairs. There was a clerk-type girl at the desk, but he didn't have to bother with her. Sam Kirby was at the water cooler.

Kirby was short and graying, his blue eyes bright in the midst of a deep tan. He crumpled his paper cup and stuck out his hand. "You never know who's going to pop up on a Monday morning," he said. "How are you, Jeff?"

Jeff took Kirby's hand gratefully. The FBI man remembered him. How much of it was friendship and how much the result of a trained memory he had yet to discover. "I wish my state of well-being were the only point, Sam."

"Official business?"

"More than you could guess. And I haven't much I time."

"Come into my office then." The office was bare and paint-peeled, but somehow it offered comfort. Kirby sat down behind his desk. "No time for reminiscences even?" he asked.

"Not today. But, I admit, I'm glad to hear you ask. It means you remember me as more than just a face."

"Sure, I do. That last Smythe party was a blast." Jeff wondered how he had missed the fact that Kirby considered him such a friend. If he ever came out of this mess, he would have to promote the acquaintance. Kirby, as he recalled, was a fine man. "Just hang on to what you thought of me at that party, Sam, and maybe we'll be able to do business. I've got some weird stuff for you, and I'll need every ounce of credence you can muster."

"I'm listening."

"What do you know about HFP?"

"Huh." Kirby plopped back in his chair. "Here—" he pointed to a stack of mail—"and here—" he pointed to a filing cabinet—"is the extent of my knowledge. I know it inside out. The mail hasn't been opened yet, but I can guess that two out of every five letters concerns HFP. Complaints mostly."

"But aside from the mail, what do you know—officially?"

"Like I said, inside and out. When there's this much mail on a subject, we investigate. HFP has a clean standing. It isn't a Communist front, if that's what you're getting at."

"You've had men up there then?"

"Checked and rechecked. Our men even go through that goofy initiation to see if they've missed anything. They come back every time with a clean bill for Wornegon. It's the same all over the world. HFP is a dangerous nuisance, but nothing more. I wouldn't bet that the motives of Montgomery Hicks are beneficent, but you can't condemn a man for being clever enough to rake in a fortune."

"And power."

"Over a bunch of fanatics? I don't call that very much."

"I didn't either, Sam. But I've just come back from Wornegon, and I've got this." Jeff broke off. He had a listener, but didn't know how to break the story. "I'm going to do the talking now. For about a half-hour. So make yourself comfortable, and don't interrupt me. I'll start with a man named Tom Sullivan. No—even farther back than that. With a riot in Bolin."

He began slowly, letting the less fantastic events of the beginning get the words flowing. He went through the Running Man, the threat, the initiation and the truth. He watched Kirby shift from interest to profound amazement.

"That's the whole thing," Jeff finished. "Right at this minute, Rogers is walking the streets looking for me. If he knew I was here, I'd be dead a few seconds after I stepped onto the sidewalk. As it is, we'll all be as good as dead in a little while. Hicks said the Big Push is ready to go and it's only a matter of time before Earth is brought to its knees."

Kirby said nothing. He stared at his hands.

"I don't blame you for thinking I'm crazy, Sam. I would, too, in your place. I thought Sullivan was crazy."

"I didn't say anything about not believing you," Kirby protested. "I know your reputation too well to think you'd make this up, and I can look in your eyes and see that you're no maniac. It's just that it's too much to take in all at once."

"You probably wouldn't even have given poor Sullivan a hearing."

"I'd hope I would have." Kirby sighed heavily, as though digesting the tale and accepting it in one breath. "I believe you. I don't know how they covered themselves so well that our men didn't get an inkling of this, but I believe you. And if time is short, we've got to move." He picked up the phone, hesitated, then put it back down. "Wait a minute. Do you actually think the initiation does something to people, and that's why our men came home with such innocent reports?"

"I do," Jeff said. "I think those Listening sessions have something to do with the Masters. The Listeners will obey anything they're told to do."

"That's just my point. If we move on our first impulse—with troops, say, and public warnings—we're liable to cause riots. World feeling is higher than you might think against HFP. They've stirred up a hornet's nest with their converting. And if the HFP-ers can't help the way they are, the riots would turn into a battle against innocents."

Jeff shivered, because before his eyes grew the shining face of Jean Tuttle. She was an innocent, led to the slaughter by Montgomery Hicks. He could envision her defending HFP and being beaten down by the feet of a mob or the guns of militia.

"We could go into Wornegon and the other centers and smash them to bits, but the HFP-ers spread around the world would be in real trouble," Kirby explained.

"I see that—too clearly. If overt action is out, what does that leave? The machines have to be smashed and HFP cleaned out." He paused. The machines. Was it possible that some kind of telepathic hypnosis was used on the converts, and thus with the machines gone, the converts would return to themselves?

"What just came to your mind?" Kirby asked him.

"The machines. If we could wreck the machines, that might be all we'd need to do. With the machines gone, the Masters would lose their contact with Earth, and the rest would be a simple mopping-up job. The little men won't be much of a problem. I doubt if they know enough to defend themselves very well."

"That simplifies it. We can go in with force then, and just get to those machines."

"Unless I'm wrong, of course, and the destruction of the machines doesn't free the people. Look, Sam, I know this is going to sound like grandstanding, but I want some time on my own. To try our idea out. I have a good, solid 'in' up there."

"So?"

"So, maybe I could get to the machines and smash them—let it look like an isolated incident. If it's successful, then you can move on the other centers. If it fails, Hicks will just think *I've* betrayed him, and you'll have a second chance to do whatever is necessary. If *I* do it, HFP won't be under attack. Only Wornegon. Failure wouldn't alert the whole organization."

"That's putting yourself in a lot of danger, isn't it?"

"I don't think so. But it does mean I'll have to make that damned speech. Otherwise they won't let me back into Wornegon."

"The way you talk, you'd think I'd already given you permission."

"Haven't you?"

"I can't on my own. Not without authorization."

"Then get it, Sam! You're killing me with every minute we waste. Rogers isn't going to walk the streets forever without getting suspicious."

"You really know how to force a man against the wall, don't you? Excuse me. I'm going to phone Washington."

Kirby left the room and Jeff waited alone. He had been hasty and brash in his suggestions, but he wasn't sorry. He was the only man in the world who could wreck Wornegon from the inside, and in any situation where there was just one possible savior, that savior couldn't refuse.

Kirby's absence stretched into a half-hour and Jeff began to sweat. When Kirby came back, he was accompanied by three men. "You've dropped a big bomb on Washington," Kirby said, "but your story was accepted. Seems the Bureau has been perturbed for a long time, trying to get an objective man on the inside of HFP and never succeeding. You're their man. They've been waiting for a story like yours to make sense out of their bits and pieces of suspicion."

"I've been given the go-ahead?"

"Yes, but not alone. You've been assigned a team to work with you. And you'd better accept their help." Kirby was belligerent.

"You didn't think I'd be crazy enough to refuse?" Jeff turned his attention to the three men. "Is this the team?"

"Right." Kirby made fast introductions. "Just remember their names and faces. The tall one is Charles Mason; the shortest one, Lawrence Terry; the pale one, Rudolph Jones."

Jeff shook their hands and cemented the names in his mind.

"Here's the plan," Kirby continued. "I'll give it to you once, then you'd better get out of here. Mason, Terry and Jones will leave immediately for Wornegon and get settled in as interested guests. They'll keep their eyes open, but wait for you. You give your speech, go back to Wornegon, join forces with them, and together you smash the machines. You'll be in grave danger at that point, Jeff, so stick by our professionals here. After the destruction, they'll send up a flare to signal me. I'll be waiting with a good-sized force far enough away to be safe. We'll come in with helicopters first, and the rest will follow in trucks. We'll mop up. And at my signal, if you've been successful, the other HFP centers will be invaded. Clear?"

"It's a simple plan, isn't it?"

"The simple ones usually work."

Jeff stood up. "I'll see you men at Wornegon then." He started for the door, then turned back. "Thanks, Sam, for believing. You've made this whole thing so much easier than I expected it to be."

"It's a job," Kirby grinned. "The way I see it, this has just about got to succeed."

"I know what you mean," Jeff said. "I feel like Atlas all of a sudden. I've got the world square on my shoulders, haven't I?"

"Don't drop it."

Back on the street, Jeff moved carefully, but Rogers wasn't in view. He slipped in the back door of a men's clothing store, surprised the clerk with his quick, no-try-on purchase of a suit, and left by the front entrance. Rogers was waiting at the parking ramp.

"Where've you been?" Jeff asked before Rogers had the chance. He lifted the suit box into view. "I've bought myself a new suit. With my position and a big speech to make, I can't look like a bum."

He left Rogers to follow and stew without any real answers. He prayed Rogers believed him. There wasn't any reason why he shouldn't.

Jeff checked in at the campus, picked up his mail, instructed one class and went home, Rogers trailing him. The class had bothered him, reminding him too sharply of the speech he had to make. Nothing could force him to make that speech; that had been his decision. But he had offered to do it. Offered.

His Political Science Club met on Tuesday nights. It always drew large numbers of students, members and nonmembers alike. His scheduled topic was HFP. Ironically, HFP. The speech was tucked in his desk drawer, nearly written; a fiery speech describing the incident in Bolin and lecturing the point of fanaticism. He would still speak on HFP, but from the opposite viewpoint.

Cory's car was in front of his house, and Rogers parked behind it. Jeff called to the skinny man, "I was going to invite you in for coffee, but I've got company. Sorry."

Cory was sitting in the porch swing. "Who's in the car?"

"Rogers," Jeff said, as he unlocked the door. "He's my bosom buddy. Follows everyplace I go." He went into the house. "He'll give up pretty soon—at least long enough to eat and sleep."

"You look like you could use some of the same."

"I'm just not used to lugging around a heavy conscience."

"Neither am I, and that's why I'm here. I've been worrying about you. We didn't say a very relaxing goodbye, you know." Cory stared at the floor, unused to making apologies. "I was an idiot to walk out on you like that, and before we get into anything else, I want to own up to it. It was a stupid action."

"I understood it. I had plenty to be sorry about myself. I never got the chance to tell you the whole story."

Cory sat down, but didn't relax into the cushions. "Do you mean that I now have the privilege of being filled in on what happened, or am I still closed off from the inner circle?"

"You're still angry with me for joining HFP—despite your apology, you're still angry. Well, rest your mind. I haven't joined anything. With words and gestures, yes, but not with heart."

"And that means?" Cory was intense.

"That I've just a few hours ago come from the FBI. I'm practically a federal agent, Cory. I've changed my spots."

"But—" Cory's one word sounded like a small explosion.

"You believed all that stuff I told you? About wanting power and riches? Come on, Cory, you're kidding me."

"No, I'm not. I could barely believe it at the time, but you were so damned sincere, and it sounded so sensible, that I finally made myself believe it. I expected you to come back with HFP literature in one hand and money in the other."

"I maneuvered, that's all. I got precisely what I went up there for. Information with a capital 'I.' If you think the other was hard to believe, wait until you hear this. Everything the Running Man said was true—and more besides."

He laid the story before Cory piece by piece, omitting only Kirby's military part because that seemed too secret. Cory's face grew whiter and whiter. When Jeff finished, Cory paced the room.

"I'm not sure I was supposed to tell you, but I thought you had a right to know," Jeff said. "You went up there with me and risked as much as I did."

Cory sighed, his back to Jeff. "And I thought I knew you."

"The knowledge that I'm working with the FBI should be easier for you to take than the thought that I was in with HFP."

"Oh, yes." Cory faced him. "But you can't expect me to be relieved when you're heading right back into the cannon's mouth. You act like a kid out on a lark. Your sense of perspective has vanished."

"Not really." Jeff lowered his voice. "There just isn't any other way to play it. It wouldn't do one bit of good for me to chew my nails or brood. It wouldn't even do any good to think too hard about it, because if I did, I'd come up against the fantastic qualities and doubt my sanity. I have to play it down or it will grow too big for me to handle."

"I think it is too big. Why don't you ever talk things over before you run headlong into them? Do you actually think this team of FBI men is going to succeed?"

"They're really icing. I'm the main issue."

"Well," Cory said firmly, "I'm counting myself in. Four men against Wornegon will be better than three."

Jeff crossed to the table to pour out two drinks. Cory was offering himself again, and he wouldn't allow it this time. "I don't think Kirby will let you involve yourself directly. Besides, I had something else in mind."

"Like?"

"Will you come with me tomorrow night when I make that speech? To stand with me and see that I don't back out?"

"You're not going to back out and you know it."

"But it's not going to be easy for me. HFP speakers have never been allowed on campus. The students have booed them out. I'm not going to have one friend in that room—unless you're that friend."

"You're not afraid of your own students?" Cory asked sharply.

"How do I know? I've never betrayed them before."

Cory took his drink from Jeff's hand and held it, watching the bright liquid swirl in the glass. "Okay, I'll go along with you on the speech. But I'm making no promises about Wornegon."

Jeff surrendered to his stubbornness. "Do whatever you feel you have to, Cory. But remember—I'm in this because I have no choice. I don't want HFP to succeed in stealing everything from me. Especially not a friend, a better friend than I realized I had."

Cory gazed at him with a strange mixture of emotion. His blue eyes held thanks for the outright declaration of friendship, and a wavering shyness that Jeff had never seen in him before. The moment was too full, and Jeff drained the emotion out of it quickly.

"Shall we eat dinner here? Or shall we give old Rogers another merry chase?"

"Let him rest," Cory said. "Where's your decency? You can't make a man's last days completely miserable."

CHAPTER NINE

THE lecture hall was full of students. Jeff held the club meetings in one of the large, tiered classrooms that normally served lectures to combined classes. He and Cory came in at the back and started down the steps between the rows of desk-seats.

"Mr. Munro," a girl called, and a hand reached out to touch Jeff's sleeve. "I was wondering about our assignment."

It was the pretty, young coed who dominated the front row of Jeff's morning class. "Miss Turner, isn't it?" he asked.

"Sally Turner. I was wondering, since we didn't have a class this morning, and there wasn't a note about outside reading…"

"Don't worry about it. Take advantage of my absence. I'll make it up in the next assignment."

As they walked on, Cory asked, "Since when are college students so worried about missed homework? It wasn't like this when I went to school."

"It isn't now," Jeff answered.

"No, it isn't," a new voice said. It was Angela Berri, one of Jeff's co-instructors. "Jeff has an ability to send the coeds into ecstasies. They're good at inventing ways of stopping him for small talk." She was smiling, but Jeff let her teasing slip by.

Cory didn't. "Maybe there's more to this business of being an ivory tower professor than meets the eye."

"Not more than your eye, Mr. Bennett, I'm sure," Angela said.

"Is that an accusation?" Cory asked.

"I only accuse you of staying away from our ivory tower as much as you do."

They were engaging in their accustomed banter, and it was usually fun, but Jeff wished they'd stop. Tonight, the students weren't just around him, they seemed to be surrounding him. There were many copies of his article in evidence. Right now they all despised HFP, and had come to hear him condone their conviction.

He went to the dais. Angela Berri had peeled off somewhere along the line, and only Cory remained with him. "I'll get somebody to move so I can sit in the front row," Cory said. "Take it easy and make it short. If you have to torture yourself, at least you don't have to prolong it."

Jeff had no notes, but he opened a manila folder and spread some papers out. Then he sat down, waiting for the hall to reach capacity saturation. Inside of ten minutes he would dishonor himself.

At the back of the hall, his roving glance came to an abrupt halt. Seated in the last row was Rogers. There was a slight upturning at the corners of the thin lips—half-smile, half-sneer of defiance—and seeing it, Jeff forgot his depression. Whatever he had to do would be done with a will, because the evil of HFP that Rogers epitomized was the fighting core of it all.

His watch said seven on the dot, and he got up, signaling to have the doors closed. With the slams, the room quieted until there was no sound, not even the shuffling of feet. He was the sudden center of six hundred intelligent eyes.

Just forge ahead, he told himself. *Get it over with.*

His voice found tone and strength as he began. "Good evening. We'll dispense with club procedures tonight, if you don't mind, because I have something of great importance to talk to you about. Actually, I have a confession to make."

Another general settling surged through the rows of students as they gathered themselves into expectancy.

"I confess this publicly, and I want it clearly heard and understood. I have been wrong!" He felt the little shock that rolled through them. "My topic tonight is HFP, as you know, but before I get into it, I must impress upon you the fact that I've been wrong.

I've just returned from Wornegon—from HFP headquarters—and it isn't at all what I wrote. Believe me, there is nothing evilly fanatic about HFP. If its members are zealous, it's only because they have every reason to be. They're supporting a great idea; they're fighting for a grand goal."

He had to stop because the quiet in the room erupted into a din of noise. He searched for a known face and found Sally Turner. She looked at him with surprise, but the surprise changed to a knowing nod as she decided he was leading them on to get them in the proper mood. She smiled at him, and winked.

"Some of you—" he shouted, "some of you have taken my opening statement in the wrong way. You think I'm trying to shock you. I'm not. I meant every word of it. HFP *is* on the march, and it's going to save the world!"

The close attention was gone. Restlessness, shuffling feet and whispered conversation dominated the hall now. Alone before the jammed-in students, Jeff felt their emotion growing into a tangible thing that crept down the tiered rows to push against him.

"There are many facets to HFP," he shouted, "but they all work together for good. And HFP needs people like you! Intelligent people, strong people."

"Too intelligent to listen to this!" shot out of the group.

"And too strong to have to put up with it!" another joined in.

Heckling. He had never faced it before. He tried the only thing he knew to try—shaming them. "Since when do you close your minds to something new? I'm here to give you a firsthand report. You owe me the respect to listen."

A figure jumped to its feet, breaking the measured rows. He was a burly boy, square-headed, his face red to the depths of his anger. "You're breaking our rules!" he called over the general din. "We voted not to allow HFP speakers on campus. You voted with us! You've said too much already."

"I've barely begun," Jeff challenged.

The hall surged with movement as, one after another, students took to their feet.

"What about the riot in Denver?" someone called.

"What riot?" Jeff answered. "I haven't heard of any riot."

"Or the ten people who died in it? HFP did that!"

"And two others killed in France!"

Had his loss of one week's news kept him from so much then? Riots? Death? The Big Push was started and this speech was more than he had bargained for. The angry mood he had expected from the students was there, all right, but more, too. Violence burned in them. Unreasoning hatred and a spur to action.

"You'd better get out while you still can," the original boy warned. "Without another word."

"No!" Sally Turner was standing. Her face held no hatred, only a dreadful fear. "Mr. Munro has never led us wrong. If he's telling us this now, it's because he believes it."

She was defending him, and that fact hurt him more than the cries of the others, because here was a girl he could win over. Here was a girl he could betray with a few more sentences, and send to Hicks to become a pawn in his galactic game. He wanted to yell at her to sit down and shut up, to listen to her friends, but he didn't dare. Rogers was watching from the back row, making notes.

He continued, for Rogers' ears. "HFP doesn't want deaths. It wants life. Life! None of you understand the—"

The burly boy was pushing his way to the center aisle. Others joined him. Cory backed away from the students to come up beside Jeff. The boys were coming down the aisle, two abreast, their jaws set, their eyes leveled. "HFP is on the march," they chanted, making it impossible for him to be heard, "but we will save the world! HFP is on the march, but we will save the world!"

"It's what they've been chanting all over the world," Cory shouted to him. "It's the prelude to violence! Quit while you can."

"HFP is on the march," came from all corners of the hall, "but *we* will save the world." It was a senseless chant, a flimsy piece of protest, yet as voices added to it, it grew into a roar and then an explosion of shouting, in cadence, over and over. It hit Jeff in waves, showering him with gooseflesh.

"Jeff!" Cory pulled at him. "For heaven's sake, don't just stand here and let them tear you apart."

He couldn't believe that they would. Not these students, not his students. The chant continued, gaining fuel, and the boys marched to it, looking at him from underneath their eyelids.

And he knew. Cory was right. Even his own students could hurt him over this. HFP had grown too hated. They had no head, no sense.

Sally Turner was pivoting by her seat, terrified, as more students joined the solid battering ram coming down the aisle. He saw her mouth form the word "Run!" as she met his eyes.

They were almost upon him and he could feel the air stir with their cadence, puffing against his skin. He wanted to run, but the humiliation of the act froze his feet.

Cory dragged him off the platform. "If you won't save yourself, then think of me. I'm not going to leave you here."

The students hit floor level.

"Jeff!" Cory tried again.

"Okay. Let's get out of here."

Cory slammed against the door and burst through it. Jeff followed on his heels. Their sudden dash repeated itself in the students, and the cadence broke as hundreds of feet ran after them. Jeff sprinted into the lead. Down the hall to the outside door, into the air and across the sidewalk, they clumped over the paved street and hit grass again on the other side.

Jeff gasped, trying to stretch his legs so he wouldn't slow Cory down. They cut around the corner of the chemistry building and fled down its wind-swept side. They were only halfway to the car, and the pack of young athletes was gaining on them. Jeff expected rocks to pour down on him, but none were thrown. The library reared beside them and they dashed the length of it.

A siren sprang up in the street, joined immediately by two others, and campus police jumped before them, giving them room to pass, then closing ranks to confront the oncoming mob. The pounding steps diminished, but Jeff ran on. The chase was over. Only the ring of angry voices carried from the mob as they exchanged insults with the police. But that sound was bad enough. Jeff drowned it with the engine roar of his car.

Cory sat in the big chair, munching on a bacon and tomato sandwich, skimming through the paper. He tossed the paper down with a grunt. "If they'd leave out some of the ads, they might have room for a little news."

Jeff glanced at the fallen paper, reading upside down. "Repeat of Night Sale," it read. "Old Fashioned Bargains. Shop Until Eleven. Free Coffee."

"What kind of deal is that?" he asked Cory, trying to keep a conversation going to cut the stifling silence that was so full of unwanted thought.

"They held it last year, too, don't you remember? They keep the stores open until eleven, thinking people will do more shopping just because it's an unusual time to be downtown. It worked last year, so maybe they're right."

"They'll stay open twenty-four hours a day next," Jeff grumbled, "if they can see an extra dollar in it."

As his statement quieted, another sound took its place—the sound of car motors, many motors; the squeal of tires; and then a hush. Jeff stepped to the front window. The curbs on both sides of the street were lined with cars.

"Somebody around here giving a party'?" Cory asked.

"Nobody's getting out of the cars."

"Teenagers then?"

"I can't see very well. I'm going out on the porch." He didn't know why he was bothering about it, but there was something off-key about the cars waiting so quietly in the street. He went onto the porch. The occupants of the cars that had parked under street lights were visible to him. Young people. Students, probably. On down to the right, under the next lamp, the figures weren't young. A mixed group of people then.

He realized with a sudden shudder that they were all looking straight at him. He retreated to the door. The street and its splotched darkness was menacing. There was a sticker attached to the windshield of a nearby car, and he strained to make out the writing. As he peered at it, the hush broke, and a low noise like the rising surge of surf trickled out of the cars. A door opened. A man and woman got out. The man bent, pulled back his arm, and a stone flew close to Jeff's ear, striking the house with a chipping crack. The whisper shouted now, jeers and catcalls, and in the new fear he made out the writing on the sticker.

"HFP!"

These were not students. They were Listeners, and they were out for his blood.

He jumped inside the door, pulling it quickly shut, and another stone hit the screen in front of his face.

"What's going on'?" Cory was beside him.

"They're Rogers' people. They've come to get me."

"But why? They think you're working with them. Why would they be after you?"

"How should I know?" Jeff shouted. He couldn't hold it back any longer. "Why shouldn't they be after me? Everybody else is! Everywhere I go, everyone I meet—they all give chase as though I'm some kind of a rabbit with a sign pinned on it. 'Chase me, I'm good fun!'" He slammed the inner door, shutting out some of the noise. "Hicks knows about me, that's all. Every move I make, he knows. I've finished myself."

"You're jumping to conclusions," Cory tried to calm him.

"There's only one conclusion to jump to. Rogers knew about the FBI, but he let me go on thinking I was free just long enough for me to give that damned speech and stir emotions up on the campus. Now he's got me in a box. I can't go back to Wornegon. My big plans to destroy HFP are finished before I even get started."

Cory had nothing to say.

The jangle of the phone cut the awkward moment in two. Jeff raised the receiver angrily. "Hello!"

"This is Rogers," the voice squeaked out of the earpiece. "I've been anticipating this moment, Munro. I've called to tell you of your situation."

"No explanations are necessary," Jeff spat. "I can see for myself." He hated the smugness in Rogers' voice, the leer he knew must be on the skinny, pinched face.

"When are you coming to Wornegon? We want you back. Back—or dead."

"It will have to be dead then."

"It just might be." Rogers let the threat spew out slowly. "Union Town is full of our people. You have a sample of it in the street. They've come to get you, Munro. They've been pouring in ever since your foolish side trip to the FBI, and they're entrenched, ready. You're going to die, Munro."

As Rogers halted and Jeff struggled for an answer, a chant grew up in the street. "Come out. Come out," it rang under the street lights. "Come out. Come out."

"Where did you get all the executioners?" Jeff demanded.

"HFP members never doubt orders given in a Listening session."

The strangers would kill him if they got the chance. They had sat entranced, and scribbled a message on their papers, and that message had said, "Kill Jeffrey Munro." And kill him they would.

"I'll be close by," Rogers said. "If I can, I'll be right beside you when it happens. This is one death I don't want to miss."

Jeff slammed the receiver back into its cradle, and leaned on the table. This was one nightmare he would never wake from. This one would suffocate him.

He breathed in deeply, as though he could defy his own written fate. "They can't stand out there and shout. Someone will call the police." He lifted the phone again. "I'll call the police."

He started to dial the number, but Cory caught his hand. "You can't wait." Cory's voice was trembling. "This house is a trap, Jeff. You can't wait for the police. Look out the window. They're coming onto the lawn. You haven't time."

Behind the flimsy white of the curtains, Jeff could barely perceive the movements of bodies on his lawn. He estimated quickly in his head. To get enough policemen here to do him any good would take at least five minutes—more likely ten. He would be dead in ten minutes.

"What do I do then?"

"Run! Go out the back and run. Give yourself a start and let me call the police. We can catch up with you."

"But, Cory, if I go into the open I'll be an easier target." He knew he was making sense. But Cory didn't agree. Cory stood beside him, white and shaking, and didn't agree. He had to trust Cory, because Cory's head was clear. Cory didn't have terror running with his blood. "They'll see me go, won't they?" Jeff asked. "They'll know I've left and follow me."

"I'll stay here," Cory said. "I'll move around so they'll know someone is still inside. They'll stay with me and you can get clear."

"I can't let you do that. They'll act before they think. They'll kill you and find out they've killed the wrong man, when it's too late."

The thump of feet on wood spun Cory around. "They're on the porch! Jeff—go now!"

It wasn't right. Something in his brain rebelled against going out into the dark. Would the people actually storm into his house after him? They were chanting, "Come out, come out." They wanted him in the open. If they killed him here, it would be murder, and they liked such things to seem accidental.

"Jeff!" Cory's shout broke his train of thought. "Now! Get out while you still can. Please."

Jeff ran to the kitchen, ignoring the stab of uncertainty that pierced him as his hands touched the back door. His brain was muddled while Cory's wasn't. He had to rely on Cory's judgment.

He leaped down the steps, wary in the dark, but the noise was still coming from the front of the house. None of the people had ventured to the back. He ran across the grass, keeping to the shadows. He took Benson's low picket fence in one leap, cut across their narrow yard and pulled himself over the five-foot chain-link fence that enclosed the Hendricks place. The chanting paced behind him, but no one was giving chase. He slowed down. Crossing yard after yard, he hit the end of the block and took to the nearest drive.

Walking on tiptoe in the gravel, he edged down the side of the house to the sidewalk. He walked as fast as he could without breaking into a trot. When he reached the corner he couldn't stand the suspense any longer. Taking a chance, he loped across the pavement, and ran, away from his own block, away from the cars, away.

He needed a destination and the only one he had was Sam Kirby. The FBI office.

He broke his course, taking a block to the right and one to the left. Kirby was his beacon. Kirby was arranging a war; he would have to be working late.

He found the street where the office was located. With his beacon in sight, he ran off the panic, using the last of his breath to fight fear. The building was dark, but he didn't let it register. Somewhere, deep inside it, there would be a light that meant Kirby. He stumbled up to the door. It was locked.

He pounded on it, the pounds cutting the night that was so still and free from chanting here, and raising echoes inside the hallway. Someone was bound to hear.

But no one came. Not even a night watchman strode the corridors or walked the creaky stairs.

He was a fool. He had let Rogers' waiting presence hurry him out of Kirby's office too fast, with no sturdy plan, not even a home phone number. And it had all been for nothing. Because Rogers had known where he was all along. How? He wanted to shout the how to the dark street. Who was it who dogged his steps, who knew his thoughts almost before he did? He had left Rogers frustrated in the parking ramp. Who had been waiting to pick him up outside?

He went down to the sidewalk again, and the night and the dark were close about him. He stiffened as he felt it. Darkness was for hiding, but this special darkness was a trap. The Listeners were swarming over Union Town, waiting in shadows, crouching, muscles ready to pounce. He had no business in the dark alone.

The sky above town was lit with a faint rosy glow. Downtown. The Late Sale. People.

He ran again, thanking God for the off-season greed of the retailers. There would be crowds downtown, shoppers, people out for an unaccustomed lark. He could lose himself among them. The Listeners would never attack him with witnesses about.

When he was only a block from the main street, he slowed his feet and fought for his breath. The lights grew brighter with each step he took, and the reassuring forms of people surged with the traffic signals: *"Walk—Don't Walk."*

Then he was among them. He stepped in with them, shoulder to shoulder, and their nearness cloaked him with security. The light changed to green and he crossed the street with them. They didn't know it, but they were a moving shield, and somewhere among them would surely be a face he knew, a hand to help him.

At the opposite curb, the crowd thinned out as people made their way into various stores. He pivoted, trying to choose a course. Had the police come to Cory yet? Until he knew, until a policeman walked up to him and gave him details, he dared not even trust a uniform. As Tom Sullivan had said when he was taking his turn at running, HFP could be anywhere.

He turned to start back across the street and stared straight into a hard, biting face. The man's eyes were brown and the glint in them was nasty.

Jeff spun from the curb and pushed through the little crowd. The brown-eyed man might as well have had HFP tattooed on his forehead, because he had murder in his eyes. Face to face with him, Jeff panicked, and hurried in the other direction. He was too vulnerable; Cory had been wrong. He would have had a better chance by staying inside his house.

He rushed along the store fronts, knowing without glancing back that the brown-eyed man was following. And where were the others? Union Town was swarming with them. Rogers had used the time from the moment of Jeff's betrayal to the speech to bring his army in. An army marching against one man. A running man.

Another hard face pushed in front of him, and Jeff sidestepped. He wanted to run the side streets again, to gain the imagined safety of his own home, but he didn't dare. It was too late for that kind of running. All he had left to defend himself was the presence of strangers and the slim hope that the Listeners wouldn't attack him in public. He couldn't be alone. Not for one moment. Because one moment was long enough to meet death.

CHAPTER TEN

HE edged into a knot of people waiting for a light. He looked over his shoulder. Two faces met his, one male and one harshly female, minus lipstick. He stood his ground. They would loom up everywhere, but he couldn't run any more. He had to keep his head. It would become a battle of nerves. If he could keep the shoppers numbering more than the HFP-ers, he had a chance.

The light flashed to green and he crossed with the crowd, then picked out a woman and a little girl to follow. They went a few stores down the street and entered a restaurant.

"Why not?" he asked himself. He was deathly tired, and thirsty. A restaurant, if crowded enough, was a good, safe place.

He squirmed between the packed tables and found one in the center. Surrounded by other tables, people sitting at all of them, he was in the middle of a tight circle of safety.

The waitress eased herself between the crowded rows and stood at his table, order pad in hand. "Just coffee, please," he told her. "And maybe a piece of pie."

"We have chocolate, cherry, banana cream—"

"Cherry," he cut her off. "And a glass of water, please."

He pulled out his cigarettes, not allowing himself the luxury of a glance around. It was enough to be sitting down and able to imagine that he was safe.

A glass of water plunked down, and he drank it before the girl was back with his pie and coffee. The pie was too sweet, but he ate it. So many people out to kill him—people he didn't know, had never seen, might possibly even like in another situation. But they were out to kill him? For trying to save the world?

And that was a total bust. He hoped the team of FBI men could complete the work for him. Even more, he hoped that Rogers hadn't picked them out. If Rogers had, then they were probably dead. "HFP is on the march," he thought, "and nothing can stop it now."

The people at the next table left. Their seats were immediately filled from the line waiting at the door. Jeff stared at his plate. He had seen the new customers sitting so close, and they were stony cold, staring at him.

He lit into the pie again. Let them stare. They couldn't touch him. People didn't die with cherry pie in their mouths. Surely, even the fanatics would see the truth in that.

The woman and little girl he had followed rose from their places, the last loud suck gone from the chocolate soda. Their places, too, were immediately filled. Now they were on two sides of him. He gulped down the too hot coffee, letting the burn of it settle the panic that nearly refused to let him swallow. How much longer did he dare sit here?

He set his eyes on a young couple. They were only concerned with each other and the pile of sacks they had accumulated in the evening's shopping. He mentally tied himself to them. As long as they remained where they were, he wasn't in a corner.

But the sacks crumpled loudly as the young man shoved them under his arm, and they started away. Jeff rose up quickly, grabbing his check, and trailed behind them, searching his pockets for change even as he walked.

He tossed the proper change on the counter. There was still a long line waiting for seats, and every third face in it was directed at him with a hard threat. Just before he went out the door, he glanced at the clock perched over it. Near ten o'clock. Little more than an hour left to him. People would start to leave the streets, the doors would darken.

He ran onto the sidewalk, then forced himself back to a walk. He wasn't alone yet; there was no need to think that far ahead. Help would come—it must come—long before the deadline.

Two figures loomed before him, and he stepped to the right, trying to avoid them. It became one of those awkward, sidewalk dances where people nearly run into each other, then apologize, reddened and feeling stupid. He started the apology, and realized this case wasn't so simple. The two men veering left and right with him were HFP-ers, and they were forcing him into a door that opened beside him—a wooden door, set in a wooden shack-like frame, covering the remodeling of a store front. There was darkness in there, and aloneness. He darted to the left, away from the opening, and stretched his legs to outdistance them. He sidestepped into a shoe store.

He stood at the crowded pocketbook counter and stared into the case, trying to regain control. Rogers was getting impatient, and his henchmen were more aggressive. He had to watch himself.

A hand slapped down on his shoulder, and he jumped, spinning around. He found a face that rang with familiarity, but in his fear, he couldn't place it.

"Sorry I startled you, old man," the face said.

The familiarity muted into recognition and Jeff breathed out a big sigh. "Bill Heller! Well, for heaven's sake." Bill Heller was a close acquaintance, never a friend, but suddenly a refuge.

Bill was leaning away from him, as though he was ready to exchange a few words and leave. "How's Marsha?"

"Fine. That's where I'm going right now. She insisted on taking in this sale, but our baby-sitter expected us home over an hour ago."

Heller moved off one step, and Jeff grabbed his arm.

"Say, Bill, I wonder—could you possibly give me a lift? Home? I…" He fumbled for an intelligible excuse. "I've come out without my wallet, and no wallet, no taxi. Do you—?"

"Sorry, old man, but I can't. Not tonight. Like I said, we're already late." Heller plunged his hand into his pocket and came up with a money clip. "Look, I'll be glad to loan you taxi fare. You can pay me back any time. Okay?" He peeled off three dollars and held it out.

"Thanks," Jeff pocketed the money. "I feel like some kind of idiot—"

He was gone. The door of the shoe store closed behind him, and Jeff was alone at the counter. He left it as the salesgirl came toward him.

On the street, he kept his eyes to the sidewalk, ignoring the people he knew were surrounding him. "Stick with the crowd," he had thought. But now the crowd was all HFP.

They walked the streets as though they had business there; in twos and threes, or all alone, and to anyone passing by, they were innocent. But to Jeff, they stood out in relief. He knew their secret and the depths of their eyes. They walked in front of the stores, alternately lighted red or green by the flashing glow of neon signs, and he walked with them, the hunters and the hunted together, gauging their chances, wearing each other out. But his loneliness was accentuated with every passing minute, for their number grew while he remained incredibly alone.

"I'm making myself as conspicuous as hell," he cursed to himself, "so why can't the police find me? The Listeners found me. Surely—"

It was ridiculous, a hunt in the open, and he wanted to give it up, to end it, but there was no opportunity. He had lost his one slim chance. How would it come? An arm pulling him into a side street, maybe, and the quick flash of a knife; or a shove at the top of an escalator, toppling him to his death; or a brutal blow in some dim, empty corner. The method wasn't important, only the result, and he wouldn't give them an opening for that result.

He nearly bumped into three of them, and the largest one caught his arm in a tight clasp, saying with an outward innocence, covered over with a syrupy slur, "Why don't you come with us for coffee?"

Coffee, stirred with death. In what restaurant? Jeff tugged his arm out of the vise of clenching hand.

"Munro!" hissed in his ear, and he widened his strides to outdistance them, sure they wouldn't hurry to keep pace and make themselves conspicuous among the shoppers.

He stepped out ahead of the light and the cop managing traffic motioned him back angrily. When the light changed, Jeff walked right by the policeman. He couldn't ask for help, and be led to a police car. That would be too easy a trap.

He tried a new tack. Since he had to stay on the main street in case Cory was looking for him, he went in and out of stores. Every store. Every door. He went in, walked down the aisles jammed with sale counters, turned around, and came back out. At any point, he might find his chance to break free. At any side door, he might find the street outside devoid of the hard faces.

But it never happened. And it was after ten o'clock.

He entered the town's biggest department store. The place was packed with slow-moving crowds. He sifted in among them. He walked to the back of the store, and then to the front again, until the floorwalker's gaze was following him, and until his feet burned and ached with a pain that shot up his legs. Fear was exhausting him. If the time ever came to run, he wouldn't have the strength.

And all along the aisles, buying unneeded and unwanted things, were the stiff, shaft-bodies of the Listeners. The clock was racing in its last round before the stores closed, and they were waiting it out.

He strode to the back again, to an area off to one side of the service desk where he had seen a public telephone booth. He had to have help—now—and the need of it panted in his lungs. He pulled the booth door closed behind him. Someone had taken the directory. Its chain hung limply by the phone. And he didn't know Kirby's number.

He dropped a dime in the slot, waited for the bell to ping and the dial tone to sound, then dialed his own number. He prayed Cory would be there.

The phone burbled three times. "Hello?"

It was Cory's voice, and Jeff collapsed against the booth in a shaking relief. "Cory," he gasped. "You've got—"

"Where the devil are you?" Cory snapped out. "We've been looking all over."

"You've got to make a call for me. Find Sam Kirby's number, Cory, and tell him what's going on. Will you?"

"But, Jeff, where are you?"

"Tell Kirby I'm in Ham's department store. I'll try to stay here. I—" he broke off as his eyes roamed outside his lighted cubicle. Coming down the aisle toward him, two abreast, were big men. They came fast, purpose in their clenched hands. "Cory! Why haven't you sent help?" the words nearly sobbed out of him.

"I told you, we couldn't find you Jeff."

"I can't stay here!" Jeff cried into the phone. "They're coming. Call Kirby. Please, Cory. *Get me some help!*"

He slammed the receiver down and slipped out of the booth. He had to go straight to them. There was a wall behind him. He went one aisle to the left, but they were there, too, coming at him, two abreast, and their lips shaped a word he couldn't mistake, "Munro!"

His knees trembled with weakness as he darted farther to the left. They couldn't be everywhere! They couldn't block all the aisles.

He found one where the two people coming at him were not so menacing. A woman and a little girl. He hurried into that aisle, and as he came close to the child, saw the smear of chocolate around her lips. The same two from the restaurant. He said a quick "Excuse me," and pushed between them. When he turned to identify footsteps hitting the floor in his wake, he saw that the woman had fallen in behind him. The child was pulled by an out-stretched arm, and the woman had deep determination in her stride.

He ran. Up the aisle, across another, down a third, until he came to the escalators. He stepped on quickly, shoving rudely ahead of two women. He heard their insulted comments behind his back, and was glad for them. They at least, weren't after him.

There was a space of ten steps between himself and the next person on the rising stair. When that woman got off, broad shoulders stepped in to fill her place. He grabbed hold of the moving hand rail, clenching it tightly to hide the shaking of his hand. They were waiting for him at the top, waiting to push him backward.

As his step on the escalator neared the top where it flowed into the floor, he braced himself, jumped off and pushed hard by the man who was blocking him. He felt the pull of a hand, but jerked free. He was on the women's ready-to-wear floor, and half-trotted to hide behind the racks of dresses.

"Could I help you, sir?" a saleslady appeared beside him.

"No." He couldn't keep a train of thought long enough to invent an excuse. "No—I'm waiting for someone."

"It's nearly closing time," she said. She was tired, and anxious to see the crowd leave, but she couldn't know how deep she stabbed him with her slight anger.

Almost closing time.

He left the dress department and went to the elevators. He could hear feet hit the carpet, off-beat with his. Why didn't someone see and question? How could they get away with this? But people stayed out of a stranger's plight. People let a stranger be murdered right before their eyes.

The elevator door whisked open, and he started to step inside, then couldn't. People bumped up behind him, caught off balance by his sudden stop. He didn't dare shut himself inside the elevator. He couldn't know if he would be with shoppers or caught inside with a whole covey of fanatics.

"Please!" a woman's voice said, and an elbow jammed into his ribs. "Are you getting on?"

He sidled away, watching the crowd slide into the car, the door close on them, and the down-light go out. He headed away blindly, letting his feet lead him, too tired to lead them.

There was nowhere left to go. They were behind him, in front of him, waiting for him at the top and bottom of the escalators, the elevators—and the store was clearing. The shoppers were complaining about their tired backs, and the aisles were less and less crowded.

He had to return to the main floor. When Kirby came, he had to be found quickly. He couldn't try the stairs. They would be too deserted. And the elevator held a terror of its own. He went back to the escalator. Down and down he went, and the ride was too fast because they would be standing at the end of it. The end came and he was in the mainstream of crowds. They had perhaps saved his life, but not for good, just for a longer duration of hell.

There was a center stair that led to the basement bargain store, and he went down. Bargain basements never thinned out as quickly as the more expensive departments.

He wandered the aisles aimlessly, exhaustion crying from his body. He passed men's clothing, and the pungent smell of leather and wax that made up the shoe department. He shuffled through household goods, his hands clinging to the cheap chenille of bargain bedspreads and the fluffy synthetics of bath mats.

And then the way before him was clear. All he could see was emptiness. No people, but no Listeners either. He stepped toward it, holding himself erect by pressing his fists on the counters he passed. Three steps to the right and four forward, and he was in a little box by himself, the tiny, empty hall that separated a store from its stockrooms. It was dark in front of him.

A bell rang—ting, ting, ting—ting, ting, ting. Closing time. Darkness ahead, and closing time.

He stared into the darkness and terror couldn't even grip him. He was too tired. He was alone. Why didn't they come? Where were they? He leaned back against the wall, rolling his head from side to side. Tears slipped from his eyes but he wasn't ashamed of them. He couldn't be ashamed of defeat when he had tried so hard.

He heard a rustle behind him. A hand clenched into his shoulder, and with his last breath of energy, he whirled to face his attacker.

"It's me," Cory said. "Jeff?"

Cory stood there, tall and blond and anxious, and Jeff let the tears squeeze out of his eyes, collapsing against his friend in a helpless mass of exhaustion and relief.

"We've got to get out of here," Jeff said, and his voice was a husky croak.

"Of course we do. Let me help you." Cory's arm went under his shoulder and then he was being led and supported, straight into the darkness. "You look like you've been through hell," Cory muttered. "Take it easy now. Let me get you out."

Jeff didn't answer. His relief was too deep to spawn words. He simply leaned on Cory's arm and followed where Cory led.

Darkness closed about them but they were miraculously alone. No one followed and no one reared up before them. They were in the stockroom, and shelves stacked with boxes and the smell of wrapping paper and glue towered over their heads.

"Hang on," Cory whispered. "It won't be much farther."

Cory couldn't know the danger. But Jeff didn't tell him. His friend seemed in complete command, and so far, even in the dark room, nothing had happened. He put all his fears on Cory's shoulders and gave over the whole responsibility.

They came to a door, and Cory opened it. No one was on the other side. Taking most of his strength, Cory helped him up a flight of stairs, then turned left and pushed another door.

Fresh air breezed out to brush Jeff's face and he breathed it deep into his lungs. They stood in an alley, a loading dock beside them.

"We're going to make it?" Jeff asked softly.

"We will. It's not much farther."

"I can't thank you enough."

"Don't, Jeff."

"But you came down, yourself—you took the chance."

"I had to come myself. There was nothing else to be done."

They walked the alley, their footsteps loud on concrete. A recessed door lay ahead, but Jeff didn't care any more. Cory was blessed with luck and safety. Cory had gotten him free.

The door was within one step, and Jeff took it. He sucked in his breath, grabbing into the flesh of Cory's arm. Four men stood within the recess. Four men. And one of them was Rogers.

"Run, Cory!" screamed out of Jeff's throat, and he let loose of the blond man, stumbling as he called on his last reserve to take him clear.

But Cory didn't let go of him. Cory's arms were around his, pinning his own, and Cory was strong, strong. Then Jeff was shoved sideways into the recess. Cory's hands left his body and Rogers' hands took over. The other men grabbed on, too, and he was pinioned.

"All right, Rogers," Cory said. "I've brought him, don't let anyone forget who did it! None of your fancy maneuvering managed to get him."

Jeff's vision blurred as he stared at his friend, his ears refusing to register the words, refusing to believe. Cory gazed back, without remorse, without sentiment of any kind. His only expression was satisfaction and a new icy glint in his eyes.

"Nobody will forget," Rogers told Cory. "Hicks plays fair."

Blackness was closing in, rushing with a silent speed, and Jeff had no strength to fight it off. His head wobbled on his neck, and he let it fall, carrying his field of vision to the cement, away from the terrible face of betrayal, away from Cory.

Rough hands pulled him out of the doorway, and he let himself be led. There was no further fight to be fought.

CHAPTER ELEVEN

HICKS was waiting in the plushness of his private office when Cory and Rogers led Jeff in. They had flown from Union Town to Wornegon, but even so the trip had consumed time, and dawn was ready to steal the sky from the terrible, flight-filled night.

Jeff was pushed into a chair by Rogers' thin hands. "Here he is, Mr. Hicks. All yours."

"Yes, yes," Hicks said. There was no gloating joy in his face. There was, instead, an odd touch of disappointment. "You gave us a very bad time, Munro. And, too bad, because it was all for nothing. Except, of course, that you proved my point. These so-called ethics and ideals that men are prone to die for are valueless and weakening. Power is all that matters."

"To you," Jeff countered. "My only mistake was trust. I was wary of Rogers, but trusted Cory. And he was the viper in my own house."

Cory, sitting close by, recrossed his legs.

"That's just what I mean," Hicks said. "Trust. That word is bandied about by many people who think they are noble: trust in humanity, trust in God. Look what it did to you."

"Only because it was misplaced," Jeff said.

"Then why did it almost ruin Cory, too?" Hicks asked. "He fell into the same trap. He trusted you enough to assure us that you were on the level. Enough to believe what you told him about coming in with us. We relied on his judgment."

"You shouldn't have. Cory never did know me. He always thought I was only out for position, for myself. I'm glad he turned on you, too."

"He has more than made up for it." Hicks folded his fat hands. "He brought you to us."

"Why?" Jeff demanded. "Why didn't you let your people tear me apart and be done with it?"

"Because we have other plans for you," Rogers said.

"You're such a fool, Munro," Hicks said. "You gave up so much in what you thought was a gallant fight to save humanity from alien hands. Earth will never fall into alien hands. Only men were made to rule men. Once things have gone our way and we have enough money and spacecraft, we're setting out on a crusade of our own. We're going to the planet of the Masters and take it over. The Masters will be the slaves, not us. The men and women of HFP will go on to conquer the universe!"

Hicks was radiant, beaming with an inner anticipation that transcended even his grossness. Power! Hicks could see it and feel it in his hands, and his fat body quivered with the vision.

"Then you're planning to double-cross the aliens as well as Earth?" Jeff shook his head at the baseness of it.

"It isn't a double-cross." Cory leaned toward Jeff, eager to explain. "It's just returning men to their birthright. Be honest with yourself. Deep inside you there's a spark that wants to command, a spark that was bred into you to rule men. I have it. I can feel it in me. Power is all there is. There's nothing greater for a man to gain than power. Ask anyone who has it. Ask anyone in public life why he went into it. To help his fellow men? No! To lead them, to hold them in his hands, to rule them."

Cory was changed. He stood taller than he had before, and his easygoing face was a mask of determination. It was a side of him Jeff had only glimpsed, and not often. Now it was no longer a side, but the whole man.

"And you betrayed me for this?" Jeff accused him.

"I didn't betray anybody. I only did what I had to do to further myself and what I believe in. I was born to be a ruler of men. HFP offers me *worlds* to lead, planets to conquer, the fulfillment of every ambition I've ever held. You could have shared in it, but as it is, all I could do was save your life. They wanted to kill you. I interceded. After you left the house, I phoned Hicks and made him agree to take you alive."

"Thanks a lot for a lot of nothing," Jeff said. "Friend!"

"More important," Rogers said, "Cory was HFP's friend. You lost me in the parking ramp, but I called Cory and he was waiting when you got home. You poured out the whole FBI story to him."

"I don't have to be told," Jeff snapped. "I know all about his betrayal. The day you were waiting for me at the fences, even that was his doing. I told him everything. But that doesn't make me a fool. It only reflects on him."

"You may as well abandon your tries to shame Cory," Hicks said, "because Cory isn't responding. He knows what he's about. He brought you to us, and he also brought your little team of FBI men. We have them under control. Mason and Terry I believe are their names. They've been dealt with. Kirby, and anyone else he informed, can be handled easily. Your fight is over before it is begun, and if I were you, I'd let that fact sink in."

The atmosphere had changed. Hicks was no longer going to accept whatever he said and shrug it off. The openness had closed down and he was just a prisoner. But the thought didn't shake him because he had caught something in Hicks' long speech that brought hope alive. Hicks had said Terry and Mason—the team of FBI men. He hadn't mentioned Jones. Jeff laughed to himself. Cory had made a mistake after all. A team of FBI men, Jeff had said, so Cory jumped at the conclusion of two, a team made up of *two*. Now he remembered Cory's grand-sounding statement about wanting to help with the destruction of HFP, that four men would be better than three. It had really been five. Jones was still free. Somewhere, Jones was waiting for him. So was Kirby, because Cory didn't know that part of the plan either.

"It's getting near sunrise," Rogers said.

"I know," Hicks answered. "We must get on with this, Munro, because you have an appointment at dawn."

Jeff looked up sharply.

"You're right to be apprehensive," Hicks said. "You've lost a lot. You gave up a world of power for a world of enslavement. As Cory said, he interceded so you won't be killed, and his point was well taken. You can still recruit for us."

Surely they weren't crazy enough to remake their original offer? "You're not asking—?"

"No! I'm not asking anything of you. I'm previewing what is going to happen to you. You were spared a normal initiation because we believed you were with us. Now you're going to get a normal initiation. Plus."

"Then there is more than hocus-pocus in the dark?"

"Much more. Normally when an initiate goes into the meditation cubicle, he is only beginning his walk into the ranks of Listeners. A gas is released into those cubicles—a sweet, perfumed gas that anesthetizes him. When the initiate is gassed, the Tobys enter, place him on the table and perform a simple operation—a matter of implanting a tiny receiver in the temple, close to the ear. The mark looks like nothing more than a pimple, and finally disappears altogether. From that moment on, the initiate is tuned to the Masters, receiving transmissions from the machines downstairs, receiving instructions at the morning Listening sessions. Those machines are capable of giving out thousands of different messages at once."

"Then your fanatics *are* just puppets," Jeff burst out.

"No, not at all. As long as they obey the commands—and they all do—they are their own bosses. However, the Masters are capable of more. I don't understand their whole power myself, but they can call up these implanted people in droves, as they did in Union Town. They can use these people as puppet armies. Mason and Terry have already been through forcible initiation, and if we let them go, they'll return to the FBI with a clean report on HFP, just as their predecessors have done."

"And that's what you have in store for me?"

"No. It would be useless for you. You wouldn't obey. There is another method, a method of full-time control, where the implanted man truly does become a puppet, as you so aptly put it. That is what we have in store for you. The Masters have a method of controlling a man, of breaking his will until he will do anything the receiver instructs him to do. It has only been attempted once before, and the implanted man died. Still, it's worth the risk in your case because we can use you well."

Jeff shot out of his chair, ready to run again. But Rogers and Cory grabbed him and he was caught tight, until only the trembling was left and that involuntary. He stared into Cory's eyes. *"You* planned this for me. You!"

"It's better than dying," Cory said. "You can still be useful."

"Useful to whom? Not to myself."

"You gave up your chance for that when you betrayed us," Rogers smiled his evil half-smile.

He was alone in a room full of monsters. More alone than he had been running the streets because then he had believed he possessed a friend. The terror of being turned into a puppet broke in him all at once and he shouted almost against his will, *"Cory, please! For God's sake, help me! You can't—"*

"Sit down, Jeff." Cory's tone was low. There was no compassion in him. "You'll only wear yourself out."

A dreadful shame spread through Jeff and he let Cory pull him back to his chair. He had shouted out a desperate plea, and because that plea was refused, he had at last become the fool he had struggled not to be.

Hicks said, "We wanted you with us, to beat the aliens with us. But you would have none of it. I'm sorry, Munro."

Jeff didn't look at him. Why should the only sympathy come from Hicks? He could feel Cory beside him, feel the warmth radiating from Cory's body and the breath puffing out of Cory's lungs, but Hicks was the only one who felt for him.

"When?" Jeff asked.

"Right away," Rogers said. "The Tobys are waiting for you now: Can we take him, Mr. Hicks?"

"Take him," Hicks said, then turned his wide back to stare out of the window.

Rogers' hands came down on Jeff's arm, and Jeff shuddered. He didn't look at Cory again.

The room was twelve by twelve and a cold, sterile white. There was a metal table in the middle of it, a smaller one beside it loaded with medical instruments, and a tiny lump of metal lying on a cushion of gauze. The receiver. The minute invader of his body that would be the whole of him within a little while, the voice that would replace his conscience and will. It would be a tinny voice, he knew.

A number of little men waited near the table. They were dressed in white like dwarfed doctors, and he wondered if one of them was Toby, the original Toby.

"Make way," Rogers ordered the little men.

The Tobys cleared a path and Rogers led Jeff along it.

The table pushed against his thighs as Rogers said, "Lie down. And don't struggle against them. They may be as stupid as hell, but they're strong."

An automatic raising of heavy, dark-skinned heads answered Rogers' remark. The many chocolate eyes lit upon him with a silent anger, but nothing was said.

"Have you got the right receiver?" Cory asked one of the Tobys.

"We have made no mistakes," the Toby protested.

"Hicks gave them the receiver himself," Rogers said. "We don't take any chances. As long as you lead them step by step, and then triple check, they manage to do what they're told."

Rogers' open contempt for the little men was insulting, and riled Jeff. The Tobys were about to destroy him, but he still felt pity for them. Stupid or not, their chocolate eyes said they were sensitive to the insults.

"Make it quick," Cory ordered them. "We want him ready for his first reception within the hour."

"But," the obvious leader of the little men stammered, "I don't understand. When he came before, we were ordered not to touch him. He is one of the special ones."

"You don't have to understand," Cory said. "You just do what Hicks says."

"But this kind of receiver is dangerous. I used it once before and the man died. Do you realize that?"

"The operation is no different from any other," Rogers said.

"But the receiver is. It has a longer range, a steady receiving stream. The Masters told me that themselves."

"Look, you dwarf—" Rogers showed his teeth in his impatience—"all you have to do is perform the operation. You're not asked to think. Now get to it!" Rogers spun his anger on Jeff. "I told you to lie down on the table. I want things settled before I walk out of here. I can't trust them to do anything right."

The chocolate eyes were on Jeff now, and he raised himself to the edge of the table. It was cold.

"Lie down," Cory commanded.

There was nothing else to do, no way to fight, not even a path to run. Jeff laid himself full length on the cold metal and closed his eyes. He didn't want to see any more. These little men would do a terrible thing to him, but it was against their will to do it. The men who were forcing them were even now leaving the room.

The door slammed behind Cory and Rogers, and the loud fall of their footsteps was replaced by the quicker patter of the Tobys. Jeff lay waiting, waiting—for the first touch of a mask over his nose, for the first clasp of a restraint around his wrists, but the dark world inside his eyelids wouldn't hold still. It spun crazily, even without sight, and his stomach revolted, pouring a stream of acid into his mouth. He had to take this staunchly. There was no other course, so he had to travel this one bravely.

"Will I really be a puppet?" he whispered into the darkness behind his eyes.

"You will no longer be a true man," a Toby voice said beside his ear. "Why you do this to each other, we can't understand."

"And why you do it, *I* can't understand," Jeff opened his eyes.

The dark-skinned face was almost touching his over the edge of the table, and the table itself was lowering, coming down to a height at which the little men could work.

"There is no choice," the Toby said. "We must have our destiny. If this is what it takes to get it, we must obey."

There was no hope of beating down that simple statement.

"Relax yourself now," the Toby said. "You will feel nothing."

A mask was descending. It touched his skin and there was a scent in it, a sweet perfume that oozed a sense of unreality. It lowered more, over his docile, waiting face, settling itself over his nose and mouth.

He threw his arms up and hit it away, leaping from the table, and falling as he misjudged the height and hit the floor too hard. He jumped to his feet and rammed against the door. It was locked.

Turning his back to it, he braced himself. The Tobys were coming, all of them, short and strong.

"Calm yourself," one of them said. "There is no use in this."

He threw himself into the midst of them, hitting out with his arms and legs, and they toppled like dominoes. He swung wildly among them, knocking them over, and cries tore out of his throat as his hands made contact with their dark skins. He would kill them all. He would better them all. He was no puppet, and he would never be a puppet.

His legs wouldn't move, and he caught his balance before he toppled with them. His vision clearing from the momentary madness, he saw what had happened. From their toppled positions on the floor, they had grabbed his legs. Three to a leg, they held fast, and he couldn't walk, or kick, or run.

More of them jumped at him, and he flailed his arms, beating them off, but the movement unbalanced him, and then the floor was rising up to meet him as he fell, his feet still cemented by the strength of those strong, short arms. He hit the floor hard, barely protecting his face, and they swarmed over him and around him, subduing his last efforts by their force of numbers.

"Give it up," shouted into his ear. "We don't want to harm you."

His struggles were stemmed at their beginnings. He couldn't move at all. He submitted, lying limp under their weight, jarring them only with a few feeble sobs that pushed out of him against his will, but couldn't even come to real fruition.

"Will you stay calm now?" the Toby asked. "If you say yes, we will trust you. Otherwise we will proceed right here on the floor. It would be best if you came back to the table."

He nodded his head as best he could, finding even that part of himself restrained by hands holding his hair. Then the hands were gone and they were raising him to his feet.

He looked at them, knowing tears were on his face, and ashamed of his weakness when he had vowed to be so brave, but they weren't laughing. He walked with them supporting him, and tried to read their eyes. Pity? Yes, pity. And regret—the same regret they had expressed before. But even more, admiration. A tiny, beginning look of admiration had come into the little men, and it was directed at him, all at him.

He stopped walking. "Have I met any of you before?"

"You have met me," one of them said. "I am Toby."

"But you're all Tobys, aren't you?"

"We are not. That is the name they call us—Tobys. But we have our own names. And they gave us others in English—Ben, Buff, Duke—names like those."

"But those are names for animals."

"We know. They think of us as work animals."

"They shouldn't. You're men! You deserve respect."

"You would say that," Toby answered gently. "Anyone who would risk what you have risked would say that."

"Then I was right and you do respect me?" Jeff asked quickly.

"As much as you respect us…You have shown courage—you have tried to save your world even in the face of giving your life. We can admire this. And understand it. We have given a lot to save our world, too. To advance it. The other special ones are nasty men who treat us with contempt. You do not."

He let himself have one last fling at wariness. "Are you telling me this only to make me submit without any more fighting?"

"No," Toby said. "In that much, Hicks is right. We are too dull-witted to fool anyone. If nothing else, we are honest."

"But why do you put up with this kind of treatment?"

"Because again Hicks is right. We live as parasites, sucking the minds of those who will help us. We must have the stars as well as you must have them. We have what we have in return for someone to help us. We have only willing bodies."

"I don't believe it," Jeff said. "You speak too well to be anything less than intelligent."

"Languages, we can learn. It is the complex and abstract things which elude us."

"But what good will it be if you gain the stars and lose your self-respect? I understand your need for racial aggrandizement, your wanting to be more than you have been. But I can't condone this crawling on the ground before men like Hicks."

"There is no other way," Toby said, and heads nodded sad agreement around him.

"There is! If you had the right allies, you could keep your dignity and still gain your goal. You've chosen the wrong friends. You had no choice in the beginning, but now you have."

Agitation stirred the short figures about him. "What do you mean?" Toby asked.

"Simply that my people wouldn't treat you like animals. We could help you as much as the Masters, but we wouldn't demand your self-respect in return. We wouldn't make slaves of you."

"Your people are like Hicks and Bennett and Rogers."

"No. They are the exceptions. My people are like me. And you claim to admire me."

Their attention swept away from him as they talked among themselves, and although the language was foreign, he saw their agitation, saw that he was making his point.

"You must see the sense in what I've said," he hurried on. "My people are just beginning to try for the stars and we have the ability to gain them. With your knowledge of spacecraft, we wouldn't even have to wait. You know how to build the ships already. The Masters taught you that."

The little group talked on within itself, listening when he spoke, discussing it when he quit. He had no way of knowing what headway he was making. He had to bring it down to concrete demonstration.

He touched the leader of them on the shoulder. "What is your name?" he asked. "Your real name."

"Ariki," the little man said.

"And yours?" he asked another.

"Coben."

"And yours?"

"Tonnard."

"Ariki, Coben, Tonnard. Please consider what I've said carefully. And quickly. Hicks is waiting for me to walk out of here a puppet, and your chance will walk out with me."

They were watching him with a strange concentration.

"Ariki?" he asked, using the proper name.

"You have made your point," Ariki said. "No one has called us by name since we arrived on Earth. It has always been Toby. You are the first to meet us as men—with souls."

"Then, if we have at last met soul to soul, you can't destroy mine." Jeff tried to dun it into them, make their slow minds grasp his point. "If you plant that thing under my skin, I'll have no soul. You can't do that to me."

"But if we don't we will suffer terrible consequences."

"Not if you cast your lot with me and my people. I promise you, we'll help. And give you the respect you deserve."

"But how?" Ariki asked desperately, wanting to believe.

"I'm going to destroy the machines. I'm going to cut the Masters off from Earth, clear Hicks and his kind out, and then we'll be free of them. If you don't rebuild the receivers', the Masters can't contact us any more. All of the people you have initiated will be free again."

"We couldn't help you in the destruction," Ariki said quickly. "Because if you failed, who knows what would happen to us?"

"I understand that. But you could promise not to rebuild the machines. And if I succeed—"

"If you succeed," Ariki said, "we could return to the planet of the Masters and destroy the transmitters we built there. Then the Masters would be as helpless as they were before they found us."

"You see?" Jeff laughed. "You aren't stupid! You've let them convince you that you are, but when it comes to direct action, you know what you're doing."

A dark-skinned hand came out to touch Ariki's arm. There was concern in the Tobys, and they spoke softly to their leader. He said, "My brothers want to believe you, and join with you, but they're afraid. They have left the decision to me."

"And they'll abide by it?"

"They will."

"Then," Jeff asked hoarsely, because so much was riding on this one answer, "what is your decision?"

Ariki stared at him with his chocolate eyes, and his square face was grave. "It would be easy if it weren't for you. But I admire you, respect you, sense something in you that speaks of fairness. And your life means so much to you. I'm afraid I'm bringing it down to emotion only, but I'm not capable of anything else. I can only do what my heart tells me, because no matter what you say in your kindness, my mind can't weigh too many possibilities. So I say—yes. We will cast our lot with you and your people."

Jeff grasped the little man's hand. "You won't be sorry."

"But now there is the immediate problem of Hicks and Rogers. We must fool them."

Jeff let the hand drop from his grasp. He had taken one giant step, only to run head on into the same wall that had dogged him all along.

The Tobys were smiling at his anxiety, and he asked them why.

"Get back on the table," Ariki commanded. When Jeff hesitated, he added, "You must either trust us or drop the whole plan."

"All right." Jeff made up his mind and walked to the table. "I'm in your hands. But why the table?"

Ariki approached him and picked up an instrument. He placed the instrument close to Jeff's ear. "This will sting a bit, but that's all," he said, and before Jeff could move to defend himself, the metal pricked his skin, a tiny searing pain arced down the side of his head, and Ariki backed off.

"That part is done," Ariki said as Jeff reared up to his feet again. "Within a few minutes, it will swell and look as though you have been implanted."

"But, I haven't?" Jeff was apprehensive.

"Of course not. We are simply fooling Hicks. Yet you won't get off so easily." Ariki's hand came out, carrying the tiny receiver with it. "You must insert this inside your ear so you can hear the instructions from the Masters. If you don't, you'll fool no one."

Jeff took the thing in his hand. It made only a small spot on his palm. "I see. I can wear this as I choose, listen to their commands and follow them so no one will know I'm not really implanted."

"And when the commands start to tear you to pieces, you can remove it."

"Tear me to pieces?"

"It happened to the other man. Something he heard— whatever the Masters said—led him about like a puppet, and he wilted before our eyes. He was dead within three days. They broke his will to act, and with it his will to live."

"Then I'm not out of the woods yet."

"Don't wear it too long," Ariki said, and it was a plea and a gesture of friendship all at once. "They will be coming for you soon. So you must tell us your plan."

"I don't really know what it is," Jeff admitted. "But whatever I manage to do will be done tonight. If you want to stay clear of implication, then keep away from the machine room tonight."

Ariki said solemnly, "Our future rides with yours now." He showed Jeff how to insert the receiver inside his ear, then explained, "Even when you are not listening, you must act the part. The other man was dazed. He walked slowly, stiff and sometimes stumbling. That is all I can tell you. Your best hope lies in the fact that Hicks doesn't know what to expect of you either. He only saw what I saw in the other man."

The receiver was weightless in his ear. It wouldn't bother him at all—until it started to speak. Before it did start, he had to set his plan firmly in his mind, so the Masters couldn't drive it out. First, he must pass the test of Hicks; then he must search for Jones. He was still in Wornegon somewhere, and Jeff needed him. He couldn't manage this alone. Once he found Jones, the plan would proceed as outlined, after curfew.

The table was raised back to normal height, and he sat on the edge of it, silent; Ariki and his brothers stood around him, silent. They were waiting for it to begin, and so was he—waiting and dreading and praying he could stand up under it. Because he must not remove the receiver too soon or too often. If he missed an order and failed to obey, the Masters would know.

A picking sound echoed in his mind, and he cocked his head. A whole new room opened up before him, but it was a world of sound, a world of spaces and machines, such as he had experienced once before when a public address system had sprung to life.

Ariki clutched at him.

"Another thing I forgot to tell you. Mr. Munro. Mr. Munro!"

"Yes."

"Don't be fooled into thinking the broadcast voice is all. It isn't. The Masters have some power that transmits with their voice. The voice isn't even real. They have no vocal chords."

Ariki's voice was blotted out by a tinny eruption from the receiver inside his ear. Jeff straightened up and listened.

"Jeffrey Munro," it said. *"You are delivered into our hands. You belong to us body and soul. Now we will prove it."*

CHAPTER TWELVE

THE tinny voice took over, and it wasn't hard to feign dazedness, because it dominated him. Its tininess penetrated the depths of his soul and spoke to his brain without going through his senses. It tore him, calling names, flailing him with insults, beating his ego to black dust. He listened, because he had to listen. He wanted to grab the voice from his ear, but didn't dare. The one time he tried, Ariki restrained his hand.

The voice was so strong and insistent that it even blotted out sight. He was a marionette, who knew his limits. If the voice ordered him to move his left hand, he would move it. He wouldn't want to move it, but he would obey, because there was more to the voice than tinny sound. There was compulsion.

His body was heavy, and his legs where they hung down from the table were shafts of cement, pulling him toward the floor. In the dimness of the voice, the door opened and he was conscious of the presence of Hicks, and another, taller figure beside him—Cory.

"I see it's done," Hicks said, his voice a faint echo against the roar of the Other One.

"We did as commanded," Ariki answered.

"You took long enough about it," Cory said.

"He was difficult. He has a strong will."

"Not any longer," Hicks said.

Ariki spoke hesitantly. "It seems cruel, sir. A man such as this, to take away his soul."

"And what do you know about souls?" Cory snapped.

Jeff saw the shape that was Ariki back off, bent into a queer sort of lump. The voice in his ear kept shouting: *You have been a fool. You are capable of nothing more. Confess it to yourself! You are nothing. You can't fight against us! Jeffrey Munro is a helpless, strutting fool. Say it! Swing—your—left—leg.*

Jeff's left leg began its cemented swing of its own accord. He didn't set it in motion. It was alive of itself, apart from him, and he cried out at it, but his cry was only a whimper.

"Ha," Hicks grunted. "They've gotten to him already. Such power. Such power!"

Something pressed against Jeff, and he stiffened. It was a softness, a fatness, with warmth emanating from it. Hicks. "Can you hear me, Munro? How does it feel, man? Is there a sensation to it?"

Jeff tried to turn from the intruding face.

"Come on Hicks," Cory said, "that's a disgusting way to get your kicks. You make me sick to my stomach."

"Then be sick," Hicks said. "Think of it, the power of it—to take a life in your hands and direct it about. How does it feel, Munro? Where did your assurance go?"

"Stop—swinging—your—leg!" The command came out of a long tirade of insults, and Jeff's leg hung limply, still without a command from his brain. *"Get down from the table!"*

How did they know he was on a table? Could they see him? Sense him? He was climbing down, clinging to the questions, determined to hang on. They could order him about and he would obey, but he would not give in.

"Walk!" The command was sharp. His body paced and he went with it, fighting for some measure of control. It was now or never. If he let go too much, the Masters would have him, removable receiver or not. Gathering a deep breath, he halted his legs, and it was a terrible fight to accomplish even that little bit of rebellion. But he halted, stood still for the count of ten, then let himself move on. Now his walk was half their order and half his will. He wouldn't be taken so easily.

"Go out on the grounds and walk the edge of the grass. Round and round. Listen! Always listen. Hear what you have become!"

He touched the door, and stepped through. Hicks laughed. "Goodbye, tin soldier." Cory joined in the taunting, but he didn't give them the satisfaction of knowing he could hear.

He went out into the early morning sun. It was still cold, and the green, green grass was dewy-damp. He obediently went to the edge of it, by the fence, and started on his first circle. Around and around he walked, on the trimmed edges of Wornegon, and the ego-beating wore on him until he could barely separate his own thoughts from the slurs of the Masters.

As he finished his second round, he forced his arm upward and plucked the receiver from his ear. The silence was a mass that fell on him.

He continued walking as he had been, bent, shuffling a little, head down. But now he was alert for voices, alert for sounds. Birds sang in the woods, cars throbbed in the parking lot and voices hummed in the distance. As he passed groups of people, he searched for Jones. He had to find Jones.

He gave himself what he estimated to be five minutes free of the receiver, and replaced it in his ear. He cut in on another tirade: *"...puny power of mind. Going against the glory of HFP is sinful, and you are sinful. Say it to yourself—your true inner self. Say, I am sinful!"* The Masters obviously hadn't sent any new orders. The voice controlled him again, and he waited until he could take another chance and cut it off.

On his tenth circuit of the grounds, he removed the receiver for the third time. His legs ached from ankle to thigh, and his back cramped. He hadn't yet recovered from the running flight of the night before, and he was being forced to walk for miles—miles of grass, miles of degradation.

He kept at it. Left foot, right foot, shuffle a bit. Left foot, right foot, stumble a little. Left foot, right—

Jones! He saw him standing by the gate, waiting for his arrival, expecting him to pull up in a car, as planned. "Jones," Jeff cried out silently, "please, man, look this way. I can't come to you!"

He walked on, slowly, stiffly, imitating himself. He was abreast of Jones, and still the FBI man didn't look around.

Jeff couldn't know if he was being watched. There was no reason even for Rogers to be suspicious of him any more, but one of them might be watching for the sheer pleasure of seeing him tortured. He had to take the chance.

He was almost past Jones, and he whispered, "Here I am, Jones, here I am. Don't follow me. Meet me at the back gate."

Jones got up and fell in beside him for the distance of three short steps. "What's the matter with you?" Jones asked.

"Meet me in the back. And make it look accidental."

Around Jeff went, walking to the corner of the clipped grass and turning to travel the side. At last the back gate was in view and Jones was dutifully waiting.

As he approached the gate, he let himself stumble.

Twelve feet from Jones, he stumbled again, and this time fell to his knees. As he had hoped, the action brought Jones at a run.

"What *is* the matter with you?" Jones tried to help him up.

"Is everything set for tonight?" Jeff demanded.

"Kirby's ready, but I've lost Mason and Terry."

"I know. We'll go it alone. Listen closely. After curfew, meet me in the machine room." He gave brief instructions as to the direction of the machine room. "I'll get there somehow."

"You don't look like you're in any condition—"

"Just help me up. Pretend you don't know me. Just one HFP-er helping another. Understand?"

Jones lifted him up and Jeff replaced the receiver in his ear quickly, because he had heard the pound of feet on the grass and knew someone was coming to check.

"What's going on here?" Rogers shouted, panting up beside them.

"This man is sick," Jones played his part. "He fell."

"Let him fall," Rogers said. "Haven't you anything better to do with your time?"

"Better than helping an HFP Brother?"

Rogers backed down, examining Jeff closely, satisfied with the glazed-over state of his eyes and the slackness of his jaw. "I'm sorry, Brother, I didn't mean that."

Jeff continued his walk, bumping into Rogers, who moved aside. "Let him go his way," he heard Rogers say. "I'll keep an eye on him. You get back to your own duties, Brother."

Rogers took off at a run for the main building, and a few minutes later the voice in Jeff's head ordered him to his room on the third floor, to walk there, pacing off the carpet.

He paced the room until his legs wouldn't hold him any more. Voices, voices, voices. If he relaxed, they grabbed him and controlled him to a terrifying degree. Just as he decided to break free again, the door opened, and Rogers and Hicks entered. He plodded on until his legs gave way and he fell headlong onto the carpet.

Rogers dragged him up.

"Let him be," Hicks said. "He's worn out."

"So? You constantly underestimate this man, Hicks. The idea is to wear him out, physically and mentally. When he does lapse into a coma, the voices will continue, and we'll have him. But first, he's got to be tired enough."

"You're going to kill him," Hicks warned.

"I don't care if I do. He'll either die or submit. There's no in-between with him any more. Personally, I'd prefer to see him dead."

"Because he outsmarted you." Cory's voice was added between the soft fall of Jeff's footsteps, counting off the yardage of the carpet.

"Please," Hicks interrupted. "I don't want to hear any arguments. We've come too far together to split now. Let's go down to dinner and leave him to the Masters."

"I'm staying right here," Rogers decided. "If he falls again, I'm going to resurrect him again. He's going to walk until the Masters say he can stop. Even if his heart gives out first."

"Which it well might," Hicks said. "The Masters don't know much about hearts since they have no bodies. They'll go too far. You'd better come along with us, Rogers. If he falls down, let him stay. They'll still be working on him."

Step, step, step. Jeff fought to hold himself erect. If he fell now, it would decide Rogers to stay, and Rogers had to leave, so he could rest. *"You've been mistaken. Say it! You are a fool. Say it!"* rang in his ear. He couldn't lapse into a coma and allow it to go on or he would lose himself forever.

"Okay," Rogers said, "but if he gets away from us, it's going to be on your head, Hicks."

Hicks answered, "How can he get away from us with that thing planted in his head? Now come along. I'm hungry."

The door closed behind them and Jeff made one more circuit of the room. Then he silenced the voice and threw himself across the bed, lying crosswise, so if anyone peeked in at him, he wouldn't be suspected. He had to sleep. The sun was setting, he had little time, and he was exhausted.

He slept, and the sleep was full of demons. When he woke, the sun was gone, and it was after eleven o'clock. He had made it then. The Masters hadn't known that he wasn't tuned in to them.

Wornegon was all stillness, since the curfew was in effect and the members were loyally tucked into their beds. He rose out of his, went into the bathroom, and doused his face with cold water. He touched the floor with his fingers a few times to limber himself, and went to the door leading into the hall.

Rogers was the real danger now. Rogers might come upon him at any time. His best chance of reaching the side corridor which led to the machines was to pretend to be following orders from the Masters. Even Rogers couldn't find anything suspicious in that.

The hall was empty. He proceeded along it quickly, running on the thick carpet to the elevator. He may as well bluff it big. The door whirred open on an empty car and he stepped inside. As the car descended, he set his expression back to dazedness, bent his body forward, and waited to be a certain target in the lobby. But

the vastness of the lobby was bare. No one watched, no one followed. He shuffled to the side door that led to the machines, and once through it, loped down the corridors, following the forbidding signs.

He was within a hundred feet of his destination with only one corner left to turn, and exultation flew through him. The tin soldier had sprung to fighting life.

He started around the corner—and stopped sharply. Cory stood before him, coming from the other direction.

Halting the startled cry that erupted from his lungs, Jeff fell back into the imitation of a man being led by the Masters. Cory was just as startled. His mouth flashed open in one surprised word, "Jeff!"

Jeff stood stupidly, knowing that his pose was too late. Cory had seen the fight in him. Cory's hand came out and darted to Jeff's temple, feeling for the raised bump of the receiver.

As his touch crawled along Jeff's head, Jeff reared up in fury. "So now you know! And we meet friend to friend—alone."

Cory only lost control for a moment. His expression hardened as he resumed his controlling hand. "I'm immune to threats. You're in my house now."

"But it's made of straw."

Cory sidestepped, a fast movement that was intended to by-pass Jeff, but Jeff blocked the way, his reflexes sharp with the danger. "No," Jeff said. "You're not going to give any alarm. This is between you and me. And this time I know which side you're on."

"I was always on your side. When it comes down to it, Jeff, *you* went against me. I didn't betray you."

"How do you figure that?"

"I tried to warn you off, didn't I? When you started with that article, I tried to warn you off."

"But then you neatly maneuvered me into coming up here. You could have talked me out of it, but instead you supported my suspicions and said the one thing that would make me come."

"I had to," Cory spoke like a man in desperate need of explaining, but his eyes betrayed him, shifting back and forth, searching for a way out. "I couldn't trust you to leave it alone after the death of the Running Man. I thought you'd be smart enough

to accept Hicks' offer. I saved your life. You'd be dead right now if I hadn't convinced Hicks he could still use you."

"If you think turning me into a robot is better than killing me... Cory, can you possibly know how much I hate you?"

"You don't hate me," Cory spoke surely. "You're not the type."

"You were wrong about me once before, remember, so don't count on your judgment now."

"That's another threat?"

"A good, big, loud one. All of your talk about power—well, I've got the power now, and *you're* going to trail after *me.*"

"You're not still trying to wreck the machines? Not alone?"

"That was another mistake you made. When those machines go up in smoke, remember it. You bungled, and destroyed HFP. You can't count, Cory. A team doesn't have to be made up of two men."

Cory went white and stammered, "There were three?"

"Three! Come along with me and meet the third one."

"No!" Cory darted sideways again, and this time made it past Jeff's clutching arms. He went down the hall at a full run, but Jeff closed in, threw himself in a flying tackle and caught the long legs, pulling Cory thumping to the floor. They struggled for position, one on top, then the other. Jeff was sore, and Cory's pounding fists hurt his body. He scrambled to his feet. He had to have room to fell this giant.

Cory faced him and they panted together, waiting for an opening. Jeff's fist flashed out, beating into Cory's face, drawing blood from the cheekbone. Then Cory was on him, and the blows were fast and cutting. With the taste of salty blood in his mouth, Jeff threw himself forward, hitting Cory with the full weight of his body, and Cory stumbled backwards, trying to catch himself. He fell against the wall, and his head cracked back with a terrible thud on the plaster. Jeff jumped on him as he fell, and pounded into his face. But Cory gave him no resistance.

A blast banged out from around the corner. Jeff crouched on top of his beaten opponent, fear coming back to him. "But no!" he shouted out loud. "That's Jones. Jones!"

He looked at Cory again and the man was too still, too pale. With his fingertips, he raised one of Cory's eyelids. The eye was rolled upward, glazed—dead.

Breath heaved out of Jeff. Dead. Cory was dead.

He whirled away, then caught himself. There was no time for guilt. Jones had just blown the inner door and was facing those machines alone. He ran. Around the corner, through the tiny, square room, and on into the immense world of the humming machines.

"Thank God," Jones cried when he saw him. "I didn't know if you'd make it."

"We're nearly home." Jeff clapped the man on the shoulder.

The room was brightly lit, but not from lamps. The light beamed out from the great machine in the center, pulsing harder until it steadied itself into a great circle that cast its glow into the corners. They approached it slowly.

"This is the heart of it," Jeff said, his voice a whisper, wrapped tightly inside his awe. "After this one, the rest will be easy."

They crept toward the light, and it illuminated them weirdly. Jones was a glowing man, sweat sparkling on his forehead and upper lip, his eyes reflecting back the light. Jeff wanted to hurry, but there was an undercurrent in the room that made him wary. It was nothing he could touch, nothing he could identify, but it hummed in the floors and beat in the air, and grew and grew.

A great slap hit him square in the face, and he froze. The undercurrent was now a physical force, and it centered in the light of the machine. The power of the Masters wasn't ready to die.

Jeff didn't understand the power, or the feel of it, but he bunched his will together into one tense ball and stood his ground.

Jones fell. A cry tore out of his throat, and he fell, sprawling on the floor. He tried to claw his way back to his feet, but was pushed down again.

"Don't give out on me now!" Jeff pleaded, but couldn't even bend to help the man. The force that had bounced out with the first slap was holding them from making any hostile move.

"There is a hostile presence in the room," the tinny voice carried out of the speaker. It was familiar, too familiar. He had heard it all day long, only then it had been small, inside his brain. Now it was deafening to his ears.

"This time you're right!" Jeff answered. He still had his voice, and still possessed his will. He could barely move, but he wasn't defeated. "I'm Jeffrey Munro."

"I have information concerning you. You are doing the impossible. You cannot be here. Return to your room."

Jeff laughed, a snort of surprise and fear together. The Masters couldn't believe he had fooled them. Their power was too great to allow for error. His laugh died abruptly. It might just as well be. He couldn't move. The alarm would be sounded, and he couldn't move. He shoved the fear back to its dark recess and drew out anger. He hated this voice. It had degraded him all day. He hated it and would destroy it.

Anger surged through him, and he managed a short step forward. Emotion against intelligence—it was a flimsy weapon, but he had to win.

Overhead a new sound came through the tinny voice. Thumping. He tried to identify it. Thump, thump, growing into a constant pound. Feet! The alarm had been sounded, the Listeners rallied from their sleep, and pointed toward him. All of Wornegon would be crashing down the hall to crush him. And he was only managing a feeble creep toward the glowing eye of the machine.

"Stand your ground," the voice commanded. "You are powerless against us. You are merely hands and feet."

"You've said that once too often—to the Tobys and to Montgomery Hicks," Jeff challenged.

"Only often enough." The voice, in itself, was mechanical, but something rode with it—the undercurrent, the force. It was so alien that he shivered inside its every word, its every pronouncement. This thing was too far apart from him. Ariki with all of his grotesqueness was a brother next to this. Across the stars this power had come, sailing through the reaches of space to command him, and it was a horror.

He took another step, and it only spanned a distance of inches. He was a worm crawling after an eagle. And the thumping over his head was louder. He had to find a way to gain a precious minute.

"I said you told Hicks that once too often, because he hates you for it."

"That is a lie!" shot back at him.

"Then," Jeff shouted it out, straight into the teeth of the light and the reverberating power, "why does Hicks plot to betray you? He has plans—plans to come to your world and enslave you! To use your ships and your transmitters for his own purposes. You're nothing to us! You can't move! You're no more than a *thing*—a tool!"

He shouted it and he didn't believe it, not when he felt the force of the Masters through his body. But the holding tension, the almost-wall that held him, softened for an instant of shock as the great mind heard his words and was astounded.

Jeff hurled himself forward, breaking through that moment of shock, running headlong, grabbing a chair as he passed it and carrying it with him. He felt the wall building again, but he drove on, letting momentum carry him, throwing himself bodily the last distance, the chair before him. He shut his eyes and made impact, falling as he did it. The chair hurtled the length of his arms and smashed into the screen. Glass crashed over his prone body, and sparks of a short circuit blew smoke into the room. In a great hiss and sizzle, the voice was dead.

The force and power were cut off with an impossible suddenness and he went limp. But there was no time for rest. The feet of the mob were in the corridor, and he had only begun his work. He groped in the new dark for a light switch. When the room flooded with the light of electricity, he ran along the banks of machines, pulling wires, smashing with a heavy hammer he found beside one of them. They sputtered themselves to death behind him, metal clanked to the floor, and the humming weakened.

The mob of people was at the door, still coming after him, but their faces betrayed them. There was little purpose there now; just confusion, bewilderment. They had jumped from their beds on command of the receivers implanted in their flesh; they had torn through Wornegon to kill him; but the machines were destroyed, the receivers were voiceless, and the people were on their own, wondering why they were here in the depths of Wornegon at all.

Jeff knelt beside Jones. The man was unconscious. He would have to finish alone. He pressed his hands along Jones' body until he found the flare Kirby was waiting to sight. He pulled it from the FBI man, and tucked it securely under his arm.

He faced the mob. They packed the hall so tightly that he couldn't get through. He rammed against them, hitting with elbow and hand, knocking them out of his way. But his progress was slow. And Rogers could pop up any time.

Still under a remembered influence, some of the people grabbed at him, but he jerked away, tearing his suit coat and shirt.

"Let me by!" He rammed into the wall of bodies again, and they fell back. He beat his path ruthlessly, not stopping to pity or understand. He had too much to do.

He went up the ramp and turned for the lobby, clawing his way around the people. They were more willing to let him pass as sense crept back into their eyes.

When he broke into the lobby, the crowd was behind him, packed into the halls leading to the basement. He by-passed the elevators and ran up the stairs, compelling strength into his weary legs. Up and up he climbed, going around in a tight circle as each flight loomed before him. Then he was at the top, and pushed out into what had to be the roof landing.

Night bloomed over his head. Stars appeared and fresh air blew over the roof edge to ruffle his hair and sting his eyes.

Before letting one stray thought come into his head, he sent the flare bright into the sky, creating a falling, lowering star of his own. It would call Kirby, waiting with troops and guns. Kirby would finish what had been started. The Tobys would destroy the transmitters, return the young, betrayed people to Earth, and it would end and be forgotten.

He sat down near the edge of the roof and let the breeze blow relief through him. He had one regret, and it wasn't Cory. It was Rogers. How he would have liked to smash into Rogers' face, just once, and see the color of Rogers' blood.

A broken-motor type of noise reached him, and he knew it was Kirby, coming by helicopter to take over, sending word around the world to attack HFP headquarters and rid the Earth of a dreadful parasite.

Jeff laughed to himself. One parasite down, and another coming up. His work still wasn't complete. He had to find some method of making heroes out of the little men, of making them acceptable as partners, so Earth could acquire a harmless parasite instead of the one Hicks had in mind.

It wouldn't be too difficult. The stars were close now, and Man would clutch them with one hand. while holding with the other the hands of the chocolate-eyed, honest-hearted, short ones.

THE END

www.ingramcontent.com/pod-product-compliance
Lightning Source LLC
Chambersburg PA
CBHW030309180626
46810CB00003B/990